Universe 10

Universe 10

Edited by TERRY CARR

DOUBLEDAY & COMPANY, INC.

GARDEN CITY, NEW YORK

1980

All of the characters in this book
are fictitious, and any resemblance
to actual persons, living or dead,
is purely coincidental.

ISBN: 0-385-15477-1
Library of Congress Catalog Card Number 79-6534
Copyright © 1980 by Terry Carr
All Rights Reserved
Printed in the United States of America
First Edition

CONTENTS

Universe 10

As the world's media become ever more widespread and pervasive, questions about the rights of public figures become more difficult. What constitutes invasion of privacy in a world full of cameras and microphones? If a politician is satirized, where's the line between fair comment and libel? And if it's legal now for a performer to have his features surgically altered to look like those of Elvis Presley, would that be true with a living actor?

Michael Bishop considers the latter question in the following novelette. His answers may surprise you.

Bishop's most recent book is Catacomb Years, *an interrelated series of stories including "Old Folks at Home" from* Universe 8.

SAVING FACE
Michael Bishop

"Get back," Rakestraw told his children, who were eyeing him curiously as he tried to chop the thick pruned branches of a holly tree into pieces small enough for the fireplace. "I don't want you to get hit."

He waited until the five-year-old girl and her slightly smaller twin brother backed hand in hand toward the mulch pile and the edge of the winter garden. Then, to demonstrate his strength to them, he swung the ax in a high arc and brought the blade down viciously on the propped-up holly branch. One half of it flew upward like a knotted boomerang, its gray-white bark coruscating silver in the December sunlight. After windmilling a good distance through the air, the severed piece landed with a thud at Gayle and Gabe's feet.

"Damn it!" Rakestraw bellowed, dropping the ax. "I told you to get back! Your mother'd kill me if I killed you!"

The boy retreated into the muddy turnip bed, but Gayle picked up the holly log and carried it to her father. Rakestraw knelt to accept it, and she reached toward his face with her small, damnably knowing fingers.

"You diddn shave," Gayle told him.

He started to catch her hand in order to rub his coarse chin in its palm, but the holly log impeded him and Gabe was running forward from the garden.

"Look, Daddy!" the boy cried. "Looka the truck!"

Rakestraw stood up and saw, not a truck, but some sort of fancily decorated imported van coming cautiously along the gravel road from town. He tossed the log among several others he had cut that morning and pulled his children to him. "Wait a minute," he said as they squirmed under his hands; "you don't know who that is. Hold still." He didn't recognize the vehicle as belonging to anyone in the county, and since the road it was traveling dead-ended only a stone's throw away, Rakestraw was as curious as the twins.

The van halted abreast of them, and a man wearing a neck scarf as big, red, and silky as a champion American Beauty rose stuck his head out the window and squinted at them. He had on a pair of sunglasses, but the lenses were nestled in his hair.

"Tom Rakestraw?" he asked.

"That's right," Rakestraw responded.

The man in the American Beauty cravat stuck his head back in the window, flipped his glasses down, and maneuvered the rear end of his van into the yard, running over several of the uncut holly branches Rakestraw had earlier dragged to the woodpile. He made a parking space between the garden and the house, where there'd never been a parking space. Another man sat in the front seat beside him, but the driver's clumsy backing maneuver delayed recognition until the van stopped and Sheriff Harrison had opened his door and climbed out.

Benny Harrison, wearing a khaki shirt with his badge half-hidden in one of its greasy folds, was a head shorter than the newcomer and a good deal less at ease. Even though he kept his thumbs in his belt, at unexpected moments his elbows flapped like poorly hung storm shutters. He introduced the man who had backed into the yard as Edgar Macmillan, an attorney from California.

Rakestraw said, "Gayle, Gabe, go play with Nickie." Nickie was the dog, a lethargic brown mongrel visible now as a furry lump in the grass below the kitchen window. The twins went reluctantly off in the dog's direction, and Rakestraw looked at Macmillan.

"I represent Craig Tiernan, Mr. Rakestraw."

"Who?"

"Craig Tiernan. Surely you've heard the name." Macmillan had his hands deep in the pockets of his blazer. The lenses of his sunglasses glinted like miniature hub caps. "Craig Tiernan."

"An actor," Benny Harrison put in. "A movie actor."

"He's placed first among male performers in three consecutive box-office polls, Mr. Rakestraw, and this year he's nominated for an Academy Award."

"We don't go to the movies."

"You read, don't you? You watch television?"

"We don't watch much television. But I read now and again."

"Then you've seen his name in the newspaper. In the amusement section, where the movie ads are. In 'people' news, in feature stories."

Benny Harrison flapped his elbows. "Tom gets the Dachies County *Journal*," he told Macmillan by way of defending his friend. "And you've got a little library of history and farming books, don't you? And Nora's magazines. Nora subscribes to magazines."

"Tiernan's always in the women's magazines," Macmillan said almost accusingly. "He's always being featured. Sometimes he gets a cover."

"I don't read those," Rakestraw confessed. "Nora gets them for recipes and pictures of furniture. She shows me the pictures sometimes."

"Has she ever told you you look like Craig Tiernan?"

Rakestraw shook his head.

"That's why I've come out here," Macmillan said. "That's why I stopped at Caracal's sheriff's office and asked Sheriff Harrison to ride out here with me." He took a piece of paper from an inside blazer pocket, unfolded it, and shook it out so that Rakestraw could see the matter printed on it.

Rakestraw recognized it as the poster he had sat for when Harrison and two or three other people on the Caracal city council persuaded him to run for mayor against the sharp-spoken, doddering incumbent. He had lost by only ten or twelve votes, primarily because he had been unable to convince the ladies of the local women's club that he wasn't too young and inexperienced for the job, which in reality was little more than a sinecure. Mayor Birkett was pushing seventy, and Rakestraw had just turned thirty-two.

"Is this you?" Macmillan wanted to know. He paced toward the woodpile, then waved off his own question. "Of course it is. Otherwise I wouldn't be here." He turned around. "Somebody in Caracal sent this to the studio. The studio forwarded it to Tiernan, and Tiernan sent it to me, along with instructions and air fare to your state capital. A friend of mine up there loaned me this van, and here I am." A sudden gust of wind rattled the pecan tree towering over the woodpile, and the

smoothed-out election poster in Macmillan's hand fluttered distract-
ingly.

"Why?" Rakestraw asked.

"To take care of the matter."

"*What* matter, Mr. Macmillan?" Rakestraw heard the twins shouting
and laughing in another part of the yard. He also heard the bewilder-
ment and impatience in his own voice.

"Your trespass on Tiernan's physiognomic rights, which he now has
on file in Washington, D.C. Your state legislature approved local compliance with the Physiognomic Protection Act last May, Mr. Rakestraw, and that makes you subject to every statute of the otherwise provisional federal act."

"Benny," Rakestraw asked, "what the hell does that mean?"

"It means your face don't belong to you anymore," said Benny Harrison, flapping his elbows. "Sounds crazy, don't it?"

Rakestraw let his gaze drift from the perturbed, disheveled sheriff to
the attorney with the crimson scarf at his throat, who was standing
among the holly logs Rakestraw had already cut.

"Let me finish these," Rakestraw said. "I'm almost finished." He re-
trieved his ax and began hacking at a smooth, gray-white holly limb
only a small distance from Macmillan's foot. The attorney backed up to
his borrowed van and watched the other man chopping wood as if witness to a performance as rare and exotic as ember-walking or lion-
taming.

"Craig Tiernan?" Nora said. "Tom doesn't look like Craig Tiernan." She dug an old magazine out of the wall rack in the den and
flipped it open to a double-page color layout.

"He does to me," Macmillan countered. "I've seen Tiernan up close,
oh, a thousand times, and your husband looks like him. An amazing
likeness, really amazing." He stubbed his cigarette out on the canning
lid Nora had given him for an ashtray. "At least you know who Tiernan is, though. That's more than I can say for your husband. I
wouldn't've believed anybody *that* uninformed or isolated, Mrs. Rakestraw. I mean, the boondocks just aren't the boondocks anymore—the
media's everywhere. Everybody touches everybody else. That's why it's
necessary to have a law like the Physiognomic Protection Act."

"Tom isn't interested in movies." Nora examined the photograph in
the magazine. "And I don't think he looks like Craig Tiernan, either. I
don't see what you see."

"That's why I'm going to drive him to the capital—so we can do a point-by-point match-up of features. This procedure isn't hit-or-miss, Mrs. Rakestraw—it's very scientific." Macmillan shook out another cigarette. "Okay. So he isn't interested in movies. But how can he be unaware? That's what I don't understand, how he can be so unaware."

"Do you know who the head of the government of Kenya is, Mr. Macmillan?" Nora asked the attorney.

"Hell, Mrs. Rakestraw, I don't even know who the President of Canada is."

"Prime Minister."

"Okay, Prime Minister. But the Prime Ministers of Canada and Kenya don't happen to be up for Academy Awards this year, either."

"Maybe they should be," Benny Harrison said. "The President, too." He stood by the double windows fronting the road to Caracal and, when a noise overhead reminded them all of Tom's activity upstairs, lifted his eyes to the ceiling.

"How long are you going to keep him?" Nora asked.

"I don't know," Macmillan replied, exhaling smoke. "He might get back tomorrow. It might be three or four days. Or a week. Depends on what the examiners report after the match-up of features."

"Well, what happens if—if they *match up?*"

"There are options, Mrs. Rakestraw. Nobody gets thrown in jail or caught out for damages for looking like somebody else. —Listen, if the test's positive, you'll be able to talk to him by telephone at our expense. It's nothing to worry about. You may even make some money."

"I don't care about that. However much it is, it won't be worth going through all this. I don't even see why he has to go. It's ridiculous." There was more noise from upstairs. "Listen to that. He's upset with me for not helping him pack."

"Nora," Benny Harrison said, turning around, "Mr. Macmillan's got a legal summons for this test. That's why Tom's going."

"What am I supposed to tell Gayle and Gabe? This is working out just as if Tom's done something wrong. And he hasn't—not a thing."

Neither the attorney nor the sheriff answered her. Sunlight fell across the hardwood floor through the double windows, and Nora tilted her head to catch the subtly frantic inflection of Nickie's barking.

After a time, Tom came into the room with his overnight case and asked if there was an extra tube of toothpaste anywhere. As a concession to the legality, if not the reasonableness, of Macmillan's visit, Nora went looking for one. The men straggled out to the van while she looked, and when she found the extra tube of toothpaste, she carried it outside and handed it to her husband with a sense of vague disappointment. Nevertheless, she kissed him and touched him affectionately on the nose.

"Take care," Rakestraw said. "I'll call you."

Back inside the house, Nora found a check for a thousand dollars on the kitchen table. Macmillan's lazy signature was at the bottom, twisted like a section of line in Tom's tackle box. Nora wanted to tear the check up and scatter the pieces across the floor; instead, she left it lying on the table and returned thoughtfully to the den.

The drive from Caracal to the state capital took four hours. Rakestraw asked Macmillan no questions, and Macmillan volunteered nothing beyond ecstatic but obtuse comments about the scenery.

"Look at those blackbirds," he exclaimed as they sped by a harvested cornfield in which a host of grackles was strutting. "There must be a thousand of 'em!" He drummed his fingers on the dashboard in time to the disco music on the radio. He filled the van's ashtray with cigarette butts.

But he was subdued and solicitous checking Rakestraw into the private sanitarium where the testing was to be performed. He kept his voice down in the gloomy but spacious lobby where potted plants were reflected doubtfully in the streaked marble flooring, and he gave the black teenager who insisted on carrying Rakestraw's bag to his first-floor room a generous but far from flashy tip. Then he left and let Rakestraw get a nap.

Surprisingly, the testing itself began that same evening. A young man named Hurd and a young woman named Arberry—dressed, but for their name tags, as if for the street—came into Rakestraw's room with photographic equipment, a scale on removable coasters, a notebook of laminated superimpositions of Craig Tiernan's features, and various kinds of stainless-steel calibrating instruments, most of which looked sophisticated enough to induce envy in a physical anthropologist. Rakestraw reflected that these two young people *were* physical anthropologists of a kind—they wanted to determine, scientifically, whether or not he looked like Craig Tiernan.

"Do I look like Craig Tiernan?" Rakestraw asked Arberry as, after weighing him and noting down his height in centimeters, she posed him for a series of photographs.

"There's a real resemblance," Arberry said genially. She smiled at him and made him point his chin for a portrait of his left profile. "Don't people you've never met before do double takes when they first see you?"

"Not that I've noticed."

"Her next question," Hurd put in, fiddling with a calibrating tool, "is whether you're married or not."

"Married," Rakestraw managed between his teeth.

"Don't move," Arberry cautioned him mildly. In the same low-key tone she added, "Shut up, Hurd, and get your own act together."

There was a surprisingly silent flash from her camera, and then Arberry was posing him face on. Like a tailor, Hurd was using a tape measure across his shoulders. Rakestraw found their finicky probing more interesting now than annoying, and he cooperated with his examiners as he was always urging Gabe and Gayle to cooperate with Dr. Meade when he took them for checkups back in Caracal. Chin up, face on, no bickering; child or adult, that was how you were supposed to do things. . . .

Arberry and Hurd were in the room with him for most of the evening, but they did give him a few odd minutes to himself as they conferred over the notebook of plastic superimpositions, flipping pages and matching features.

Rakestraw began to feel like a pretender to the name, title, and person of the Grand Duchess Anastasia. Those fervid women had tried to prove their claims by a variety of methods, including the assertion that their ears had twelve or thirteen or fourteen positive points of identity—out of a possible seventeen—with the ears of the infant Anastasia, as revealed by photographs. The difference, of course, was that he didn't wish to establish himself as Craig Tiernan; he certainly didn't want his examiners to find enough points of similarity to make his resemblance to the actor a trespass against the Physiognomic Protection Act. Where had such legislation come from, anyway?

But Rakestraw was fascinated by the procedures Hurd and Arberry were using to determine the extent of his resemblance. Even when they weren't touching his jaw or forehead with cold metal instruments or trigonometrically surveying the pyramid of his nose, he hovered behind them, looking over their shoulders and eavesdropping on the cryptic verbal shorthand they used to communicate their findings to each other. Toward what decision were their measurements leading them?

Rakestraw's powerful curiosity was not strong enough to overcome his natural reticence, though, and he sat down on the old-fashioned tufted bedspread to wait them out. As he waited, indignation seeped back into him, and a painful sense of separation from everything that was important to him.

At last Arberry said, "Mr. Macmillan will be in to see you in the morning, Mr. Rakestraw. Jeff and I are going to report to him now."

Rubbing his frighteningly cold hands, Rakestraw stood up. He refrained from asking the question that even they expected him to ask. He was sure that the pressure of his self-control had to be visible in his face—the face they had clinically savaged for almost three hours.

Two polite, well-groomed, amiable technicians. . . .

"Mr. Macmillan will give you the results in the morning," Arberry said, opening the door to his room.

Hurd pushed the scales through the door. "Good night, Mr. Rakestraw—hope you get a good night's sleep." He had an equipment bag over one shoulder. Arberry smiled pleasantly and followed her colleague into the long, darkened, palm-lined corridor.

They were gone.

An hour or two later the telephone beside Rakestraw's bed made a faint buzzing noise. Rakestraw picked it up.

"Turn on your TV," Macmillan said through the line. "They've got cable here, and there's a Craig Tiernan movie on channel twelve. A good one, too. Tiernan plays Robert Pirsig in *Phaedrus*. It got great reviews five years ago but bombed out at the box office—strange how those things happen."

"Did you talk with the examiners?"

"Yeah. I'll tell you about it in the morning. Turn on the boob tube, Mr. Rakestraw, and catch the flick." Macmillan hung up.

It took Rakestraw a good thirty or forty seconds to find the television set, even though it was in full view and he had been in the same room with it since late afternoon. The set rested on a gilded stand in the corner beyond the dressing table, and a large potted rose geranium obscured most of the stand. The eye of the television set was cold and empty, camouflaged mysteriously by its own nakedness. Rakestraw crossed the room and turned it on.

Opening titles rolled up and over a barren early-morning landscape of cattails and marsh water; a pair of motorcycles moved silently along the highway bordering the marsh. Rakestraw sat down on the bed.

The film turned out to be full of flashbacks and flashforwards, as well as several wrenching exchanges about metaphysical matters that Rakestraw had trouble keeping straight in his head. *Phaedrus* was beautifully photographed, however, and he felt a grudging but genuine sympathy for the complex personality Tiernan was re-creating. Everybody in the film was suffering, everybody was on the edge of madness, and Rakestraw *felt* for them. An hour later he could take no more of their suffering—he got up and turned the set off.

"I don't look like that man," he said aloud. "I don't think we resemble each other at all."

•

Macmillan came for him in the morning and escorted him down the corridor to a dining room furnished with huge rattan chairs and tables with wrought-iron legs. They took coffee and Danish pastries from a serving board at one end of the room and found a table of their own.

"Your face belongs to Craig Tiernan," the attorney said a few minutes after they had sat down. "That's the verdict of the data that Hurd and Arberry came up with."

Rakestraw laughed humorlessly.

"It's true, I'm afraid. The resemblance is acute and actionable."

"If I've got Craig Tiernan's face, Mr. Macmillan, then he must be walking around California with all the expression of a hard-boiled egg."

"He lives in Oregon. When he isn't working."

"Then why the hell is he worried about Tom Rakestraw's face? I'm not going to Oregon. Who the hell does he think he is?"

"He may live in Oregon, Mr. Rakestraw, but he's a personality in every state of the union and more than a dozen foreign countries. Your infringement on those rights whereby his recognition is—"

"Please, Mr. Macmillan. No more legal double-talk. Just tell me what 'actionable' means if Tiernan can't win damages from me."

"It just means he can press suit, which is what he's doing. Don't worry about that, though. Here are your options under the law."

Macmillan took an envelope from his blazer pocket and began to write on it with a disposable plastic pen. Finally he pushed the envelope across the table to Rakestraw, who picked it up and hastily scanned what the attorney had listed as his options.

1. Co-ownership of the rights in question, through either purchase or grant.

2. Authorization as a legal impersonator of the licensed owner, 10 percent of income derived from this source to accrue to plaintiff and his appointed agents.

3. Voluntary self-sequestration, with the owner of the rights in

question retaining to himself and his agents the means of checking and ensuring compliance.

4. Immigration to a country to which legal distribution of the public works of the owner of the rights in question has either not yet been approved or not been taken advantage of.

5. Permanent alteration of those features trespassing most conspicuously on the proprietary rights of the plaintiff, to be accomplished without appeal or delay.

"Six," Rakestraw added, placing the envelope in the middle of the table. "Voluntary self-annihilation of the offending party."

Macmillan laughed. "Oh, come on, it isn't as bad as that. The thing you forget is that in the case of suits under the Physiognomic Protection Act, it's the plaintiff who's responsible for court costs and all the financial obligations arising from the defendant's choice of an option. This is the only law on the books, Mr. Rakestraw, dictating that a victorious plaintiff must compensate his defeated court opponent for emotional suffering and any expenses following upon the action."

"But I haven't been in court, Mr. Macmillan!"

"You're there now, in a manner of speaking. Hurd and Arberry are testifying for both you and Craig Tiernan—or their data is, I should say. And the verdict of the data will be the verdict of the court. Our case seems to be a solid one, Mr. Rakestraw."

Rakestraw picked up the envelope again. "Let me see if I understand this," he said, glancing over it at the attorney. "Number one means that I can buy my face from Tiernan if he'll agree to sell. Or that he can give me part interest in it if he wants to be . . . generous."

"That's right. He won't do either, though."

"Okay. What's number two about?"

"The law permits three legal impersonators. Tiernan already has three, I'm afraid. Two perform movie stunts for him and one's a double at functions he doesn't wish to attend."

"Like the Academy Awards?"

"Oh no—he'll be there in person this year. He's got a good chance to win."

"I've got my fingers crossed." Rakestraw took a sip of coffee, which by now was cold and scummy-tasting. "Three means that I can become a hermit and that Tiernan's lackeys have the right to make sure I'm staying indoors in my hair shirt and sandals."

Macmillan nodded. "More or less."

"Isn't Caracal hermitage enough for Craig Tiernan's purposes?"

"I'm afraid not. Your election poster went up all over Dachies County, the sheriff told me, on telephone poles and fence posts. That's an infringement of Tiernan's—"

"Number four seems pretty clear. What countries might Nora, the twins, and I hope to immigrate to, Mr. Macmillan?"

"I'd have to look that up. Great Britain and Western Europe are pretty much out, though. Tiernan has big followings in those places. —Not many people choose this option, I'm told. Once you get a job and get settled, the plaintiff's financial obligations to you begin to taper off really drastically."

"Which brings us to number five?"

"Plastic surgery," Macmillan said.

"Plastic surgery," Rakestraw hollowly echoed the man.

"Right. On the house. We've got the facilities for it right here in this lovely sanitarium, they tell me."

A week later, Rakestraw rode home on a bus. Benny Harrison met him at the little town's only grocery store, which also served as its bus depot, and drove him out to his house in the Caracal sheriff's car.

"Do you want me to go in with you?" Benny Harrison asked.

"No thanks. Go on back to town. I appreciate the ride."

Rakestraw watched the car float away from him in a backboil of thrown gravel and drifting dust. Then he saw the door to the house open and Nora and the twins come out.

Nora was carrying a wreath of holly leaves. The berries on the wreath were like excruciatingly crimson drops of blood. Rakestraw's face tightened in reminiscence.

Gayle and Gabe looked toward him, and when Nora said, "Tom?" in surprise and evident doubt, the twins heard only the name and started to rush to him—as they had always done when he came in from the fields or back from a solitary trip to Caracal.

At that moment Nickie came banging out the kitchen door, loped madly past the children, and halted at the edge of the road in front of Rakestraw. Wagging its tail dubiously, the dog soon began to bark—a sonorous and violent heaving from deep within its chest. The hair on the dog's back stood up like a fan of porcupine quills, but it was clearly of two minds.

"Goddamn it, Nickie! It's me! Shut up, you dumb cur!"

Nickie kept barking, and when Rakestraw looked over the dog's ugly, persistently jerking head, he saw that Gayle and Gabe had re-treated toward Nora and the house. How often, after all, had he warned them against taking up unquestioningly with strangers?

In the kitchen, Rakestraw spoke to and embraced his children. By picking up his suitcase again, he avoided allowing Nora to put her arms around him, for he was alert to the fact that she wished to do so not only to welcome him home but to prove to him that the change didn't matter. It hurt to realize how fully Nora understood the trauma of his homecoming. It hurt even more to realize that he was not yet ready to accept the simple *kindness* embodied in her love.

"I'm going up to the guest room," he said abruptly.

As he swung out of the kitchen and began climbing the stairs, Gabe began to cry and Gayle to expostulate with her mother in bewildered, high-pitched tones. Rakestraw could hear Nora patiently declaring that she had told them their father would look a little different and wasn't it shameful to be making such a fuss when inside where it counted Daddy was exactly the same person and couldn't they understand that he was probably even more confused and uncertain than they were.

Upstairs, Rakestraw threw his suitcase into the guest room, angrily followed it in, and slammed and locked the door.

Long after the children had gone to bed, Nora knocked lightly and spoke his name. Knowing that she would be surprised to find him naked in the dark, he nevertheless opened to her, oddly indifferent to the pathos of his own behavior. This was not Tom Rakestraw acting in this unmanly, self-pitying way but an amazing, if imperfect, duplicate. Only the faces had been changed, to protect . . . well, some self-obsessed S.O.B. he had never even met.

Nora closed the door and embraced him. "Aren't you cold? It's not even spring yet, and here you are walking around in your birthday suit." Her hands moved gently up and down his back, as if to warm him, and Rakestraw surrendered to the extent of placing his chin on her head and embracing her chastely in return.

"I don't feel naked before you, Nora."

"You're not supposed to. Clothed or not, we're naked to each other almost all the time. We're married."

After a long silence Rakestraw said, "What I meant, Nora, is that I don't feel naked *at all*. I think I could walk through Caracal like this without feeling any shame. It wouldn't be me, anyway."

"Because your face is different?"

"Exactly."

"You're still the same person, Tom."

"I heard you tell Gabe and Gayle that, Nora—but it isn't true. I'm becoming someone else. It started the moment I saw myself in the mirror after surgery. And it's continuing even now."

Nora's fingers caressed the hair in the small of his back. "Maybe we'd better hurry, then."

"Hurry?"

"Before our lovemaking becomes adulterous."

Rakestraw kissed his wife, disengaged from her embrace, and walked to the bed to turn back its coverlet. This was a kindness for which they were both ready, and he could deny neither himself nor Nora.

"I don't care if they do have school tomorrow," Rakestraw told Nora at dinner several evenings later.

"But they need their sleep, Tom, and you really don't care who wins what. At least, you never have before."

"This year I care."

"Because of—"

"That's right. Because of Tiernan."

Gayle and Gabe were observing this exchange like spectators at a heated Ping-Pong match. The victor would determine their destinies between the approaching hours of nine and midnight.

"But it's everything you used to despise," Nora persisted, "if you thought about it at all. Is this Tiernan business enough to make you want to expose your children to the whole gaudy rigamarole?"

"They know what we think of that rigamarole. That's our parental guidance, their knowledge that we disapprove."

"They're first-graders, Tom. *First*-graders."

Rakestraw put his fork down and looked at each of the twins in turn. He had even more authority with them than he had had before. They listened to him now as if he were a policeman or a school principal.

"Do you think you can stay awake for the Academy Awards program?" he asked. "You certainly don't have to stay up if you don't want to."

"We want to," Gayle said.

"Yeah," said Gabe, wide-eyed and anxious.

"Lord, Tom—"

But Rakestraw, as he had known he would, prevailed. Nora did win a concession of sorts: she made pallets on the floor in front of the television for the twins.

By ten-thirty Gabe had fallen asleep with his stuffed paisley dog and Gayle was staring bravely, glassily, at a group of gowned women and bearded, tuxedoed men holding Oscars aloft for the polite approval of a Hollywood audience of celebrities and other film industry people. But because no camera had yet picked Craig Tiernan out of the crowd, even Rakestraw was growing impatient with the program.

Nora said, "Are you sure he's even there? I think I've read that he usually boycotts these things."

"He's nominated this year. Macmillan, the attorney, said he'd be on hand. He was in a film called *Yeardance*. Yesterday's paper listed him as the favorite for Best Actor."

"Can't we at least put the kids to bed?"

But the orchestra began playing a well-known movie theme and Rakestraw saw Tiernan, a lanky black starlet on his arm, descending a monumental tier of steps to the presenters' lectern.

"There he is, Nora. Wake up Gabe."

Nora shook her head in simultaneous refusal and exasperation.

"Wake him up, Nora!" Rakestraw got down on the floor, shook the boy by the shoulders, and pulled him to a precarious sitting position. "Who is that, kids? Tell me who that is!"

On the tiny television screen Tiernan was all glittering teeth and windswept coiffure. The young black woman at his side exuded a sultriness that seemed almost to mock his innocent good looks and bearing. Applause filled the auditorium. Then the couple went immediately into their clumsy, ghost-written repartee.

Gabe was jolted fully awake by the novelty of seeing his lost father in the company of a half-naked woman. Gayle, meanwhile, looked back and forth between the television set and the man who had just eased himself back onto the couch beside her mother.

"That used to be you," the girl said.

"That was never me," Rakestraw responded.

Tiernan and his sultry companion presented two awards for documentaries. The Rakestraws watched both presentations without speaking, fascinated by the eerie spectacle. Daddy was—or had been—a famous movie star.

"All right," Nora said. "They've seen him. Can't they go to bed now? Upstairs, I mean."

Rakestraw insisted that the twins stay for the Best Actor presentation, and Gayle and Gabe importuned their mother so enthusiastically that she had to relent. Tiernan's appearance on the program had dislodged the sleep from their eyes.

Another forty minutes passed before the Best Actor nominations were read, at which time a camera located Tiernan in the crowd and focused on him for almost half a minute. Then the screen was filled with that scene from *Yeardance* in which the title character comes face to face for the first time with the "lepers" under his care. It was a gruesome bit of film, but quickly over with. Tiernan, spotlighted again among his applauding colleagues, suddenly looked tense and uncertain. His smile was a rictus of counterfeit calm. Rakestraw could not recall ever having exercised the facial muscles that would produce such an expression.

"He really wants it."

"They all do," Nora said. "It's natural that they should."

The other nominees were shown, along with clips from their films. But the winner was not Tiernan. The winner was an eccentric Hollywood leading man who had made his first film during the early years of World War II. The auditorium rang with shouts and applause, and a television camera dollied in on Tiernan, cruelly, as he feigned a self-effacing grimace and then waved heartily at the victor threading his way to the stage.

"There's the Academy Award performance," Rakestraw said.

"Are you happy now?" Nora asked.

"Not yet," Rakestraw confessed. "Not yet."

The next day he drove to Ladysmith, a good-sized textile town about thirty-five miles south of Caracal, and purchased a videocassette recorder. In several different record and television shops he informed the clerks or sales managers that he wanted to buy videocassettes of all Craig Tiernan's movies.

"All of 'em?" asked a young woman with an unattractive blond Afro who was clerking in a shop at the Ladysmith Mall.

"That's right—all of 'em."

"Well, you can buy some of the early films legit, but the most recent ones—you know, *Yeardance* and the remake of *Dark Passage*—well, you're not likely to find those anywhere but on the black market."

"I don't mind. Can you help me?"

"Hey, are you a cop?"

"No, I'm just a Craig Tiernan fancier."

The girl tilted her head and gave him an appraising look. "I might be able to help you if . . ."

"If what?"

"Take out your wallet and let me go through it," the clerk challenged him.

Rakestraw took out his wallet and laid it on the counter. Surprised, the girl picked it up, glanced at Rakestraw, and then began folding out the laminated cards and photographs until she came to his driver's license.

"Cripes," the girl said under her breath. "You've got Craig Tiernan's picture on your driver's license. You *ain't* a cop, are you? How in holy Christmas did you manage that?"

"I've got a friend at the Highway Patrol station." The lie made Rakestraw infinitely happy. Three or four weeks ago he had taken an intense private pride in his truthfulness, even in situations where a small distortion of the truth would have saved him either time or embarrassment.

"All right, mister. I guess it also looks like you can pay for what you want."

The clerk sold him the two black-market cassettes at steep prices, found five or six old Tiernan films in inventory, and helped him fill out an order for seven other Craig Tiernan vehicles. That was the whole shebang. Tiernan was still a young actor and, Rakestraw had learned, he was notoriously picky about the roles he accepted.

"That's the third time today you've watched *Dark Passage*," Nora told Rakestraw one midnight shortly after his visit to Ladysmith. "Bogart was twice as good in that part, too. What do you think you're accomplishing?"

"I never saw Bogart in the part. I think Tiernan does a pretty fair job, really."

"It's a pretentious and outdated movie, Tom. Using the camera as a character was fine the first time around, but in this remake it just seems silly. Self-conscious. The girl isn't as good as Bacall, either."

"How come you know so much about it?"

"I used to watch all the late movies on TV . . . until you started asking me out. Come to bed, Tom."

Rakestraw leaned forward, propped his chin on his fists, and continued to stare at the low-quality tape he had bought in Ladysmith. "You've got both critics and moviegoers on your side, Nora. Everything

I've read about this one says it was a bomb. Tiernan and what's-her-face got panned, and no one went to see it until *Yeardance* was released a couple of months later. Then, they say, *Dark Passage* suddenly got hot at the box office."

Nora, standing in the doorway, looked with angry compassion at her transfigured husband. "The story fascinates you, doesn't it?"

Alerted by the cryptic tone of her voice, Rakestraw looked toward her. "A man with a past he has to overcome has plastic surgery and takes off to make a new life. Sure it fascinates me. It doesn't take a genius to figure out why, either."

"I'm going to bed, Tom. Do you want me to turn on your half of the electric blanket?"

When he shook his head, Nora left him in the den and walked through the dining room to the staircase.

Later, Rakestraw also went upstairs. But he strode down the hall to the guest room, turned on the light, locked the door, sat down at the antique vanity, and removed a small tape recorder from its drawer. Then he began contorting his altered features back toward the shapes he had known them to have only a few short weeks ago. Silently, hunching his shoulders and then straightening them again, he mimed the gestures that were Tiernan's hallmark as an actor. After a time he began to speak as Tiernan had spoken in *Dark Passage*. It astonished Rakestraw how easily and successfully the impersonation came to him, but he kept his voice down in order not to awaken Nora.

Two days later, Nora was surprised to look out the kitchen window and see parked on the edge of the yard an automobile bearing on its left-hand door the insignia of one of the state capital's major newspapers. Then a young woman with a camera case slung over her shoulder and a notebook in her hand knocked for admittance. Daffodils were growing in the grass between the kitchen door and the dirt road, and the young woman, her dark hair pulled back and tied in a navy-blue scarf, looked sunny and efficient.

"Is this the Rakestraws' residence?" she asked when Nora had opened the heavy Dutch door. "I'm Michelle Boyer, with the *World-Ledger*. I've got an appointment to talk with your husband."

Nora led Michelle Boyer into the den, where Rakestraw was intently watching Craig Tiernan in *Good Country People*, one of his early major films. Rakestraw turned off the videocassette and shook hands with the reporter, whereupon Nora, angry that her husband had said nothing to her about expecting a visitor, prepared to leave the two of them to whatever business they might have.

"Stay," Rakestraw said. "I think she'd like to hear what you have to say too, Nora. It's very important that she hear it, in fact." Finally Nora permitted herself to be persuaded.

Over the next two hours Rakestraw submitted to several photographs, and he and Nora detailed for Michelle Boyer the changes that had occurred in their lives because Craig Tiernan had invoked the Physiognomic Protection Act against him.

"I was the first defendant in this state," Rakestraw said, "and I lost on the basis of physical measurements of my skull and facial features. The data went to court, but I didn't."

"You're being compensated handsomely for the trauma, aren't you?" asked Boyer, taking the devil's-advocate role and writing in her notebook.

"Five hundred dollars a month. Which Tiernan, out in Oregon, writes off his income tax as a business expense."

"Are you looking for a larger settlement?"

"I'm not," Nora put in. "I don't know what Tom's looking for. The monthly check from Tiernan has turned him around. He spends all his waking hours doing what you found him doing when you came in. Two months ago he would have been chopping wood, preparing the ground, ordering seed."

"And now he obsessively watches Craig Tiernan movies?"

"He's a changed person, and I'm not just talking about his face. He's different inside. He admits it himself."

"What do you want," Boyer asked Rakestraw pointedly, lowering her notebook, "if it isn't more money?"

"Do you think this is fair?" Rakestraw asked her in turn. "Giving up a portion of myself because of another man's vanity?"

"You didn't have to opt for surgery, did you?"

"Not if I didn't mind moving to a war zone in Africa or an A-bomb test site in the Marshall Islands."

"What's been the effect on your children?"

"They're distant. They don't really believe I'm their father. They obey me without question." Rakestraw laughed.

"You don't sound like Craig Tiernan," Michelle Boyer observed. "How closely did you resemble him? Do you have any photographs?"

Nora took a padded leather photo album from one of the bookshelves and also found the infamous election poster. These she gave to the reporter, who glanced at the poster and then began turning the pages of the album.

"I think the resemblance is uncanny," she said after a while. "I can understand why Tiernan would have been alarmed. The danger of exploitation and overexposure is a real one to a celebrity who's worked his or her entire professional life to create a viable public image. Do you remember the Presley imitators? In those days death put Presley in the public domain, but then came the·impersonators of *living* celebrities. Those exploiters didn't merely *imitate* their famous victims, Mr. Rakestraw, they had their faces surgically altered to resemble the President's or Bob Dylan's or Barbra Streisand's—while those people were still alive. Often they could libel and rip off their victims at the same time. Court cases proliferated, and a great deal of time and money was wasted. Hence, in states like New York and California, the Physiognomic Protection Act. It was probably overdue getting *here*, if you want my opinion."

"But Tom didn't surgically alter his face to resemble Tiernan's," Nora said. "It was his to begin with."

"That may be, Mrs. Rakestraw—but your husband's face wasn't essential to him in his livelihood. Tiernan was only trying to protect his livelihood."

"Tom Rakestraw was never a threat to Craig Tiernan's livelihood," Rakestraw said. "Never."

"Your voice isn't at all like his," Michelle Boyer observed again.

"No, it isn't," Nora said.

As if trying to make out the lineaments of the face that underlay his old one, the reporter looked at Rakestraw. "Why exactly did you call me down here?" she asked. "What did you want me to do for you?"

Rakestraw went to the VCR unit, turned it back on, and wound it forward to the loft sequence in *Good Country People*. The three of them watched as Craig Tiernan, playing the Bible-selling mountebank Manly Pointer, seduced Lisette Corley as Joy-Hulga Hopewell in the scene that not only solidified Tiernan's status as a rising beefcake star but earned him his present reputation as a formidable actor. It was impossible to watch Tiernan in this role, a piece of brilliant against-type casting, without laughing helplessly. As Nora and Michelle Boyer laughed, Rakestraw stepped forward and froze the motion picture on the screen at the precise point where Tiernan scrambled out of the loft with Corley's artificial leg in his Bible case.

"Is that why you had me come to Caracal?" the reporter asked. "To give me a private screening of the Great Leg Heist?"

"Partly." Rakestraw, facing the two women, set his feet apart, hunched his shoulders, and magically transformed himself into Craig Tiernan as Manly Pointer. When he spoke, the voice was Tiernan's Manly Pointer voice; and when he moved, the illusion of Tiernan as a callow but caustic redneck salesman was overwhelming. That illusion obliterated the commonplace reality of the den and its homely furniture.

" 'I may sell Bibles,' " ranted Rakestraw in his Tiernan-Pointer voice, " 'but I know which end is up and I wasn't born yesterday and I know where I'm going!' "

"Incredible," said Michelle Boyer, applauding him enthusiastically when he was finished. "No props, either. Very, very good."

Nora was staring at him as if he had just stripped naked at a Methodist covered-dish dinner. She was almost beginning to wonder if Macmillan had sent home to her from the sanitarium the same man he had taken.

Then the young reporter's eyes narrowed suspiciously. "That's it, isn't it? You're going to try to milk your connection with Tiernan. You want notoriety, and you think the *World-Ledger* can give it to you."

Rakestraw let himself slump back into his own persona, which, over the past several days, had grown more and more protean and tenuous. Nora was conscious of a firm purpose somewhere inside him, but also of the fact that this purpose was one of the few phenomenological constants remaining to him. Twice recently he had wakened at night and sleepily asked her what his name was. Sometimes, when they had looked through the photographs she had just been showing Boyer, Rakestraw had failed to recognize himself. And although he always recognized Nora's features in the faces of their children, he said he could never—anymore—discern the imprint of his own. . . .

"That's right," Rakestraw said. "Don't you think there's a story here?"

"Oh, undoubtedly," Boyer acknowledged. "But you may not like the one I'm formulating."

"Balance it, or unbalance it, any way you like—but get in the violence done to both me and my family."

"Not to mention your burgeoning talents as an impersonator?"

"Why not? I think they're pretty goddamn pertinent."

"Tom!"

"Good-bye, Ms. Boyer. I appreciate your driving down." Rakestraw shoved his hands in his pockets and stalked out of the den.

Nora led Michelle Boyer back through the kitchen and then walked with her out to her car. Daffodils fluttered alongside the gravel road, and the breeze was silken.

"Try to remember," Nora told the reporter, "that he was never like this before. That means something, I think. It definitely means something. I hope you're smart enough to figure out what."

Under the headline CARACAL MAN LOSES FACE TO CRAIG TIERNAN, / MASKS HURT WITH RARE IMPERSONATIONS, the story appeared in the Sunday *World-Ledger*. The Rakestraws were surprised to find themselves reading a sympathetic human-interest feature, for, despite Michelle Boyer's sunny good looks and her short-lived delight in Rakestraw's impromptu performance, she had seemed something of an apologist for the Physiognomic Protection Act and Rakestraw had ended up swearing at her. But the story—complete with side-by-side photographs of Tiernan and the "new" Thomas Rakestraw—was a virtual paean to the Rakestraws and a forthright assault on the arrogance of legislation expressly designed to protect the privileged.

"I'm proud of her," said Nora. "I'm really proud of her."

"The sympathies of the thing aren't as important as the fact that my story made the paper," Rakestraw said. "This just makes it a little nicer, a little easier."

The following morning the telephone began to ring.

Rakestraw spoke to the editor of the Ladysmith *Times*, to news personnel from three different television stations in the state, and to a man with a booking agency in Nashville, Tennessee. Although he discouraged this man on the grounds that he wasn't yet ready to leave Caracal, he made appointments with several others; and over the next three days just that many television camera crews invaded the Rakestraw house to film him doing, sans props or makeup, the loft scene in *Good Country People*, the metamorphosis of Karst in *Singularity*, and the self-blinding of the title character in *Yeardance*. A different scene for each camera crew. These mini-performances were shown on evening news programs in Ladysmith, Fort Lanier, and the state capital, each with an adulatory commentary and a brief interview with Rakestraw in his obsolescent persona as a wronged country boy.

A wire service picked up Michelle Boyer's story from the *World-Ledger*, and it was reprinted in newspapers nationwide.

In the wake of these events, a clip of Rakestraw's Tiernan-Pointer performance, originally filmed by the CBS affiliate in Fort Lanier, appeared the following Friday evening on network news, after which a rash of new telephone calls struck the house. Nora, after talking briefly with a woman in Lebanon, Kansas, who said she wanted to touch Rakestraw's perfect body with her mind, unplugged the telephone jack in the den and then went upstairs to lift the phone in the bedroom out of its cradle.

"This is certainly the week of Thomas Rakestraw," she said disgustedly, coming back down the steps.

Rakestraw was standing in the foyer beneath the staircase. "I've plugged the phone in the den back in."

"Why?"

Assuming a languid Craig Tiernan posture, Rakestraw aped the actor's gestures and voice. "Because," he said insouciantly, "it's more than a tad likely we're going to be getting a very important call, m'lady."

"Tom," Nora said softly.

"What?"

"Knock it off, all right? Please just knock it off."

As well as he was able, Rakestraw knocked it off. "It's just that I'm pretty sure Tiernan is going to try to get in touch," he said. "That's all."

"To let you have your face back?"

"Probably to threaten to cut off our monthly compensation."

"That might be almost as good as the other." Nora turned clumsily and went back up the stairs.

Four calls and two and a half hours later, Rakestraw reached over from his easy chair and uncradled the telephone in response to its renewed ringing.

"Thomas Rakestraw?" said a voice through the wire.

"Yo." Was this old army slang or Spanish? Rakestraw didn't know. The word gave him a comfortable degree of distance from the apprehension he had begun to feel.

"This is Edgar Macmillan. Am I speaking to the same Thomas Rakestraw whom I met several weeks ago?"

"No."

"I'm sorry. I—"

"You're speaking with a different Thomas Rakestraw—whom, however, you did indeed meet several weeks ago."

Macmillan, after a silence, said, "You probably know why I'm calling, Mr. Rakestraw. Craig Tiernan has directed me to get in touch with you to point out that because you're presently in violation of the terms of our settlement, we intend to—"

"Halt my compensation payments."

Macmillan chuckled, maybe in surprise. "Of course."

"Well, Mr. Macmillan"—Rakestraw spoke into the phone with the authority of a prosecutor—"it's my opinion that you're just trying to steamroller me. I've had occasion to read the Physiognomic Protection Act very carefully, as well as the terms of our settlement, and nowhere in either is there any mention of the illegality of my impersonating the former plaintiff if I don't happen to resemble him facially. I no longer resemble him facially. My impersonations arise from an innate talent for mimicry that is exclusively my own, and Craig Tiernan has no lawful right to attempt to restrain the expression of that talent. Impersonators have long been a part of this business. Craig Tiernan himself is an impersonator, and if he denies my right to practice, he also denies his own."

Macmillan's subsequent silence led Rakestraw to believe that Tiernan was perhaps in the same room with his attorney. Were the two conferring because he had put a hitch in their assessment of his likely response? He hoped so.

"Mr. Rakestraw," Macmillan tentatively resumed, "it still remains the case that you're exploiting the talent, the work, and the personality of Craig Tiernan, and this infringement on his career is an actionable matter which may result in your having to *pay* damages rather than simply receiving them."

"Well, Mr. Macmillan, my 'infringement' on the career of Mr. Tiernan is a direct consequence of his infringement upon my life. I'd never even heard of the bastard before you came to Caracal. It's an accident of his own making that I'm impersonating anyone. Please tell him that I started with Craig Tiernan for pretty straightforward reasons, and that if I wanted to, I could do just about anybody I damn well choose, including his own most recent mother-in-law."

"We intend to sue for—"

"And I intend to countersue for unconscionable harassment after the indignity of having to forfeit the face I was born with."

"Mr. Rakestraw—"

"And when I press suit, you might remind Mr. Tiernan, he'll have to come to court. His plastic overlay photographs and my cranial measurements won't be able to speak for him. Craig Tiernan and Tom Rakestraw will occupy the same courtroom, and the publicity generated will be more than he bargained for and quite distinctive in its thrust as far as he and I are concerned."

"Mr. Rakestraw, you're . . . you're whistling in the dark."

"How much hate mail has Tiernan received this week?"

"Hate mail?"

"How many people have written to tell him what a jerk he is for depriving an innocent man of his own face?"

"I don't read Craig Tiernan's mail, Mr. Rakestraw."

"But it hasn't all been sympathetic gushings this week, has it?"

"No, it hasn't," Macmillan confessed. "But that's neither here nor there when—"

"It's there, Mr. Macmillan. Here the mail and telephone calls are mostly favorable. That's how I know what kind of communications your employer's been receiving."

"What exactly do you want?" Macmillan asked, a trace of desperation in his voice. Michelle Boyer had asked very nearly the same question more than a week ago, but the only honest reply Rakestraw could frame was one he could not bring himself to voice.

"I want to speak to Tiernan," he said instead.

"On the telephone?"

"In person."

"Do you propose to fly out here for that purpose?"

"Why doesn't he come here? It's all tax-deductible, after all. For him, anyway."

A silence, during which Rakestraw felt sure that Macmillan and Tiernan were discussing this turn of events. Maybe the attorney had a long-distance hookup with the actor, too, and maybe his, Rakestraw's, voice was being broadcast to Tiernan over a speaker in the attorney's office. If they were in the same room together, Rakestraw could hear none of their conversation.

Finally Macmillan said, "Mr. Tiernan has directed me to tell you he'll be happy to meet you at a neutral location within your own state. Maybe in a nearby community, if that's all right."

"Neutral location? Are he and I football franchises? Why can't he come here? We've got plenty of room."

"Think about that one a sec. or so, Mr. Rakestraw. You just might be able to come up with an answer."

"My family," Rakestraw said suddenly. "The effect on my family—Tiernan's worried about that."

Macmillan didn't reply.

"I'll make the preparations for his visit," Rakestraw said.

The owner of a theater complex in Ladysmith agreed to open one of his auditoriums at ten-thirty on a weekday morning so that Tiernan and Rakestraw could meet in a setting both private and apropos. Having these two people in his establishment, one of them an up-and-coming local boy, was incentive enough for the owner, but Tiernan had also consented to kick in an honorarium.

Rakestraw was the first to arrive. When he entered the drapery-lined theater, he found that *Phaedrus* was unraveling silently against the high, canted screen. The owner, ensconced in the projection booth, was paying homage to Tiernan with a showing of the most acclaimed and probably most neglected motion picture of the actor's career. Perhaps this homage encompassed Rakestraw as well, for the film—the first of Tiernan's that Rakestraw had ever seen—bore strangely on the terrible change in his life.

Even without the aid of the soundtrack Rakestraw could recall every word of Tiernan's voice-over narration for the dream sequence now unfolding. Halted midway down the left-hand aisle of the theater, he allowed himself to repeat these words under his breath: " 'My hands sink into something soft. . . . It writhes, and I tighten the grip, as one holds a serpent. And now, holding it tighter and tighter, we'll get it into the light. Here it comes!' "

Aloud, at the dream sequence's climactic moment, Rakestraw cried, " *'Now we'll see its face!'* "

Whereupon he heard the real Craig Tiernan say quietly, from the aisle opposite his, " 'A mind divided against itself . . . me. . . . I'm the evil figure in the shadows. I'm the loathsome one. . . .' "

Rakestraw turned to face the double whom he no longer resembled. Craig Tiernan was dressed from head to foot in white; a fine gold chain circled his neck and glinted in the diffuse illumination thrown by the movie projector. He hardly seemed real.

"That's been your basic assumption from the beginning, hasn't it? That I'm the loathsome one."

His heart thudding wetly, Rakestraw stared across a row of shadowy seats into a face he had often seen in his own bathroom mirror.

"Here I am, then. Direct to you from Oregon via Southern California. And this little tête-à-tête is holding up the production of a thirty-million-dollar epic. I'm supposed to be in Nairobi. Or Cairo. What do you have to say to me, Rakestraw?"

Rakestraw continued to stare.

"This is petty and self-indulgent," Tiernan said. "But the surgery's reversible. It's designed to be that way in case anything happens to the owner of the physiognomic rights in question. If you'll return to your own home and agree to stay there without any further infringement on me or my work, I'm prepared to grant you co-ownership of those rights. Macmillan will take care of the details. We'll even continue your emotional-hardship compensation."

"What happened to me is irreversible," Rakestraw finally said.

Tiernan took a step down the seat aisle toward Rakestraw. "You'll be all right when you get your face back. Some people just don't adjust very well to that sort of surgery. Even money doesn't help much. You're one of those people, I guess."

"I don't want my face back."

Almost as if dumbstruck, Tiernan halted. On the movie screen, Rakestraw noted peripherally, a man and a boy on motorcycles were climbing toward a stunning mountain lake. Crater Lake, probably. The man on the motorcycle was Craig Tiernan.

"What, then?" the actor himself said. "*Is* it more money?"

Rakestraw didn't respond.

"I'll up the payments if that's really the problem. Lord knows, I've brought this on myself. Just don't push me too far, Mr. Rakestraw. You're treading dangerous ground with these publicity-seeking impersonations."

"But I'm not breaking any law." Rakestraw was conscious of a shift of settings on the screen. Now Tiernan and another actor in a coat and tie were arguing mutely in a university classroom. Outdoors, indoors. The film was schizophrenic. "And it isn't money," Rakestraw added distractedly. "Not entirely, anyway."

"Goddamn it, man!" Tiernan suddenly raged. "What am I doing here, then? Did you have me come all this way just to show yourself you could do it? Just to prove you could get me in the same building with you?"

Rakestraw returned his eyes to the real Tiernan. "I thought you ought to see me," he said. "And vice versa."

"Why?"

"Listen, when Macmillan arrived to tell me I was violating your rights, we had nothing in common. Absolutely nothing, despite your long-distance concern about my face. Well, now that I no longer resemble you facially, we have a great deal in common. I find that I like that. If I took my old face back, people outside of Caracal wouldn't know who I was. They'd think I was you, and I'm not. We're more alike today than we were before you had me altered, and although there remains a difference that's important, I'd just like to . . ."

Tiernan, gripping the back of a theater seat, waited for him to conclude.

"I'd just like to thank you for opening up my life."

That night, in bed, he rehearsed for Nora for the fourth or fifth time the details of his meeting with Tiernan. Moonlight came into their bedroom from a dormer window, and Gabe, across the hall, moaned and twisted audibly in his bedding. The nights were growing warmer.

"It frightens me," Nora said when he was finished.

"It should," Rakestraw said, stroking his wife's hair. "It's always a little frightening, a new life. You never know where it's going."

"Where *is* it going, Tom?"

Rakestraw lay back and stared at the ceiling. When he closed his eyes, he seemed to see the ganglia of his own feverish brain, like roads branching in a hundred different directions.

"Nora," he said, without opening his eyes, "I feel filled with power. It came on me slowly, opening up inside me after the surrender that took my face. It's been like climbing out of a well into the light. I still don't recognize myself, but what I see isn't displeasing."

There was a small hitch in Nora's otherwise regular breathing.

Turning toward her, Rakestraw said, "What would you think about leaving Caracal? About selling the farm and going somewhere else?"

"This is all I've ever wanted, Tom."

"It was all I ever wanted, too—until Macmillan showed up and I surrendered to him. But I'm different now, for good or for ill. Something that was pent up has been set free, and I don't think it's going to go willingly back to where it came from."

"I'd have to think about it," Nora said evenly, turning her own eyes to the ceiling. "Where do you want us to go?"

"That's something *I* still have to think about, I guess."

Conversation failed. They lay side by side in the familiar bed, their hands touching, thinking toward tomorrow.

A spaceman home from the stars, haunted by Something he's seen . . . is this just a cliché, or perhaps an archetype? Maybe there's something out there that we fear to find, even as we search; maybe we've always suspected this.

It needn't be anything awful. In fact, perhaps quite the opposite. . . .

A SOURCE OF INNOCENT MERRIMENT
James Tiptree, Jr.

His eyes did not bear the look of eagles, his skin was not bronzed by the light of alien suns. Like most astro-explorers, he was a small, sallow, ordinary figure, compact and flexible, now sliding inconspicuously to paunch. His face, from the distance he had been pointed out to me, seemed ordinary too: boyish and a trifle petulant. He was sitting alone. As I came toward him through the haze and spotlights of Hal's place, he glanced up, and the very bright blue of his eyes was striking even in the murk.

"May I join you for a moment?"

He started to say no, and then looked me over. I'm not young and I never was Miss Galaxy, but I still have a companionable smile.

He shrugged. "If you want."

I sat down puzzled and wary. Clearly this was no situation to mention my being with GalNews. After what I hoped was a relaxed silence, I told him I was a historian—which was also true.

"I'm collecting data that will be lost forever unless somebody preserves it now. The scouts, the men and women who are the first humans to set eyes on an alien planet, sometimes have experiences so bizarre or improbable that they never get into the official records. They have no witnesses. If they report honestly, it's put down to cabin fever or nitrogen poisoning. Mostly they don't report. And then if some of it comes out later, it becomes barroom gossip, and the facts are soon lost in hype and garble. You know? . . . Some of the stories may be nonsense, but some of them have to be true, and very important. I feel deeply that someone should get it all down straight, while there's still time. I'm trying."

He grunted; not hostile, but not forthcoming either.

"Hal said you had quite a story."

Instead of answering, he shot a blue gleam of fury at Hal behind the bar.

"I use no names, by the way; I protect identities every way I can. My records are under numbers, which refer to other numbers, and the master set is in my safe on Pallas. Also I can disguise all the nonessential detail you want. . . . You did experience something extraordinary, didn't you?"

He really looked at me then, and I saw in the depths of the blue eyes a pain eating at him, a loss barely to be endured.

"Hal says you don't take the first runs anymore, after . . . whatever happened."

"No. I stick with the follow-up teams, where it's safe."

He had a good, patient voice, underlaid with obscure self-mockery. I saw he was drinking Hal's blue doubles, but they hadn't affected him yet. I knew he didn't mean physically safe; the teams going in to set up bases on Earth-type planets have an unpleasant casualty rate.

"Could you tell me why?"

He was gazing beyond me.

"Please, if you can. It's so important."

"Important. . . ." He sighed; I sensed he really wanted to let it out, but the self-discipline of silence was strong. "Well . . . we were way outside the Arm, see, checking out a cluster of promising-looking second-generation stars— Did you mean that, about the codes?"

I showed him my notebook: nothing but numbers. "Somewhere in here is a woman who saw a flight of winged hominids take off into empty space. And singing, where of course no sound could carry. Another is a man who fought a huge invisible hand in his cabin. They put the wreckage down to space paranoia: he'd been out twenty trips. You see, I can't tell who they are myself until I get back and go through the locked safes routine. Does it matter, so long as the facts are there?"

He sighed again, yielding. "Well, all right. . . . Anyway, we didn't find anything useful, just gas giants. I took the last run, out to a GS at extreme range. And I saw it had two inner planets in the life zone. One of them was nothing but a cinder, the atmosphere read solid CO_2, with the runaway heat effect. But the other was cool, it read out fine. I don't mean habitable yet, I mean it had its permanent atmosphere, nitrogen and water vapor, with the CO_2 going down fast, being taken up by calcium silicate rock. Not a trace of free oxy, of course—or rather, just a twitch from zero. Big ranges of volcanoes blowing like mad. It had to be changing fast. I hadn't heard of anyone catching an Earth-type planet right on the edge of atmospheric flip-over, so I decided to run on in for a look. I had plenty of fuel. The problem was air. Those scouts don't have a bionic regeneration like the big ships, maybe you know that."

"I thought you had some sort of catalytic recycler."

"Oh yes. Just enough to let you die slow after the tanks are empty. You have to figure close. But I had enough for two orbits easy. And the thing was, as soon as I got within tight scan range, I *knew* I had to get closer. There was . . . activity."

"The vulcanism?"

"No." He was staring past me, with his teeth bared. I was afraid Hal's specials were getting to him, but he went on very lucidly.

"It was a half-and-half planet, you see. All the landmass on one side, and the other all ocean. Not like our ordinary oceans, of course, not water. Hot and shallow and mephitic. What they used to call the primordial soup. Lot of electrical storm action going on. My readout showed that ocean was loaded with protolife, bits and pieces of proteins and nuclear material—the precursors of our kind of oxygen-based life. Anaerobic, methanogenic—are those the words? I'm no biologist. The primitive stuff that doesn't use oxygen. . . . People think of it as dumb, nothing, like a lot of clay that hasn't made bricks."

He drained his glass, signaled Hal for another.

"It was . . . beautiful. Not the land side, that was just silicates where it wasn't igneous. The ocean. Like a sea of jewels, like a sunrise in the water—oh hell, anything I say sounds stupid. I can't really describe it. The atmosphere there had a kind of ruby cast, lit up blue-white from tremendous lightning bolts, and in between the storms you could see the surface swirling with colors—gold and sapphire and coral and lavender and lemon and dark purple, all changing. No true green, of course. Except in one place where there was a great round rosette of floating algae. It was photosynthesizing, making oxygen. I'd really caught it just as the change was starting, you see."

"Was that the, what did you call it, the activity?"

"No. I mean activity, movement. Not like wave action, not like boiling. When the clouds cleared off I saw that all over that huge ocean the surface was formed up into unnatural-looking shapes that moved and pulsed and transformed into others. At first I saw only the big ones, like towers and ridges and crevasses. And then I saw they were covered and intermixed with smaller and smaller shapings—hillocks, lines, dark fuzzy patches like forests, clusters of geometrical blobs. And everything moving, changing, some slow, some fast. The whole thing—well, it was like flashes of a populated landscape. If you took a still shot of it you'd swear it was inhabited land, with cities, roads, dams, traffic—although I was too high up to have any idea of the details. It was never still. A couple of times there were glimpses of what looked like great battles, with organized masses and weird objects surging, and fires and explosions—and then peace again. I realized that it was exactly as if you were running a film of the history of a whole planet at incredible speed. Centuries, millennia of history flashing by. I couldn't keep track of it, I couldn't imagine what it was. All I knew was that it was alive, and I had to get down closer. And then just as I was passing over the far shore onto the rocky side . . . it hit me."

His breathing had quickened almost to sobs. I kept quiet.

"The joy," he said at last, in a heavy, dead tone. "Oh, God. That whole crazy sea of poison was exuding it. Radiating joy. At a thousand km up I was grinning like a fool, happier than I'd ever been in my life. It faded some while I was over land, and then came back stronger than ever as the coast showed over the horizon. I'd backfired down lower by then. . . ."

For a moment he seemed to be lost in pure wonder, and then noticed me again.

"You have to understand it wasn't anything we would call life that was doing it, see. It was some kind of prelife, the transient forerunner. Doomed to die—in fact it was starting to die. *And it knew it.* Somehow I was sure of that. And yet it was broadcasting this innocent gladness, this contagious, childlike glee. All alone by itself, it was *playing.* And when I came over the shore again I began to suspect what it had found to play with. . . . Say that somehow it could foresee the oxygen-based life to come, the life that would kill it. And it was amusing itself by running through a show of the whole damn future history of that planet."

"But—"

"I know. It's impossible. But I became absolutely certain, although I kept telling myself it was just a brew of mindless molecular fragments.

By that time I was down to one-fifty km; my scope showed me the flickering forms of alien animals and people and their artifacts. If you could have *seen* it—the momentary panoramas of empires spreading out and falling, the huge engineering structures flashing into being and back to dust again, and everything growing more complex as it evolved and changed and vanished away—and always with this aura of delight, a great joyful play."

"You mentioned film—"

"No. I said 'if.'" His tone was abruptly savage. I understood that something had happened there. If his cameras had been running he must have destroyed the film. Why?

"You couldn't catch the essential thing," he said more quietly. "The incredible harmless happiness, the acceptance. It was enchanted just to be, to play its game of foreseeing, even if what it saw was based on its own death. It wasn't afraid or saddened at all, it was even using that damn lethal patch of oxygenating algae in its structures . . . and sending out its joy. To me, to the universe. . . . I can't tell you what it felt like, all pain gone, all fear gone, all the crap—just deep, total joy, that's the only word. Nothing like sex or drink or drugs, nothing like anything you've ever known, except maybe in dreams. . . ."

He fell silent.

"Well, I do thank you." I started to close my notebook. "That is something I shall always remember."

He gave a short, harsh laugh. "There's more," he said painfully.

"Oh?"

"As I was on my second pass over—that should have been the last one—I saw a new change. And I realized it was becoming aware of me, of me personally, I mean. Suddenly an Earth-type spaceport formed below, and a familiar lake, and the flash of a house I knew. Like signals. And an increase of delight, as if it was discovering a fine new game. And then glimpses of more and more personal stuff—the lab, my aircar, the ship, roads and places from my childhood, all mixed up. It seemed to be reading me deeper and deeper, and it loved it. Believe it or not, I loved it too—I heard myself laughing. Ever notice how pretty a traffic tower is? . . . And people's faces, friends, even a guy I hated, big as a mountain—you must understand, the scale of sizes was chaotic, and things dissolved into each other. But all suffused with this gladness. . . . And then my folks, my family, covering half the sea, and lit with this glow, this sort of sweet playfulness as if it was proud of itself and wanted me to share. . . . Funny, I've always felt better about what happened to Dad after that. . . . But I was coming over the shoreline, and then . . ."

"Then?"

He took a deep drink.

"Well, I had to cut out and go back, see. The oxy. But I couldn't. The last glimpse I had of that ocean, it seemed to be building up a big cliff of foamy white stuff, I couldn't figure what it was. It didn't change and vanish like everything else as long as I could see it. I *had* to find out what it was. . . . And, oh hell, the truth was I couldn't bear to leave that wonderful happiness. Couldn't. So, over the land side, I refigured everything and decided I could make one more orbit if I didn't mind getting back to the ship half-dead. . . . Mind? What I really wanted was to stay and go round that planet until I strangled. Or even to dive down in and die in bliss. . . . How the goddamn training tells; I reset the program for automatic kickout after one more turn. Oh, God, I wish I hadn't."

He seemed to be out of words, looking at me as if I were an ape or a robot who couldn't possibly understand.

"You wish you hadn't gone back to the ship?"

"No. Yes, that . . ." he said blurrily. His voice was getting very low. "It was . . . that last orbit, see."

"What did you find?"

"Find? Felt—got burned forever, I guess." He started to take another drink and then seemed to become aware of what Hal's blues were doing to him. He put the glass down and straightened effortfully in his chair. When he spoke again his words were flat and clear.

"When I came around again, I saw that whole deadly sea was edged with this beautiful creamy white lace. Joyful, like—like as if you could see laughter. And as I came over it, it opened. It was a goddamned gift box."

He did take a drink then, looking far away.

"Most men don't have it, I guess. The lucky ones. But some do—maybe women too, God help them. I'm one of those that have it. The *dream*, you know. The ideal. Quite explicit, vivid. Your perfect, ideal woman. The one you long for, seek for, knowing it's hopeless. You take other women because they seem to remind you of her, body or soul, for a time. Body and soul . . . there she was."

He was forcing his voice, the words coming out harshly.

"She was lying on that lacy stuff, naked. Flawless. Perfect and flawless. And absolutely alive. I could see her sweet belly breathe, her wonderful breasts blushed a little. Her long thick lashes—her eyes were closed—were trembling on her cheeks. . . . She was as big as a planet, of course, and I was a midge in the sky, but it didn't seem that way. She seemed normal-sized, or rather, we were both the same. . . . I slowed down as far as I dared, just drinking her in. She stirred a little, I could see every intimate part of her. Totally exposed, totally innocent. . . . The sexual impact was unbelievable. I wasn't laughing anymore. They—it—whatever had created her had even used that deadly algae rosette to make a sort of flower bouquet in the crook of her arm, I could see it hurting her beautiful skin. . . ."

His face creased with pain.

"Yes. . . . It—they—didn't mean to hurt me, you know. It just read what I wanted and gave it to me, in delight, as well as it could. And I think I could have stood the physical thing, the violent sexual lust . . . I think. But as I came over her she opened her eyes and looked directly up at me. And the deepest, wildest bliss a man can imagine enveloped me. All the joy that ocean could project was looking from those huge eyes into mine. Sex? God, it was ecstasy. She *knew,* you see—she knew all about me, and about herself, and we loved. How shall I say? A marvelous fond complicity, as if we had lived all our lives together. I tried—I tried to tell myself it was just a hundred billion shreds of proteins and viruses somehow reflecting me, but I couldn't. She was a living person, a living, loving person. And *mine.* . . . Then she smiled, the most beautiful smile, with a sweet quirk of playfulness. Total sharing . . . oh, God, I was in heaven. If I hadn't been paralyzed with wonder I would have killed the orbit and gone down to her. But she wasn't calling or luring me down in any way, you understand, it wasn't any dumb siren stuff. She was just so happy I was there. . . . And then my orbit carried me to the coast. I saw her raise her head and push back her floating hair to look after me. And then just at the very last her expression changed. It only lasted an instant—it was like being mortally cut with a razor, you don't feel it at the time. One heartbreaking look of sadness—love and loss and good-bye. As I say, it was over in a flash, and all was joy again . . . and the lovely smile. . . . But I—I—it nearly—"

He drank again, and then again more deeply.

"I had to leave then, of course. If I hadn't laid the course in on automatic I couldn't have. Couldn't. I almost punched it out. . . . If I had it to do over again, I would have. Just to keep tasting of heaven. . . . As I left the system I could feel it dying away, the joy; the hell we call life coming back. I tried to hold on to it. I was still imagining I could feel it when I did run out of oxy. . . . When the scout docked and they peeled me out I remember the human air smelled like poison, and I tried to punch Grober, the crew chief. . . . Later on I told them there was nothing there."

He was silent a minute. Emotion seemed to have burned the drink out of him, but his eyes were sick.

"I keep wondering, do you suppose that happens everywhere? The forerunners, a strange unliving life, knowing it's transient and doomed, but foreseeing all, accepting all—and laughing? The most beautiful thing in the universe, existing only for cosmic seconds. Do you suppose it happened on Earth, happens everywhere before the dull bloody grind of oxygen life begins? . . . The sweetness . . . and I left it."

He noticed me again.

"Do you see why I'm through scouting?"

"You mean, in case you run into another?"

He sighed; I saw I hadn't quite understood. Maybe no one could. "That. Yes. Dreading, wondering if there're more." Fatigue and liquor overcame him then, his head sagged into his fists. "I don't want to know," he mumbled. "Let somebody else get burned. God help them. . . . God help them . . . I don't want to know."

For some time now, R. A. Lafferty has been writing stories about the four men who know everything. A tricky subject for someone who doesn't claim to know everything himself, but . . . well, maybe Lafferty knows things that you and I don't know. (And perhaps he makes some up.)

AND ALL THE SKIES
ARE FULL OF FISH
R. A. Lafferty

I.

> Beware aesthetics throwing stones
> (We state it here prologgy).
> Oh by our fathers' busted bones
> We'll fight with dint and doggy!
> —"Rocky McCrocky" comic strip

Austro was still only twelve years old, and Chiara Benedetti had just had her thirteenth birthday and so had to resign from the club. She nominated Austro to take her place.

Ivan Kalisky had also turned thirteen and would have to get out of it. He nominated his little, fat, freckled, glasses-wearing sister Susie Kalisky to take his place. Susie Kalisky looked a lot like the Susie Kalusy in the "Rocky McCrocky" comic strip.

There was another vacancy in the gang. One small boy who shall be nameless had been expelled when it was discovered that he was as yellow as a daffodil. Austro, as soon as he was confirmed as a member, nominated his dog for this other vacant place.

"People will laugh at us if we have a dog for a member," Dennis Oldstone said.

"People won't laugh a whole lot at a dog that can swallow them in one swallow," Austro argued.

"And there *is* a certain prestige in having the biggest dog in the world as a member," Lowell Ragswell supported Austro. So they accepted the dog into their club. And they had gotten their membership in shape just in time.

There was another group of young people around; these were pure-hearted and aesthetic, and they had psychokinetic powers that reflected their pure-heartedness. They danced willow dances and they wore sweet-gum leaves in their hair. And it had been announced that they would give a public demonstration of their powers. There was quite a bit of scientific interest in the demonstration.

But the gang that Susie and Austro and the dog had just joined was more known for its fish fries than for its pure-heartedness. And it was known for its harassing of those aesthetic kids. In its reorganized form, it now took the name of "The Local Anaesthetics" to show that it was at war with the aesthetic kids. It had never had a name before this.

Along about this time, Barnaby Sheen was opinionating to some of us.

"We deal in facts at our place," he said. "We are open-minded, but we do not let just every wind blow through. We respect the new as well as the old, but we do know that some things must be rejected instantly. There are people around here who still haven't rejected the pretensions of those willow-dancing, rainmaking kids. Austro, you have assured me twice that you don't belong to that whey-witted bunch of squid kids, but I keep hearing tales about you. Assure me one more time that you're not a member of them."

"By the busted bones of my fathers, I am not a member of the willow dancers," Austro swore the oath truly. And that was the start of that.

The willow-dance children were to give a "Sunshine and Showers" presentation right in the Civic Center Area to show their powers and to promote science and inquiry. They had the full support of the city magistrates in this. Our magistrates were all proud of those talented and scientific children, and we were all proud of our magist—

"We sure do have good-looking magistrates in our town," Barnaby Sheen would say with that forked tongue of his. "They're not as competent as we'd like. They're not as dedicated as we'd like. They haven't much integrity. They bumble and they stumble, and they're just not very smart. But they *are* good-looking."

"And it will be a good-looking show that they put on," George Drakos said. "We are all for pure-hearted and aesthetic children with a scientific bent, and we are all for willow dancing (what is it anyhow?); we are certainly for 'Sunshine and Showers' in proper proportion. I, at least, do not reject the weather-making powers of these children instantly. If they do it, then it can be done. Let us see the presentation."

"The weather influences me a lot, and maybe I influence the weather a little bit," Harry O'Donovan stated. "If I had my life to do all over again, I believe that I could influence the weather and many other things much more than I did. Well, these children do have lives to do all over again. They start where we left off. Children aways did have special powers. We tend to forget about it, but even we had a smattering of powers once."

"Ah, peacock pug, we did not!" Barnaby Sheen argued. "There are no special powers."

"I myself haven't any doubt that humans do influence the weather," Cris Benedetti said. "The ideal system is to let the towns go dry-shod in their sunshine, and let the farmers enjoy their needed rain. As a general thing, that has always been the real as well as the ideal case. There are records to confirm this. Cities do have (from the viewpoint of cities) more pleasant weather than do the countrysides: milder in summer, milder in winter also, dryer most times, and more sunny and more smiling than country places. This is because, in the cities, there are greater numbers of minds working for fine weather. The people of a town, by their desires and sympathies, can literally hold an umbrella over a town and protect it from inclement weather. But in the country there is need for great falls of rain and for, ah, sometimes showers of proteid matter also."

"Into each rain some albuminoid must fall," said Austro. "That's a proverb."

"Prayers for rain have been part of the furniture of the Church from the beginning," George Drakos commented. "They have always been effective, but perhaps they were more effective when the majority of the people were rural. Dozens of great historical droughts have been broken by the fervent prayers of the peoples."

"I don't doubt the efficacy of prayer," Barnaby said. "But I will doubt the efficacy of this weather-making pseudo-science that has been shoveled into tender children's minds by certain mentors. And I doubt the efficacy of the little fetish magic that the children themselves contribute to it."

"The fetish magic of children *is* a form of prayer," Cris said. "And both prayer and fetish magic have scientific backing (read Manolo

Grogly and others). Prayers are legitimate scientific requests, and they do often receive scientific answers in the form of rain from heaven, and even in the form of bread and fish from heaven."

"Aw, porcupine pellets!" Barnaby barked.

"Consider our two weathermen on the evening broadcasts," said Harry O'Donovan. "What they really present is ritual, scientific prayer. And, as is always the case, one of them is of good influence and the other one is evil. Dean is a good-weather man. Keen is a bad-weather man. And they defer to each other. One of them will give a listless presentation on the evening that the other one gives a passionate show: and the sense of the situation goes out to the people. With a good-weather feel in the air, seventy percent of the clients will tune in on Dean, and the good weather for the morrow will be even better. With a bad-weather feel in the air, seventy percent of the clients will tune in on Keen, and the bad weather for the morrow will be even worse."

"Aw, turtle dirt!" snapped Barnaby Sheen.

"The four men who know everything," jeered the twelve-year-old Austro, "and they don't know weather from wolfmagite!"

(Barnaby Sheen, George Drakos, Harry O'Donovan, and Cris Benedetti were the four men who knew everything.)

Amelia Corngrinder, one of the aesthetic children, was making it rain a very local shower into Donners' front-yard birdbath. She did this by mental and spiritual powers alone. Several persons were watching her and admiring. One lady (well, it was Amelia's own mother, Ellen Corngrinder) was admiring Amelia out loud.

"This is angelic power!" Ellen was crying out. "This is a miracle that my girl performs by sheer mentality and grace and goodness. This is controlled and pure rain from the sky. It's wonderful."

"What's wonderful about it?" asked Austro, who was watching. "It only has to come a mile, and it's downhill all the way."

"Buzz off, fuzz-face," the angelic-powered, willow-dancing Amelia told Austro out of the corner of her mouth. It was a controlled and directed remark that was heard only by Austro and by that fat little freckled girl Susie Kalisky, who also happened to be there.

"It just seems that something is lacking," Susie said. "There is something wrong with empty water, and there is something lonesome about uninhabited rain. Nobody lives in your rain, Amelia."

"Broom off, crack-eyes," the pure-hearted and aesthetic Amelia hissed a controlled hiss at Susie. And then she willow danced some more and drew down still more rain. It was absolutely pure rain.

"I like there to be some *body* to the rain," Susie said. Then she cupped her mouth and her voice skyward and bawled out, "Does anybody live in that house?" And there was either a slight clap of thunder or a hoarse murmuration of cold-blood voices above.

"I do believe that you two are envious," said the mother, Ellen Corngrinder, to Austro and Susie. "Why must you be like that? You two could hardly be called 'beautiful children' in any sense of the term."

"Your glasses are cracked, lady," Susie said. And Ellen Corngrinder's glasses were indeed cracked. Austro and Susie walked on up the street.

How long does it take a sarcodic mass to fall a mile? From the time that there was either a slight clap of thunder or else a hoarse murmuration of sky voices, it took—just that long! A very large and lively body smashed out of the sky into Donners' birdbath and shattered the thing into shards of Granite Mountain Simulated Pressed Stone of which it was made. And, with this distraction, Amelia Corngrinder lost control of the little shower, and it unfocused and dispersed into a thin sprinkle over several blocks.

"Your glasses are cracked, sir," Susie said to a gentleman in the next block, and sure enough they were. Susie always noticed cracked glasses before the owners did. The Susie Kalusy of the "Rocky McCrocky" comic strip would shatter the flint-glass lenses out of folks' spectacles for pure malevolence and leave the rock frames hanging empty on the mortified faces. But Susie Kalisky was a slightly different person, and how could she smash eyeglasses by thought alone?

It rained foreign matter that night all over the south part of town. It was very strong sarcodic substance and it offended everyone within nose shot.

"There's something a little bit funny about this!" Barnaby Sheen bellowed when he saw it the next morning. "Austro, did you make it rain? —Oh, what's gone wrong with my wits? How could the kid make it—well, I already have the words in my mouth and I'm not going to swallow them again. Austro, did you make it rain that—ugh—stuff?"

"What a strange question, Mr. Sheen! All I will say is that I did not do anything to prevent it raining that stuff. Is that a good enough answer?"

"No it isn't. Say, that's about the strongest I ever smelled! You could hardly praise it for its downwind flavor, could you?"

"It wouldn't be so bad, Mr. Sheen, if it were seasoned with just a few bushels of wielandiella fronds."

"Is that the stuff your dog eats?"

"That's some of the stuff that he eats."

Austro's dog came then. It had slipped in from the country for an early-morning visit. It was, as you know, a very large creature. It had been clearing blackjack oak trees and thickets off of a few sections of land forty miles to the west. Flamethrowers and eight-way power saws and the strongest bulldozers in the world wouldn't clear those blackjacks very well, but that dog could get rid of them; and he got his needed roughage doing it. Now he wanted a little bit of more satisfying fare. And that more satisfying fare fell down for him with a muted but heavy jolt. It was 180-foot-long crinoid stems, and it was huge fronds of macrotaenopteris ferns.

Austro told the dog that he had been accepted for membership in the smoothest club in town, and the dog croaked pleasure. Barnaby patted that biggest-dog-in-the-world of Austro's, and then he went about his daily business.

2.

The world's a blast (Ka-whoosh! Ka-whish!)
With healthy soul and belly,
And all the skies are full of fish,
And all the fish are smelly.
　　　　—"Rocky McCrocky" comic strip

The weather happening was scheduled for one o'clock that afternoon in the Civic Center Open-air People's Area. Press people and university people and scientific people would be there. And all the city magistrates would be present: Arthur ("It's pretty but is it Art?" Barnaby Sheen used to say about him) Topmann, the mayor. Topmann really was a good-looking man, and he liked to serve the people, and he liked almost all children. Almost all of them.

"Your glasses are cracked, Mr. Mayor," said that little, fat Susie Kalisky, who just happened to be there. And the mayor's glasses *were* cracked as soon as she said it.

There was Gaberdine McPhillips, the lady commissioner of playgrounds and sewers. Gaberdine was offering, from her own funds, a money prize to the young person who could make it rain the purest rain. Gaberdine had a thing about pure water.

"Your glasses are cracked, madam," Susie told her, and they were. But had they been cracked just a moment before?

There was George H. Corngrinder, who was commissioner of streets and who was also the father of Amelia Corngrinder, who was one of the willow-dance youngsters who had now seized the scientific community by the ears.

There was Peter Kalisky, the police commissioner, who was a gruff man.

"Austro, get that sign out of here or I'll pitch you into the pokey," he called now.

"You can't," Austro said. "I'm a juvenile, and besides I belong to an alien species. Your anti-poster ordinances don't apply to me."

Austro belonged to the species *Australopithecus*. The sign or poster that he was putting up there in the area read:

COSMIC, FREE FISH FRY! WE REALLY KNOW HOW TO FIX THEM! COME TO SHEEN'S RAVINE AT ONE-THIRTY TODAY (IMMEDIATELY AFTER THE DEBACLE). EVERYBODY COME.

"Get it out of there, Austro, or I'll put the police dogs on you," Commissioner Peter Kalisky thundered.

"The dogs are all afraid of me," Austro said. "They know I own the biggest dog in the world."

"Your glasses are cracked, Mr. Commissioner," that fat, freckled little Susie Kalisky said. And Peter Kalisky's glasses were cracked. They were cracked so recently that glass slivers were still tinkling to the pavement.

"Dammit, Susie, I'm your father!" Commissioner Kalisky roared, and with shocking cruelty he swatted that little girl where she was biggest.

"Oh, wah, wah, wah," Susie blubbered. "I keep forgetting. How'm I supposed to remember everyone?"

The willow dancers were gathered and they were ready for it. They were effective from the very start. Little clouds began to form and to dance in the sky with the same shape and motion the willow dancers showed. It was winding into the most graceful rain that anybody had ever seen.

"It's a fraud all the way," Barnaby Sheen gruffed. "There is no way

that such an empty-eyed aggregation of kids could make it rain. I
wouldn't believe it if I drowned in it."

"Your glasses are cracked, mister," Susie Kalisky said.

"Susie McGoozy, you know I don't wear glasses."

"Then get some, and we can enter into a whole new relationship."

Barnaby Sheen and Susie Kalisky liked each other.

"There is no way that they can make it rain," Barnaby said again.

"There's a dozen ways they can do it," said that young Roy Mega
who worked as an electronic genius for Barnaby. "There's half a dozen
ways that I could do it myself, and I've almost left off being a kid. I
could set up a simple astasis voltage grid, and I could add a bleeder cir-
cuit with one reflecting nexus located just above the predominant cloud
layer at five thousand feet. Then I'd build up a hysteresis shield to a
point just short of coronal discharge. Then, by the addition of almost
any Keefe-Minsky equation, I could—"

"No, no, Roy," Barnaby protested. "I mean that there's no way that
a person could make it rain by use of the mind."

"This would be by use of the mind. I'd arrange all those things by
use of my mind."

"By your mind alone, Roy; not by tools of the mind."

"Oh, that's like saying that one may use his hands but not the
fingers of his hands," Roy Mega complained.

Those aesthetic children—Amelia Corngrinder with her controlled
grace and goodness; Aldous McKeever with his exquisite pallor and his
high psychic threshold; Horace Wickiup, who was an Indian (and you
know how full of rain they are); Margaret Grainger; Adrien Chastel;
Alice Whitetoken (who was very spiritual, as her mother had been
also); Rolland Clatchby—they were all doing the rain-willow dance.
They were rolling their eyes; they were breathing hard (but always in
good taste): and their seven clouds in the sky had turned into seven
sparkling showers that began to spill down, under absolute control, into
the Civic Center fountains.

"I'll not believe it," Barnaby Sheen said sourly. "It isn't scientific."

"Let's say that it is prescientific," Roy Mega suggested. "It works, but
we don't yet know how it works."

"I bet that's the biggest dog in the world over there," a woman
among the spectators said to her husband.

"Yes, I heard that some monkey boy in town had the biggest dog in the world," the husband said.

"Oh, but now it's gone. I can't see it anywhere. Instead of it I see a big hairy hill over there. I bet it's thirty feet high. What would a big hairy hill be doing in the middle of the Civic Center Plaza?"

"I imagine that the city fathers had it put there for the children to play on," the husband said. But when you are as big as that dog, and you live in a world as small as this one, you learn the art of camouflage.

"Let's say that it's pseudo-science." Barnaby still balked (and there were now seven pretty good showers of rain coming down all asparkle into the fountains). "It works, yes, apparently, and for the moment at least. But I bet it can be unworked. Austro, can you unwork it?"

"What do you think all our huffing and puffing's been about? We're on your side, Mr. Sheen. Parascience will beat pure pseudo-science every time. Local Anaesthetics, come get with it! Susie! Dog! Dennis! Lowell! They're leading us on points!"

"Your glasses are cracked, sir," Susie remarked to a gentleman as she hurried to the assembly of the Locals. And the gentleman's glasses *were* cracked.

"Oh, look, Reggie," that woman among the spectators said to her husband. "Now that big hairy hill is getting up and walking off."

"They're probably not going to use it today, what with the rain-makers and all."

But those pure-hearted and aesthetic children with their rainmaking willow dances were far ahead of the Local Anaesthetics on points. The Locals would have to play catch-up ball. Those were plumes and sheens of the purest rain that anybody ever saw.

It was now or never. The Locals put their heads and their hearts together to generate what power they might. A fish crashed to the pavement there amid the throng.

That was a crash? You couldn't have heard the sound of it a block. That was a fish? Why, that thing wasn't more than three feet long.

"We might as well let the empty-water people have it if we can't do any better than that," Dennis said.

An anomalous frond of macrotaenopteris fell down there with a muted but heavy jolt. That was a heavy jolt? Why, that frond wasn't twenty feet wide, and it wasn't twenty million years old. That was the biggest dog in the world with his snout in this business? A little Great

Dane could do that well. The Local Anaesthetics would have to muster more power than this.

"How are you going to get the fish out to Sheen's Ravine, Austro?" Roy Mega asked.

"I never thought of that," Austro admitted. Austro was panting already, and the battle looked bad for the Locals. "Maybe Dog would carry them out there in his mouth," Austro said.

"Fish?" Barnaby asked. "What fish? Will there be many fish?"

"Quite a few, I believe," Mega said, "though I'm not sure quite what the kids have in mind."

"Better go get the twelve-ton truck, then, Roy," Barnaby said. "Some people might be fussy about the dog carrying the fish in his mouth." So Roy went to get the heavy truck.

A few of the larger fish fell, but most of them weren't much longer than a man. Quite a few of the long crinoid stems swacked down to earth, and many really big wielandiella and macrotaenopteris ferns from the ancient days. The dog was getting with it now. He was drawing bigger stuff down from the Tertiary skies. He was doing a better job than the kids in the gang were.

(Several persons, George Drakos and Roy Mega among others, have said that Austro's big dog was really a hairy dinosaur. You can believe this if you want to, but you should notice that there are points of poor correspondence between them. Go look at the anklebones of a dinosaur, for instance. Then look at the anklebones of Austro's big dog. How about it?)

There were bigger and more weird sky falls now, but the Local Anaesthetics just weren't stealing the initiative from the willow-dancing, pure-water kids. The limpid showers of the dancers were just doing too many sparkling things. And yet there was real talent to be found among the L.A.s. There was Austro. There was Dog. There was Susie.

"Almost every time the world is turned around it's a little trick that does it," Susie said. "I'll just try a little trick." And she went boldly into the area of the enemy, into the lair of the pure-pseudo-science, rain-dancing young people.

"Your glasses are cracked, kids," Susie told them. And the glasses of all seven of them were cracked (all aesthetic, willow-dancing children wear glasses). And something else about them cracked at the same time. It was their protective psychic carapaces. It was their science itself.

The tide of battle swung to the Local Anaesthetics. Something else was falling to the pavements of the area now. It was the scales from the eyes of the people. Now the folks were able to see the monstrous crashing ichthyoids that had been, or would be, or maybe already were fish. Ancient sorceries will whip modern fetishes every time, and it was a case of that.

Man, that's when they pulled the stopper out of the drain and let it all come down!

People loaded up the twelve-ton truck that Roy Mega arrived with then. And then they brought in a number of really big trucks and loaded them with the gloriously smelling old fish and the earlier-age crinoids and giant fern fronds. And a great number of loaded trucks as well as several thousand people went out to Sheen's Ravine for the enjoyment.

"My magic can whip your magic and my dog can whip your dog!" Austro called to the aesthetic remnant.

Out at the ravine, it was fun to cut up crinoid stems with axes and crosscut saws. It was fun to bruise the fronds of large and early ferns and palms (Ah, that was a palmy hour!) with pneumatic hammers. And then to use that royal vegetation to garnish the big and powerful fish, to bring out the nobility of their strong smell and taste, that was to know what an enjoyment and a banquet were all about.

"Where those rain dancers and the big people who sustained them made their mistake," Dennis Oldstone was lecturing like an even younger Roy Mega, "was that they didn't understand the vastness of the universe. They—"

"Duck, everybody! There's no way he won't think of it!" Susie wailed the warning.

"—they only understood the half-vastness of the universe. Luckily, enough of us with enough scope to handle the situation happened to be around."

"I suppose that I'll have to accept it," Barnaby Sheen was saying. "It's a fractured plane of reality that is introduced here. I can brush up on my fractured-plane equations, or I can have Roy Mega review me on them. Ah, I find that little shower rather refreshing. And the fish really isn't bad, Austro."

Susie Kalisky (or Susie Kalusy; it depends on which part of the fractured plane you are on) was focusing a shower of inhabited rain right on the head of Barnaby Sheen. The shower was inhabited by frogs and fish and eels and claw-feet that bedecked the wet head and shoulders of Barnaby as he ate (along with five thousand other people) the fried and garnished fish.

"It's not really bad fish the way it's fixed," Barnaby admitted. "The garnish is so strong that one can't taste the fish, and the fish is so strong that one can't taste the garnish. But where did it really come from, Austro?"

"There's a pool about a mile from here, Mr. Sheen. It's plain loaded with those big old fish. And the banks and bottom of it are loaded with those big old plants. It was Dog who first discovered it."

"Your glasses are cracked, mister," Susie Kalusy said to a fish-eating man there.

"That's all right, little girl. They never did fit me. I don't look through them. I look over them." He was a nice man.

"The pool's only a mile from here, Austro?" Barnaby Sheen asked. "Which way?"

"Up."

With the advance of technology, the range for artistic endeavors also widens: new art forms are invented, existing forms are augmented by new techniques. Humans, of course, remain central, for it's they who must interpret and use the new artistries.

Lee Killough, whose novels include A Voice Out of Ramah *and* The Doppelganger Gambit, *writes of anomalies and dangers in one new art form, in this colorful novelette set in her future artists' colony of the Aventine.*

BÊTE ET NOIR
Lee Killough

On gray days, when the clouds hang in heavy pewter folds and the wind comes down cold and sharp as a blade, I think of Brian Eleazar. We stand facing each other in the sand garden, surrounded by the elaborate and alien patterns of rock outcroppings in a score of minerals and dunes of a dozen different colored sands. The sand underfoot is fine and white as sugar over a deeper layer of red. Across it, between us, a trail of footprints shows scarlet, as though they were stepped in blood.

Gateside was still thawing out from winter when I arrived at the Blue Orion Theater to join the cast of Zachary Weigand's new play. Leaden clouds shrouded Diana Mountain, hiding the stargate above the city. The wind blowing over the remaining traces of snow and ice left me shivering, despite the efforts of my coat, which fluffed itself and clung to me like a frightened cat. For as long as it took me to pay the cabdriver and hurry across the sidewalk into the theater, I thought with regret of the movie I had turned down to take this part. It was being made in southern Italy, where the sky was almost certainly clear and the sun shining.

As I pushed through the doors into the Blue Orion, a guard came out of his station, ready to turn back anyone who did not belong here. "May I help—" He broke off, a smile of recognition spreading across his face. "It's you, Miss Delacour. Mr. Eleazar said you'd be coming. Congratulations on the Tony nomination for *Silent Thunder*. I hope you win. Are you going to play Simone in the movie, too?"

I smiled back at him. "If my agent has any influence at all I will."

"I'll keep my fingers crossed. Before you go in, may I have your autograph?"

He brought a book from his station. I took it and thumbed through looking for a place to sign. I would be in Olympian company, I saw. The pages already signed carried the signatures of the theater's greatest, personalities like Lillith Mannors, Eden Lyle, Walter Fontaine, and Maya Chaplain. I found a new page and signed it in a precise hand with ornate capitals: Noir Delacour.

It reminded me why I was here instead of in southern Italy. Zach Weigand's name on a script was enough to fill a theater opening night, but when it was accompanied by that of Brian Eleazar, who had directed in almost every medium in his career and earned himself a shelf of Tonys and Oscars to prove how competent he was at it, the play was sure to draw the attention and acclaim of every major critic. *The Sand Garden* had the additional attraction of being a *théâtre vérité* production. Improvisation and scriptless drama had become very fashionable in the past few years, but *théâtre vérité* was the most popular. It was playing to huge, enthusiastic audiences all over the world.

And of course I could not overlook the fact that Brian Eleazar had asked me to be Allegra Nightengale.

"He was almost on his knees begging for you, pet," my agent said when he relayed the offer.

However histrionic he sounds, Karol Gardener rarely exaggerates. There was no real agony over which contract to sign, then. It meant a great deal when a director of Brian's stature begged for a particular actress. The director of the movie had not begged.

I returned the guard's autograph book. "Can you tell me where Mr. Eleazar is?"

"He's onstage with the rest of the cast. Go right on through there."

Warmth was seeping back into me. My coat loosened its grip on my arms and chest as the heat soothed and settled it. I could also feel my hair loosening from the hairpins. To the despair of hairdressers everywhere, it has the texture of quicksilver. I did not need a look in the lobby mirrors to know the wind outside had ruined thirty minutes of Raoul's best efforts. I pulled out the hairpins and let the whole pale, slithery mass fall free down my back as I went into the auditorium.

I love theaters. Full ones are best, of course, but I have a special fondness for empty ones. I love the sensation of hearing the ghosts of a thousand past performances still whispering in the musty silence, and of feeling the magic of performances yet to come waiting in golden expectation.

I listened to the ghosts as I made my way down the sloping aisle toward the stage in the center. Halfway down, though, I switched my attention to the three men standing in the pool of light onstage. Two were familiar faces. I had worked with both before. Tommy Sebastian's classic profile and lamb's-wool curls looked copied from a Grecian vase. With the help of cosmetisculptor surgeons, they probably had been. In contrast to Tommy's beauty, Miles Reed's face was so unremarkable it disappeared instantly from memory. He hardly existed as a person offstage. Miles was a blank canvas on which he painted every role with a new and different brush. I noticed he had shaved his head for this part.

The third man must be Brian Eleazar. He was smaller than I had expected. His head reached barely higher than Tommy's shoulder, but he radiated a presence I felt even from where I was. Above the turtleneck of his sweater, the craggy irregularity of his face, which the gossip columnists liked to describe as "Lincolnesque," had a compelling magnetism.

I had reached the stage without any of them noticing me. I made my presence known. "Good afternoon, gentlemen."

They turned. Miles shaded his eyes to peer past the lights. He grinned. "Noir." He came over to offer me a hand up the steps. "Congratulations on the Tony nomination."

Even Miles's voice was subject to change. Last time we met, it had been deep and rich. Today it was a sibilant hiss.

Tommy blew me a kiss. "Darling. 'She walks in beauty, like the night.'"

I squeezed Miles's hand in thanks before I let go and looked past him to lift a brow at Tommy. "That's nice, but do you ever learn more than the quotable bits?"

Tommy grinned, unabashed. "That's all it takes to impress most people."

Brian Eleazar nodded to me. "Good afternoon, Miss Delacour." His voice was unexpectedly deep, rumbling up from the depths of his chest.

I smiled at him. "I'm delighted to be here. I've been looking forward to working with you."

I extended my hand. He managed to ignore it and I pulled it back,

feeling annoyed and foolish. Once Brian had been legend for romanc-
ing his leading ladies. That had ended when Pia Fisher became a
fixture in his life, and apparently her influence remained even though
it had been a year since her death. After a few minutes, amusement at
my own reactions overcame the annoyance and disappointment of
being held so clearly at a distance. Only then did I discover that Brian's
cinnamon-colored eyes were fixed on me with searching intensity.

Before I could examine that expression, he turned away to four
chairs in the middle of the stage. "Now that we're all here, shall we
begin?"

A thin loose-leaf notebook lay on each chair: our playbooks. I found
the one with "Allegra Nightengale" printed on the cover and sat down.
The playbook would not be a script, of course; *théâtre vérité* uses no
scripts. The notebook contained the biographical history of Allegra
Nightengale.

The biography is what makes *théâtre vérité* unique. Instead of
merely ad-libbing from an opening situation, as in most improvisation,
or playing roles, as in conventional drama, actors in *vérité* learn the histories of their characters, absorb them until they know how the characters will think and feel and react to any given situation. Then, with an
angel's help, they *become* the characters. The action of the play
emerges from the natural response of the characters to each other.

And because many factors can affect a response—a variation in another's tone or inflection, a distracting sound, the normal day-to-day
difference in outlook—no two performances are ever quite alike. There
have been numerous examples of *vérité* productions with endings that
changed from night to night. The dynamic nature of the form, the
limitless possibilities in each new performance, are what brings in the
audiences.

I opened the playbook. The first page was a scenario of the opening
and a tentative outline of the action. Authors have some idea what they
want to happen. They design their characters to produce personalities
that will react in the desired manner. They also hedge their bets by
stating their expectations. No matter how involved the actors become in
their characters, then, the professional subconscious steers a course in
the right general direction toward a satisfactory climax.

"Read over the outline and opening scenario, please," Brian said.

I had seen the outline before in Karol Gardener's office when I
signed the contract, but I read it again. Brian paced while we did so,
and on every turn I felt his cinnamon eyes come back to me.

Allegra Nightengale and Jonathan Clay were lovers, the sun, moon, and stars to each other. Jonathan was also a speculator. He had an option to buy a cargo brought back by an exploration team from a planet the stargate had touched once and lost. Because the planet had no receiving gate, reestablishing contact with it was virtually impossible. That made the cargo priceless. Jonathan went to a Shissahn living on Earth for financial backing. Hakon Chashakananda was a careful businessman and demanded some security to insure the return of his loan. The opening scenario had Hakon, played by Miles, telling Jonathan, Tommy, to leave Allegra with him as a hostage until the cargo was sold and profits distributed.

I went on to the plot outline. If Zach Weigand had tailored Jonathan's character correctly, Jonathan would agree to the arrangement. Allegra would also agree, out of her love for Jonathan. She would be repelled by the alien, because of both his inhuman appearance and his demand for a hostage, but gradually she would find aspects of him to admire. He would be drawn to her in turn and eventually release her. On returning to Jonathan, however, Allegra would find herself looking at him with new eyes. She would find flaws in him she could not accept, and she would leave this once-beloved man of her own kind to return to the alien.

"All right," Brian said. "Study the bios tonight and start learning your characters. Do you all have your angels?"

Miles and I nodded. Tommy shook his head. Brian handed him a vial of minute white pills. "Don't take more than one. I don't want you to settle in too deep. Tomorrow we'll begin scenarios and bio alterations as necessary. I shouldn't need to, but I remind you not to discuss your bios with each other."

We all nodded. We knew not to. Too much knowledge of each other could interfere with the validity of the reactions. We should not know more than the characters naturally would.

"And in the same spirit," Brian went on, "I don't want you socializing with each other offstage." He looked at all of us but it seemed to me he stared hardest at Tommy.

We stared back. Not socialize? That was unheard of.

Tommy's eyes rounded in dismay. "Are we supposed to become hermits until the run is over?"

The cinnamon eyes looked through him. "I'm sure you can find friends among the locals."

"But casts traditionally spend time together offstage," Miles said.

"Théâtre vérité is not traditional drama." Brian paced down the line of us, like a drill sergeant before his troops. "It's my firm belief that when there's no script to follow and your reactions must all come up out of yourself, personal relationships inevitably affect those of the characters you're becoming. How can Allegra be repelled by Hakon the first time she meets him if Noir has been Miles's close companion?"

I have sometimes experienced personality bleeding during *vérité* productions, so I realized Brian had a point, but I thought his precaution against it was extreme. We were experienced actors, not amateurs, practiced in living with multiple personalities and keeping them separated. What bleeding there might be would not affect the performance noticeably.

Tommy said, "During *Rainbow Man,* Giles Kimner said he thought antagonistic characters should keep their distance offstage to avoid diluting the hostility, but he had no objections to sympathetic characters mixing, and even with the antagonists he never insisted—"

Brian cut him off coolly. "I'm not Giles Kimner, so I *do* insist that the only contact between you be here in the theater. Our job is to produce *The Sand Garden,* not party. Anyone who cannot live with my direction is free to leave the cast. In fact, I'll insist on it. Is that clear?"

Tommy shrugged. "Youse is da boss, massa." He sighed dramatically. "I hope I can find a friendly female soul somewhere in this bleak city to comfort me in my solitude."

"Do you two understand?" Brian looked at Miles and me in turn.

Miles nodded. I frowned—I liked Miles and Tommy and had been looking forward to spending free time with them—but I nodded, too. I could always hope Brian would relax his rules later, and until then I needed the time alone to learn who and what Allegra Nightengale was.

"That's all for now. Don't go into the substage until I give you permission to use the sets. I'll see you here ready to work tomorrow morning. Noir, I want you at nine o'clock; Tommy, at ten; and Miles, at eleven. We open in one week."

Tommy groaned. "The thing I hate about working up a play is getting up in the middle of the night to do it."

Brian's cinnamon eyes flicked over Tommy and passed on. He turned away. As he did, he looked at me one more time. His eyes remained fastened on me even while his body continued turning. He stepped forward beyond the circle of lights and disappeared.

Tommy brightened. "We're free. Anyone for a drink?"

Miles shook his head. "I'm not ready to buck the boss just yet."

"Noir?"

I waved my playbook at him. "Bio, Tommy. Study."

"I'm going to drink first." He stood and headed for the steps. "I saw some delectable creatures in the Beta Cygnus Café when I came by on my way here. Perhaps they're still there. *Au revoir.*" He blew us a kiss before he left.

Miles and I sat for a moment longer, just looking at each other. "Well, it was nice to see you again, Miles. I don't suppose we'll be doing any practice scenarios, since our characters have never met."

Miles stood. "We can at least walk to the door together. That's still in the theater." He offered me his arm down the steps.

I tucked my hand around his elbow. "Isn't Brian over-worried about personality bleed?"

I kept my tone noncommittal but Miles must have heard the irritation under the words. He said, "Not bleed. It's character carry-over that worries him. Don't you know how Pia Fisher died?"

"I know she drowned."

"It's how she came to drown." We reached the lobby. He stopped beside one of the aquarium benches and looked down through the transparent top at the fish swimming in bright flashes through the water and greenery inside. "Pia was the mermaid in *Rainbow Man* while it was touring in Hawaii. One afternoon she went out and tried to swim around one of the points along the coast. The trouble was, Pia couldn't swim."

I shuddered at the thought of that lovely young actress so caught in the grip of her angel-produced hallucination of being a mermaid that she had walked into the ocean. It explained Brian's attitude. We were much more likely to fall into carry-over characterization with each other than around unconnected outsiders.

"Poor Brian. Thank you for telling me." I waved to the guard as we left the theater. "Where are you staying, Miles?"

"The Diana Radisson."

I smiled. "Really? So am I. Much as I want to follow our director's orders, I think it would be a waste to call for two cabs, don't you?"

We shared the one Miles hailed. Despite Brian, we talked all the way to the hotel, catching up on where we had been and doing what with whom since the last time we worked together. I enjoyed every forbidden moment of companionship.

At the hotel, though, we went to our separate rooms. I changed into a comfortable robe and ordered hot tea from room service, then curled up in a chair with the playbook. I am a quick study. I read twice through Zach Weigand's notes on Allegra Nightengale and laid the playbook aside. Then I went to my bag for my angels. I took one.

I can never remember the full chemical name of the angels. They are a derivative of PCP, though. Government research developed it, the story goes, for use in espionage and the witness protection program. With it, spies could assume an undercover identity so completely they could not be blown even under drug or hypno interrogation, and the previous identities of hiding government witnesses would never be betrayed by old habits or mannerisms. Not only could the government guarantee a new identity; it could provide a personality to match.

Inevitably, the drug had leaked out onto the streets where trippers, ever on the lookout for a new high, gobbled it in high expectation. They were bitterly disappointed. It did not magically turn them into someone else. The angels are only a tool. A new personality requires study while using the drug. So eventually the trippers forgot about it, and actors started using it.

There's a new saying in the theater these days: that ordinary productions take one kind of angel, the one with an open checkbook; *vérité* needs two angels.

I began to feel the first effects of the angel. My head went light. It seemed I was looking at the room through binoculars, and that I heard sound from a great distance.

I lay back in my chair and mentally read the bio again. The words appeared printed across the inside of my eyes. While I read, I tried to visualize the people and scenes the words described. I created faces for Allegra's parents and friends. I built the houses, towns, and schools of her life. I looked at it all as it would be seen through Allegra's eyes, and included fine details, right down to the contents of her school locker.

As the images developed, I could feel myself slipping into Allegra. It is a feeling I enjoy, rather like pulling on a body suit. When I was finished she would fit me like another skin. The images would become "memories," and she become "I, Allegra," rather than her present "she, Allegra."

The phone rang. Even at its distance, I recognized the sound as part of the real world. I groped through the angel mist in my mind to reach for the receiver.

Tommy Sebastian's tenor voice sang over the wire with a slight lilt of intoxication. "I'm alone in a golden city with no one to properly appreciate my company. Come relieve my desolation, Noir. 'How do I love thee? Let me count the ways.'"

The sound of my name opened a hole in the angel mist. I became myself. I frowned. "Tommy, you're incorrigible. You heard what Brian said about seeing each other out of the theater."

"We can't possibly see each other. It's far too dark in this bar."

"How did you know where to call me?"

He assumed a British accent. "Elementary, my dear Watson. I called your agent and asked him."

I had to smile. "I'm sorry to put you to so much trouble when I can't accept the invitation. I'm working."

There was a pause, then, petulantly, "You take old Brian seriously, don't you?"

"I always take my work seriously."

"All work and no play—"

"No work makes a poor play," I came back. "Why call me? Surely there are some sweet things who will swoon in pleasure at the sight of your profile."

"Any number of them, I'm sure, but it's you I want. 'If I were king— ah, love, if I were king—/What tributary nations I would bring/To stoop before your sceptre and to swear/Allegiance to your lips and eyes and hair.'"

I sighed. "Tommy, please go away and let me study."

"'Had we but world enough, and time/This coyness, lady, were no crime.' You'll miss a terrific evening."

"So I will. Good-bye," I said firmly. "I'll see you tomorrow." I hung up.

I waited a couple of minutes to be sure he was not going to call back, then I let the angel mist wrap around me again and resumed pulling on Allegra's character.

Carry-over let me wear her to the theater. She looked back at me from the mirrored walls of the Blue Orion's practice hall, all pastels and soft focus, dressed in clinging baby blue, hair hanging down her back in a single braid, except for the escaping locks that curled in feathery wisps around her scrubbed face.

Over the shoulder of the image I saw Brian appear in the doorway. He regarded me critically, then nodded. "I see you're into her. Take another angel and let's try some scenes."

He opened his playbook and glanced through the notes on Allegra.

He chose random incidents from her life prior to the play's opening and played the roles of other people as we acted out the scenes. That is, he acted out the scenes; as Allegra, I lived them. The practice hall became a schoolroom, my home, an office, and Brian wore the faces of teachers, adolescent loves, and bosses. I, Noir, watched from the back of my head, evaluating my performance. Some of the emotions I felt and words I used amused me. Others made me wince. They were not what I would have said or felt. They seemed right for Allegra, though.

A little past ten, Brian laid his playbook on the piano and came back to my chair. "That's all for now, Noir."

I shook my head to clear out the angel mist and, with a mental somersault to fold Allegra away, resumed being Noir Delacour. "Evaluation, Mr. Director? Criticism? Applause?"

Brian stared at me with an expression so intense I felt as though I were being dissected.

I raised brows at him. "You don't agree with my construction?"

He blinked. "What? I'm sorry; I was thinking of something else for a moment. No, I've no objections. You've made her a warm, loving woman who will certainly do anything for Jonathan and find goodness in Hakon." He smiled. It was a tight gesture, quickly gone.

He had not intended to stare me apart, then. He had merely been looking my direction. I wondered what he had been thinking about. Had something Allegra said reminded him painfully of Pia?

Brian looked past me to the door. "You're late, Tommy."

Tommy sauntered in, yawning, unaffected by the reprimand. "You're lucky I'm here at all. This isn't my best hour of the day."

The cinnamon eyes swept down him. "It should be Jonathan's. What's the matter? Did you leave him in your hotel room?" Brian turned away to get his playbook from the piano.

Tommy sidled over to me. "You missed one of my best performances, sweetheart," he said out of the corner of his mouth in a Bogart accent. "I was super, and it was all wasted on a cocktail waitress who kept her eyes closed the whole time because she thought love should be made in the dark."

I put my finger to my lips. If he were not careful, Brian would hear.

He blithely ignored my warning. "I can't guarantee a repeat, sweetheart, but why don't we give it a try tonight?"

Brian's back was to us at the piano, but he was facing a row of mirrors. His reflected eyes shifted toward us. He must have heard. I held my breath, waiting for his reaction, but he only regarded Tommy's reflection thoughtfully for a moment, then picked up his playbook and turned back to us.

"Good session, Noir. Let me see you again about one o'clock. If Tommy does as well as you did, we'll set up scenarios for the two of you. See the wardrobe mistress while you have time."

I left them and went exploring around the rest of the theater. I found my dressing room and the wardrobe mistress. She took my measurements and promised to have some costumes for me to choose among by tomorrow. Mindful of Brian's warnings, I stayed out of the substage, where the sets were being built on the lowered sections of the stage carrousel. I did go up into the auditorium and watch a gaffer work on an empty raised section programming one set's walls.

It looked as if it might be the horizon for an exterior. The holographic projection was circular, cutting the corners of the stage, and the section visible to me had the outline of low hills. On my far right was the possible early blocking of a building. The gaffer, wearing a microphone headset, walked in and out across the projection line, consulting a chart in his hand and talking into the mike to his colleagues at the computer in the lighting and projection control booth high on the back side of the theater. Piece by piece, details were added and the scene built on the projection.

A theater projection wall has a limited depth—it's more a bas-relief than three dimensional holo—and a one-way image. From the inside looking out, it appears opaque, but someone outside always perceives the closest side as transparent. It solves the problem of giving complete visibility to all members of an audience in the round while providing the set boundaries necessary for verisimilitude and the illusion of peering in on private lives. It does cut off actors from the audience, however, which I have always regretted, even though a *théâtre vérité* cast is supposed to react only to one another and not to observers.

I walked on around the stage to see the rest of the projection. It was becoming unmistakably an exterior backdrop. The added details identified the building as the outside of a house. The hills remained puzzling, though. There was no grass or any flowers on them, and the few trees showing were stark and twisted. Then I realized it must be the sand garden of the title.

Someone called my name. I looked around and saw Miles waving to me as he cut across the auditorium toward the stairs to the practice hall. His walk was a sinuous glide. Miles was wearing Hakon Chashakananda to the theater as I had worn Allegra. He was a bit like the projection wall, adding new details to his characterization each time I saw him. I looked forward to seeing the total Hakon onstage, even though Allegra would have to dread it.

My watch said eleven o'clock. Brian did not want me again until one. What should I do with the intervening two hours? I remembered Tommy mentioning a café down the street. I could pass the time by drinking tea and practicing Allegra on waiters. I could people-watch, always an enjoyable pastime in a city like Gateside.

I went after my coat.

At one o'clock I walked back into the practice hall, and into an atmosphere so charged the tension arced almost visibly between the three men in the room. Tommy sat in a folding wooden chair staring at his nails while Miles stood over him and Brian paced in front of them with a face hewn of ice-rimed granite. My coat is supposed to be only temperature-sensitive, but its fibers stood straight on end, then flattened and clung so tight that taking it off was like skinning myself.

Brian saw me. His chin dipped in a brusque nod of greeting.

I peeled the last arm free and dropped the writhing coat on an empty chair. "When does the massacre begin?" I asked. "And do I have to attend?"

Cinnamon eyes blinked. Brian took a few deep breaths. "No massacre," he said. "It's just that we have a small problem with Jonathan, or more to the point, with Mr. Sebastian."

He looked around at Tommy. Tommy's eyes remained fixed on his manicure, but his jaw muscles twitched.

Brian sighed. "Miles, you can go. Thank you. See you tomorrow."

Miles headed for the door, smiling at me in passing. It was a tired product. "Have fun."

Brian resumed pacing. "Tommy is *playing* Jonathan Clay, not *being* Jonathan Clay."

"I'm doing what I always do. Giles Kimner didn't complain in *Rainbow Man*."

"I'm not Giles Kimner, as I pointed out before." Brian's voice remained even, but every syllable crackled like breaking ice. "I do not believe one can produce valid *théâtre vérité* by *playing* characters. Jonathan Clay has depth. He has layers of feeling and behavior. If he didn't, Allegra would have realized what he was long ago. He has to be done as more than a veneer over your own facade."

"*I'm doing what I always do.*" Tommy followed his rising voice until he was standing, glaring down at Brian, only centimeters from the director's face. "You've seen me work before. You know what I do. If you don't like it, why the hell did you come asking me to be Jonathan!" He whirled away and kicked his chair.

The chair collapsed and skidded across the polished floor.

"Very good," Brian said.

I blinked. He sounded delighted.

"I've got you feeling real emotion now. Before, you've just played at it, as you've just played at *vérité*. You've never bothered to learn how to work with angels, only waited for them to do the job for you. I'll teach you how to use them, though, with Noir's help. You are Jonathan. I want you to be him onstage for the whole world. Noir." He turned and looked at me. "What I'll do is set up scenarios for the two of you, and you'll live as many as necessary for as long as you need to, until Jonathan becomes real to you and us."

We swallowed our angels and started to work. After the first hour I could see why Miles had been exhausted. Even with angels, remaining Allegra and seeing Tommy as Jonathan was an effort when the words and reactions coming from him were all Tommy Sebastian. Though we had never worked in a *vérité* production together before, I knew Tommy had done several. I wondered how. I also wondered why Brian wanted him for Jonathan. There were plenty of more gifted actors with profiles just as beautiful as Tommy's.

We must have lived nearly fifteen repeats of the party where Jonathan and Allegra first met, and that was only one of seven scenarios Brian had chosen for us. When Brian finally let us quit, it was nearly dark outside. I was too tired even to eat. I took a cab back to my hotel and collapsed into bed.

The next day was a repeat of the previous afternoon. Brian let me take short breaks to choose my costumes and be fitted for the alterations while he worked Tommy with Miles, but most of the scenarios were between Jonathan and Allegra. It was wearing, and wearying. I stayed in character for so long I started to feel that Allegra owned my body and Noir was someone who lived in the back of my head. The blitz worked, though. Somewhere in the middle of the afternoon, Tommy visibly changed. I found myself talking to someone unmistakably Jonathan Clay. The easy chatter and poetic quotes disappeared, replaced by warm, adoring eyes that said more than words and lingered on me wherever I went. Finishing the scene, we came out of the angel mist and were actually startled to find Brian there.

He measured us with his eyes, nodding. "He's got it." He grabbed me and danced me across the practice hall. "By Jove, I think he's got it."

I started to pull away. I did not want any man touching me but Jonathan. Moments later I recognized the carry-over. I grinned sheepishly and relaxed in Brian's arms. "Does he have it or does it have us?"

Brian did not reply. His head was turned, watching our whirling reflections in the mirrors. No, I saw a moment later, not our reflections; he was watching Tommy.

Tommy preened himself, grinning. "You should be dancing with me, Brian; I'm the one who's done something marvelous."

Abruptly, Brian let me go. A frown rippled across his forehead. He ran back toward Tommy. "No, don't quit; don't lose it again. Let me work with you on some other scenes and we'll zip you into Jonathan once and for all. Thank you, Noir," he called back to me. "We'd never have done it without you. You're through for the day."

I picked up my coat and escaped before he could change his mind. I treated myself to a long walk to clear Allegra and the angel mist out of my head. I needed it. I kept finding myself looking in shop windows at dresses that, while beautiful, were not my style. When I felt like Noir again, I took a cab back to the hotel and soaked in the tub, reading a book. I was debating whether I wanted to bother dressing to go down to the hotel dining room or have room service bring something up when the phone rang.

It was Tommy. "How would you feel about having dinner with me tonight?" His voice was quiet, without its usual flippancy.

"Has Brian given permission?"

There was a pause. "Of course not, but our characters are supposed to know and enjoy each other's company. Please, Allegra?"

I frowned. "Don't try that on me, Tommy Sebastian." Even as I said it, though, I could feel Allegra nudging me, responding to Jonathan's voice. I fought a minute, then gave in. Why not? What was the harm? "Pick me up in half an hour."

He knocked on my door in exactly half an hour. I shook my watch in disbelief. Tommy on time? But he was, and he looked me over with approval. "Lovely." He squeezed my hand as he tucked it under his arm and led me toward the elevators. "I thought we'd eat at The Caverns."

That was fine with me. We chatted while we waited for the elevator and I noticed that he did not once check his reflection in the mirrored wall. In The Caverns, which was paradoxically on the top floor of the hotel, he continued to be attentive while we sat on a stalagmite-supported bench seat at a stalagmite-supported table beneath dim stalactite lamps.

"I thank you for the dinner," I said, "even though I'm having it with Jonathan Clay and not Tommy Sebastian."

Tommy rubbed his forehead. "I'm sorry, but I can't seem to shake him off."

"I can sympathize." I leaned my head against his shoulder. "How did the rest of the afternoon go?"

"More of the same. Well, not quite. Brian made some changes in my —in Jonathan's bio, then he put me through the hoops with the changes. Would you like to take a walk after dinner?"

I would. We did. Hand in hand, we strolled down Gateside Avenue. The clouds that had been drooping overhead the past two days were gone. Through the clear, crisp night we could see the towering bulk of Diana Mountain and, high on it, the lights of the buildings housing the stargate.

"I always thought there should be a shining arch filled with stars," I said, "not just flat, dull buildings."

Tommy squeezed my hand. "Why, you're a romantic."

I thought about it. "Allegra is."

The stargate and the international jetport put Gateside on a crossroads of the galaxy. The avenue was lined with shops whose brightly lighted show windows displayed the products of a hundred worlds. We examined fabrics, gems, artworks. In one window stood an intricate painting made by pouring colored sands into the narrow space between two sheets of glass.

I pointed to it. "Isn't that from Shissah?"

Tommy peered at the tag just visible under the edge of the glass. "Yes. Would you like it? I'll come back tomorrow and buy it for you."

I stared at him. "You really *are* stuck in Jonathan's skin, aren't you? Snap out of it, Tommy."

He shook his head like someone dazed. "This is weird. I know I've got just Jonathan's personality, not his money, but for a minute there I was thinking I could write a check for that sand painting, no matter what it cost."

I nodded. "There can be a lot of carry-over when the character resonates with your own, or when it's the first time or two in deep involvement. What's the matter?"

Tommy was shivering. "I wonder if this is how Pia felt."

"Pia Fisher?"

He leaned his forehead against a window. *"Rainbow Man* was her first part in a *vérité* production. If I'd understood then what that meant, I would have made sure she knew what she was doing going into the water."

The skin on my back prickled. "You were with her the day she died?"

He stared broodingly in at a bright collection of fabrics in the window. "I was doing Adoni in the show. We had a free afternoon. I rented a car and talked her into coming for a drive with me. She'd been shut up for days on end, never going anywhere except to the theater, just waiting for Brian to call her during breaks in that movie he was directing in Africa. We stopped for a walk on the beach. She started pulling off her clothes and daring me to a race around the point. I'm not a strong swimmer, so I told her I'd drive around and meet her on the far side." He bit his lip. "She never got there." He turned so his back was slumped against the window. "I didn't know she couldn't swim at all. I never thought to ask her if she knew what she was doing."

Of course he hadn't. It was not Tommy's nature to question people's actions. He would have waved to her as she waded into the warm Hawaiian ocean, then merrily driven off to meet her on the far side of the point.

"You know," he said, "I feel worse about it now than I ever have before. In fact, I'd almost forgotten about being there until just now."

I took his hand. "You couldn't have known how much of her was carry-over. Come on. We haven't finished our walk."

We were ourselves the rest of the way down the avenue and back. Pia had dissipated the last of the angels' effects. We were subdued, though. Not even Tommy could find his usual light humor. When we reached the hotel, he left me in the lobby without once extolling his virtues as a night-long guest.

He was still quieter than usual at the theater the next day. I wondered if I should be concerned, but Brian was obviously pleased. "Jonathan is coming very well. Tommy, I want you and Miles to work together this morning. I have some errands to run, but I think you're capable of working by yourselves. Do some early meetings between Jonathan and Hakon."

Tommy's eyes were on me. "Can't I work with Noir?"

"Later. Here comes Miles." He repeated his instructions to Miles, then picked up his coat and started for the door. "Noir, will you walk to the street with me, please?"

Leaving, I saw Tommy's face. He looked displeased.

Brian was a fast walker. I had to stretch my legs to keep up. "Is there something you want me to do?"

"Yes. Button your coat and come with me."

I raised brows at him. "What?"

"I have to go over to Aventine. You've been working hard and deserve a little bit of holiday." His hand was under my elbow, urging me forward. "A cabletrain leaves from here in fifteen minutes. We just have time to make it if we hurry."

I stopped. I would love to see Aventine. That retreat of the rich and famous was legendary, but . . . by cabletrain?

He pulled me forward again. "It's so high you'll lose the sensation of height, I promise you. You'll enjoy the trip."

I let myself be dragged with him. "How did you know I was afraid of heights?"

He shrugged. "I suppose I heard it somewhere. Come on."

Aventine. The name had a magic ring. Why not? "All right."

The hour's ride on the cabletrain was not as bad as I feared. With Brian holding tight to my hand, I allowed myself to be talked into looking out the windows. The mountainside fell away hundreds of meters below us, a patchwork of melting snow and new spring green. As Brian promised, there was no sensation of being *up*. The scene could have been a projection wall mere centimeters below the bottom of the train. Brian offered to take me up to the observation platform where coin-operated binoculars let passengers who cared to, take a close look at the bear fishing in the streams below and the deer grazing in the meadows. I declined. The sway of the train was enough to remind me we were suspended over this chasm on just a cable. I felt more secure sitting down.

"What do you have to do in Aventine?" I asked.

"Pick up a prop. Jonathan is a wealthy man with impeccable taste in women and possessions. I thought we should have some first-class art for his office. Xhosar Kain is creating a sonic sculpture just for the play."

Xhosar Kain? I was impressed. "You're going after it yourself?"

"Would you trust a Kain piece to a delivery service?"

The conversation lapsed for a few minutes. I looked out the window again. Clouds were starting to move in, some so low they were under the train. I hoped that did not mean the ride back would be minus the scenery. I could feel Brian's eyes on me, measuring, searching. What was it he was looking for in me?

"What are you doing with your evenings?" he asked.

I could not stop the sudden guilty flush that went up my neck. "Reading, mostly."

"Not going out with Tommy?"

He knew. His voice was neither accusing nor judgmental, but it was clear the question was rhetorical.

"I did last night." There was no point in denying it. I looked at him. "Why shouldn't we? Jonathan and Allegra are lovers. Our togetherness offstage should strengthen the bond onstage."

The cinnamon eyes were focused past me. "Were you Allegra and Jonathan last night?"

I wished I could read him better. I could not guess how far he intended the question to go. "I reacted to him a bit as Allegra while he was very much Jonathan. He had trouble getting out of the character. He went to his own hotel for the night, however."

There was a brilliant flash in his eyes. I wondered for a moment if it was anger, but then his face lighted in a smile of satisfaction. "We may make a real actor of him yet."

Minutes later the cabletrain pulled into the Aventine station. I climbed out, rubbernecking with unashamed curiosity. I found the retreats of the rich and famous were not immediately visible. The station was at the edge of a shopping square. Off it were streets with apartments and studios. Long ago, Aventine had begun as an artists' colony, and that still dominated its center.

Brian led the way up one of the artists' streets. He stopped at a studio with a sculpture in front that was an X elaborately wrought in sonic vanes. The wind set it vibrating in a pleasant if repetitious pattern of chords. Brian pushed open the door of the studio.

I am not sure what I expected Xhosar Kain to look like—a bear-like blacksmith, perhaps. I did not expect the thin, twist-spined man who put down his welding torch and mask to come slowly to meet us. The body was frail, but the hand that took mine was large and strong, I noticed, and his eyes were warm.

"Noir Delacour. I'm a great fan of yours."

"And I of yours. I saw *I, the Living* when it was on exhibit in New York and felt like I'd had a religious experience."

He grinned. "You are obviously a woman of outstanding judgment. I'll love you to my death." He looked at Brian. "Come after the lady, have you, Eleazar?"

Brian nodded.

"Just a minute."

He limped into the depths of the studio and came back carrying a small sculpture. Once he set it down I could see it was not all that small, but it was still less massive than most of his work. It was right for a table or desk.

"I call her *The Fury*. Is she what you had in mind?"

I could see why he called the sculpture "she." My first reaction was that it was a bird with wings spread to fly, but it could also have been a woman. The rising vanes looked as much like flowing sleeves as wings. The piece was beautiful, and at the same time somehow frightening. The air currents in the studio set it off in a sound that was now a hum and now a keening wail.

Brian touched the edge of a vane with a tentative finger. "It's just right."

Kain wrapped the sculpture carefully and laid it in a box. He gave the box to Brian. "Watch out for her."

He followed us to the door of the studio. "Come back and let me do a sonic of you one day, Miss Delacour. It will sing as fair as the angels."

I promised I would.

Outside, the sky was still lowering. Leaden, waterlogged clouds rolled across the blue, cutting off the sun. The wind was coming up, too, setting off discords in the sculpture in front of the studio. My coat fluffed and tightened around me.

Brian looked up. "It's no day for sightseeing, after all. Let's go back to the station."

The weather changed his mood entirely. Eating lunch at the Gallery Café in Aventine while we waited for the next train, and during the ride back, Brian sat silent, lost in thoughts that looked as brooding as the sky outside. From time to time his cinnamon eyes rested on me or the carton he carried, but for the most part he looked past me, focused on some bleak otherwhere. We were back at the Blue Orion before he could shake free of the mood.

He gave me an apologetic smile. "I'm sorry I was such poor company."

I shrugged. "That's all right."

He opened the door of the practice hall. Miles and Tommy stood by the piano drinking coffee. They looked around.

"We're back." Brian had forced a gay, almost playful tone into his voice. "Thank you for coming with me, Noir." He kissed me full on the mouth.

Tommy set down his coffee. His eyes traveled from Brian to me. "You went somewhere together?"

"Aventine . . . to get this." Brian opened the box and took out *The Fury*. "I'll show you where it goes."

He led the three of us into the substage area. The sections of the carrousel were dressed, waiting to be turned to position beneath the stage opening and raised into place. Light came down from the auditorium through the stage opening, falling on the stage section immediately beneath. The other three sections remained in shadow. The one lighted section was an interior. It looked oddly naked without the projection wall that would be around it when it was in place up top. Brian stepped up onto the platform and placed *The Fury* on a massive desk there.

"This is Jonathan's office. Starting tomorrow, we'll send the sets up top in turn and let you work on them. I want you to familiarize yourselves thoroughly with those you need to know. For you, Noir, that means just this office. You still need to keep away from the sand garden and the interior set of Hakon's house. How did the scenes go this morning, Miles, Tommy?"

Tommy's forehead creased. "Why did you go to Aventine with him?" he asked me.

I looked quickly at him. His voice had a note I had never heard in it before, a hard, controlled evenness. I frowned. "That's hardly your concern, but Brian asked me along."

"The period of mourning is over, then, Brian?"

Brian did not respond.

I rolled my eyes. "Really. It was hardly an assignation."

Tommy stepped toward me, his fist clenched. My heart leaped in my throat. For a moment I thought he was going to raise it to strike.

"Tommy!" Fear sharpened my voice. "Tommy, stop that! Tommy Sebastian doesn't care where Noir Delacour goes or with whom. You're letting Jonathan keep too tight a hold on you. Shake him off."

Tommy's mouth opened and closed several times, without letting out a sound. He shook his head hard. After a bit his fist relaxed. "God, I don't know if I can take this." He whirled away and ran out.

Miles went after him. "I'll see if I can help him."

I bit my lip. I leaned against Jonathan's desk. "You may make Tommy a good *vérité* actor, but you're also making him an unhappy, confused human being, Brian."

"He's doing beautifully, just beautifully." Brian looked in the direction Tommy had gone, a fierce joy in his cinnamon eyes.

I frowned. "Do you really want Jonathan acting like that? It isn't how he usually is around Allegra."

His eyes came around to me. "That's because she's always been so completely, faithfully his. When he finds her admiring Hakon, though, and enjoying the alien's company, it will bring out a side of his character she has never seen before. Sit down, will you? I was thinking about Allegra on the way back from Aventine and I've decided I'm not quite satisfied with her. I think we need to make a change in her bio."

My brows went up. "Now? We open in just three days."

"That's time enough to incorporate the change. We need a dissonant element in her early life. Up to now, she has always been loved. She's had no reason to distrust anyone. I think she'll work more effectively if there's an element of fear as well as loathing in her initial reaction to Hakon. Let's say that her father died when she was eight and her mother met a man that loneliness caused her to think she loved. The man, though, proved to be very jealous and possessive, and one night he accused Allegra's mother of seeing someone else. He struck her in his rage. She broke off with him and soon afterward married a man who became a gentle, loving stepfather to Allegra."

My skin pimpled. I shivered.

Brian cocked his head. "What's wrong?"

I pulled my braid over my shoulder and toyed with the end. "Something very much like that happened to me. I was ten and my mother was divorced, not widowed, but—didn't you know that?"

The cinnamon eyes flickered. "No. Why should I?"

"You knew about my fear of heights."

"That was just chance. I didn't know anything about this." He sighed. "That's going to make it very painful for you, isn't it?"

He had known. I felt it with chilling certainty. He was lying. Why? "Can't we introduce someone unpleasant into her life another way?"

He thought, rubbing his temples. "I wish we could, but I'm sorry. I have to have it this way to achieve exactly the effect I need. If it helps, we won't work through a scenario of it. You find a name for the man and a way for Allegra's mother to have met him. Visualize the rage scene and include it in Allegra's memories. All right?"

He said it as though he were offering a concession. I started to protest, to refuse, but his eyes caught mine, steady and compelling. Without ever meaning to, I found myself nodding agreement.

He patted my shoulder. "Good girl. Well, I think I'll see if I can find Tommy and Miles."

I could have left the substage with him, but I stayed, somehow reluctant to step out of the light slanting down through the opening above and into the darkness of the cavernous room around me. I sat down in the big chair behind Jonathan's desk and stared at *The Fury*, trying to sort out my emotions. I could see the face of my mother's boyfriend before me, ugly and inhuman in its rage. I could see him crumple as my mother struck him with a lamp. I could also see Brian's cinnamon eyes, flickering past me when he denied knowing about that incident in my past. Later, though, he had looked into me with unwavering directness. It shook my conviction that he had known. Perhaps, after all, he had just chanced to hear about my fear of heights and it was coincidence he gave Allegra one moment of history in common with me. Perhaps he did need just that incident to create dramatic conflict in Allegra's character.

I started looking around the office. It was so like Jonathan, all flashy chrome pole lamps and chrome-framed designer furniture . . . expensive, handsome, sterile. In it, *The Fury* was the single spot of life and emotion. I leaned across the desk to touch a sonic vane. The motion stirred the air and set the sculpture keening. The sound plucked at my nerves. It was like a wail of grief, sharp and unrelenting. It carried after me out of the substage and followed me all the way back to the practice hall.

The last three days before the opening were hectic. The costumes were ready, and Tommy and I started wearing ours while we practiced in Jonathan's office. Miles disappeared. I never saw him except in glimpses coming and going. The once I saw him long enough to ask him about his costumes, he only laughed in a long, sibilant hiss, and winked.

"It's more of a body makeup. You'll like it. It's spectacular."

Tommy and I learned to know the office so well we could cross it in the dark. I came to recognize the feel of every piece of furniture, the location of every holographic book in the projection-wall bookcases. Tommy seemed to have recovered from his upset the day I went to Aventine. He was a gentle Jonathan on the set and almost his old self offstage, only a little subdued by his character's persona.

We were all developing first-night nerves. In a sense, every night of the run would be an opening night, but we were products enough of conventional drama to find something special in the very first night. Also, in spite of the practice scenarios, we could still not predict exactly how the characters would react. The course and end of the play were no certainty. The agony of anticipation was almost unbearable.

"Think about Zach Weigand," Brian said the afternoon of the opening. "He's going to be in the audience tonight chewing his knuckles, wondering if we'll dispose as he has proposed. He's much more nervous than any of you." He herded us toward the door. "Go rest, or meditate, whatever you need to do to be at your best. Be back by seven at the latest. The lights go down at eight."

I took a cab back to the hotel. I always think I'm going to take a nap before an opening, or lose myself in a light novel. I had the book ready. But I ended up doing what I always do. I paced, nerves singing like high-tension wires. I fought to keep from biting my manicure into ruin. Inevitably, I picked up the phone and called Karol Gardener.

His voice came laughing back at me over the wire. "Very good, pet. You held out fifteen minutes longer than usual. I have a drink in my hand. I raise it in a toast to you."

I kept pacing, taking the phone with me, phone in one hand, receiver in the other. "You'd think I'd learn to have more faith in myself, wouldn't you, but here I am lost once more in the dreadful broody 'what-ifs.' Tell me I'm not going to lay an egg."

"My darling Noir, there is no way in this glorious galaxy you can lay an egg. You'll be superb as Allegra Nightengale. Remember, Brian wanted you and no one else for the part. Do you doubt Brian Eleazar's judgment?"

I stopped. I felt cold. "Wanted me and no one else? Where did you hear that?"

"Prying into the affairs of other agents, pet. Vonda King and Maya Chaplain had their agents wooing him for weeks, but after he had asked around, Brian came after you. He wouldn't hear of anyone else."

Why did that disturb me so? "Asked around where?"

"Well, he talked to Charlotte DeMetro, for one."

Charlotte DeMetro? Why would a director talk to a gossip columnist when he was looking for someone to take a character? Because, a small voice in me whispered, gossip columnists know things like who has what phobias and what kind of family histories. Charlotte knew more skeletons than any other five columnists put together. Why should gossip be important in finding an actress, though?

I did not have time to think about it. Karol chattered on, giving encouragement and relaying inconsequential gossip. The words ran through my head in a murmuring stream, sound with just enough sense to distract and calm me. My answers could not have been much more than monosyllables, but Karol read them with precision. He knew to the second when my stomach stopped churning and my pessimism lifted but the keen edge was still on my nerves. That was the moment he broke off.

"You need to get ready to go now. Break a leg, pet. I'll call you tomorrow and see how it went."

He sent me off to the theater at a peak of emotion. I considered asking Brian what he had talked about with Charlotte, but did not have the chance. I did not see him until a few minutes before eight, and then only as he stuck his head into my dressing room to warn me about the time. His face was shuttered and his cinnamon eyes focused on otherwhere. I had taken my angel and was busy slipping into Allegra along with the first costume. It was the wrong time to ask anything. I shrugged. The question would keep until afterward.

The lights went down in the auditorium and up on the stage. The first scene was between Jonathan and Hakon. I waited in the substage.

The scene ended and the stage was lowered. Above, I knew, the projection wall would have gone completely opaque and become a swirling storm of opalescent colors. The stage reached floor level. With a smooth hum of motors, the carrousel revolved, bringing Jonathan's office into position. Tommy leaped from the first set to the office. A stagehand helped me up onto the platform. Slowly the stage began to rise. We went up into light, where the audience was a warm animal smell and a sigh of collected breathing beyond the opalescent projection walls.

The sound of the audience retreated to a great distance, beyond the angel mist. I looked at Tommy . . . Jonathan.

The walls resolved into windows, paneling, and bookcases. I looked at the dearest man in the world and saw he was in pain. My heart went out to him. "Jonathan, what's the matter?"

I, Noir, retreated to the back of my head. From there I watched

Allegra critically but without interfering except for a nudge here and there to keep the action and dialogue dramatically interesting.

The action went very much as Zach Weigand outlined in the play-book. As Allegra, I was distressed and horrified by what Jonathan had let Hakon force on him.

"How could you agree to it, Jonathan? It's . . . barbaric."

Jonathan slumped in his chair, a picture of misery. "He tricked me. I was committed to handling the cargo before I knew the Shissahn's conditions. God, if I'd known what he was going to demand, I would have cut off my arm first. I'd have let the Corbreen syndicate take the option."

I could not stand to see him in misery. I threw myself at his knees. "It's all right. I'll go."

The walls went opalescent. Jonathan's office sank into the substage. The next set rose. I found myself in the Shissahn's sand garden. Allegra was horrified by it. It was desert, desolation, nothing but rock and sand, no plant life except an occasional cactus or Joshua tree. Noir was entranced. I had never seen anything like it before. I hoped real Shissahn gardens were like it. The rock outcroppings were of many varieties, too many to be occurring naturally. They gleamed with veins of gold and silver, glittered with crystal and semipolished gems. They studded dunes of a dozen colored sands. The main section of the set was a double layer of sand, heavy red under fine silver-white. Mixed together, they made a shimmering pink, then slowly separated into two distinct layers again. Walking across the sand, my feet sank through the topsand to reveal the red beneath and leave scarlet prints that remained a few minutes, bright in white sand, then disappeared as the topsand sifted into the depressions. The projection wall made the set look as though it stretched for acres.

I was standing in that miniature wilderness working up the courage to go to the house when I heard a sound behind me. I turned, and screamed. The creature standing on the top of the dune looked generally humanoid but it was hairless and earless. Its mottled green, brown, and slate-gray hide had the texture of old leather. A leather kilt wrapped its hips and a long curved knife hung diagonally across its chest.

"You are the Clay female?" Its voice was the dry hiss of sliding sand. "I am Hakon Chashakananda."

Miles had been right. I loved his makeup. It was spectacular. If I had not known for sure it was Miles, I would have sworn a genuine Shissahn had been rung in for the part.

I backed away, clutching my suitcase, then stopped and forced myself to stand, chin lifted high. I would not run from this creature, no matter how fearsome he looked. "I am Allegra Nightengale." I tried to keep my voice from trembling. "Be so good as to direct me to my room."

Friendship with Hakon came slowly. It developed through the next scenes, beginning with impertinent questions: "Why does a supposedly civilized being run around in nothing but a leather loincloth and that hideous knife?" Hakon had his reasons, which he gave me, but in deference to me he began wearing loose caftan-like robes. Then came curious questions: "What does your name mean in your language?"

His answer began with a grin, almost a human gesture. "It has no meaning. You could not pronounce my actual name. Hakon Chasha-kananda is what I have adopted for the benefit of your people."

I blinked. "Then why not use a simple one?"

He blinked, too, in a slow saurian gesture. "What? Would you have an alien named John Smith? Humans expect us to have long and difficult names."

That broke the ice forever. From there, the relationship grew quickly. The I that was Allegra began to see the beauty in the sand garden, and the equally fine qualities in the garden's owner.

Soon after that, he sent me home to Jonathan.

Jonathan was startled but overjoyed. He hugged me until I thought my ribs would crack. "How did you do it? I'd have thought he was impossible to move."

"You just haven't had a chance to know Hakon well enough. Today he said, 'I have come to know you well and find you a person of trustworthiness. If you say your Jonathan is a man of honor, I believe he must be. Then I do not need a hostage.' And he let me go."

Jonathan drew back, frowning. "What did he mean, he's come to know you well?"

Inside the angel mist, Noir started. Tommy had used that tone when asking why I had gone to Aventine with Brian. Allegra did not hear the change in voice. "We've spent a great deal of time together in four months. I couldn't very well sit in my room alone day after day. I'd have gone mad. It's exhausting to hate, so we became friends. He's really a very fine man."

Jonathan's eyes narrowed. *"Man?"*

I nodded. "Any intelligent being is a man. That's what his people believe. Isn't that a fine concept? It binds us together instead of separating us into alien and human, Terran and Shissahn."

"Have you adopted Shissahn philosophy and discarded human beliefs, then?"

There was no mistaking the displeasure in that question. Allegra reached out to touch his hand. "Of course not, but they do have some ideas worth considering. Are you disturbed by that?"

The muscles in his jaw twitched. "What do you think? I've spent four months in hell, working as hard as I could to sell off the cargo so I could redeem you. I was scared to death for you. I didn't have any idea what that creature might be capable of doing. Now you come back singing his praises and spouting alien philosophy. Exactly how friendly have you been with him?"

His implied accusation shocked me. "He's never touched me. You are my beloved, Jonathan. I have been faithful to you."

He hugged me fiercely. "Thank God. And now we're back together again, we can forget this whole incident and continue where we left off."

We did not, of course. I had been changed by the months with Hakon. I looked at Jonathan through eyes grown a bit alien. I saw things in him I had never seen before, things that deeply disturbed me. When I realized Jonathan was preparing to cheat Hakon out of part of the profit due him, I had to speak out.

Jonathan was brusque. "This is none of your concern."

"It *is*. I promised Hakon you were trustworthy. It isn't right for you to do this."

His anger was not the flaming kind. Outwardly, he remained calm. His voice stayed level, his face clear, but the muscles twitched in his jaw as I talked and his voice took the tightness of careful control. He refused to discuss his business and ordered me out of the office.

I looked at him in great sorrow. I had been afraid it might come to this. "Very well. I'll go pack."

"Pack?" He was on his feet. "What do you mean, pack?"

"I'm leaving you."

He came flying around the desk. "No. You can't."

I felt as if I were being torn apart, but I refused to yield to him. I tried to explain how different I felt about things now, how differently I saw. He could not understand.

"I knew there was something between you and that alien."

I shook my head emphatically. "You're wrong. Perhaps there could have been, but I remained faithful to you and he respected my choice."

"Is that so?" His voice was rising. "You think he's a wonderful *man*. You bargain in his behalf in business matters that are none of your concern—bargain against *me*, the man you claim to love. Now you want to leave me. And you expect me to believe it isn't to go back to *him?*"

"I expect you to believe that, yes."

"You're lying." He said it through clenched teeth. His hands flexed.

Panic went through me in an icy wash. He was going to hit me! I backed away, feeling helpless and eight years old.

One of his hands drew back, open, poised for a slap. "You're lying to me. Don't you dare do that. Admit there was something between you and the alien. Admit it!"

"No, Jonathan." I tried to back farther, but the desk, that huge, solid desk, blocked my retreat. "There was nothing! I swear it!"

In the back of my head, Noir was screaming, too. Jonathan wore the face of my mother's boyfriend. The hand swung forward. Allegra groped behind her. I needed something to fend him off. My hand closed on the base of the Kain sculpture.

Noir protested, struggling against the angel mist inside me. The play was not supposed to go this way. Allegra should drop the sculpture, should let him hit her once if necessary, and reason lovingly with him. Once I might have, but now Jonathan's hand was headed toward my face and the terrifying memory of another hand and another man paralyzed me. Noir Delacour should have resumed control, but that same image held me snarled in the angel mist. I swung the sculpture at him.

It slashed across his face. The vanes were like dozens of knives, cutting and tearing through cheeks and nose and eyes. Somewhere beyond the walls of the office, there was a shriek, and the sharp stench of sweat and fear. Jonathan screamed and clawed for me. I swung the sculpture again. This time it crossed his throat.

As he went down I realized what I was doing. I dropped the sculpture and fell on my knees beside him. I tried to stop the bleeding with my hands.

"Jonathan, Jonathan, why did you do this to me? I never wanted to hurt you. I loved you."

Through the angel mist, Noir watched with dull horror and realized it *was* supposed to happen this way. It had been orchestrated. Brian had chosen me for Allegra because of my mother's boyfriend. It was to keep me from stopping Allegra's panic reaction to Jonathan's anger. I was not the only one chosen, though. Brian had asked Tommy to be Jonathan . . . poor foolish, irresponsible Tommy. Brian had commissioned the Kain sculpture, so appropriately named after those Grecian instruments of revenge.

Allegra cried, "What are we? I found humanity and compassion in an alien, and monstrosity in my beloved. Even I, for all my pride of being gentle and civilized, become a clawing animal at the first threat of attack."

Beyond the projection wall the crowd murmured in excitement. The sound came through the angel mist. My head cleared. I looked down at Tommy. He lay slack and still.

The blood delighted the crowd. Suddenly I understood them as I never had before. This was why they loved *théâtre vérité*, what they really came hoping to see . . . modern Romans at a modern circus.

I looked at my hands, red with Tommy's blood. "Who are the men, Jonathan, and who the beasts and aliens?"

I huddled over him. I did not look up when the projection wall was shut off. I would not stand to take a bow. Someone picked me up. It was Miles. He kept an arm around me, holding me against his leathery chest while the crowd screamed its pleasure and the stage carried us down out of their sight.

Miles helped me off the stage in the substage area.

Brian pushed through the crowd of gaffers and stagehands to us. "Noir, how terrible, but don't worry. I'm sure the inquest will find it was an accident, death by misadventure."

I looked around at him, not letting go of Miles. "What a pity," I said bitterly. "Then you can't take proper credit for the most brilliant directing of your career."

He stared at me one flicker of time, then patted my shoulder. "Poor Noir. You're upset."

"What does that matter? Pia is avenged, and that's what it's all been about, isn't it?"

"You'd better take her to her dressing room to lie down, Miles. I'll call a doctor."

I let Miles lead me away, but in the doorway I stopped and looked back. Brian had picked up *The Fury* from where I'd dropped it and stood holding the sculpture. The light slanting down from the auditorium reflected off the vanes onto his face. It caught his eyes, and as he lifted his head to look back at me, the cinnamon eyes glowed red, like an animal's by firelight.

On gray days, when the clouds hang in heavy pewter folds and the wind comes down cold and sharp as a blade, I think of Brian Eleazar. We face each other in the sand garden, and between us lies a trail of footprints, scarlet in the fine white sand, as though they were stepped in blood.

*Science fiction is an unpredictable literature, and you can trust How-
ard Waldrop to be more unpredictable than most anyone. Remember
the stories about lost valleys in the Amazon or islands in the South
Pacific where adventurous scientists discovered living dinosaurs, mas-
todons, or saber-toothed tigers? Those were only a few of the strange
creatures from Earth's past that have long been extinct. . . .
For instance, there was the dodo.*

THE UGLY CHICKENS
Howard Waldrop

My car was broken, and I had a class to teach at eleven. So I took the
city bus, something I rarely do.

I spent last summer crawling through the Big Thicket with cameras
and tape recorder, photographing and taping two of the last ivory-billed
woodpeckers on the earth. You can see the films at your local Audubon
Society showroom.

This year I wanted something just as flashy but a little less taxing.
Perhaps a population study on the Bermuda cahow, or the New Zea-
land takahe. A month or so in the warm (not hot) sun would do me a
world of good. To say nothing of the advancement of science.

I was idly leafing through Greenway's *Extinct and Vanishing Birds
of the World*. The city bus was winding its way through the ritzy
neighborhoods of Austin, stopping to let off the chicanas, black women,
and Vietnamese who tended the kitchens and gardens of the rich.

"I haven't seen any of those ugly chickens in a long time," said a
voice close by.

A gray-haired lady was leaning across the aisle toward me.

I looked at her, then around. Maybe she was a shopping-bag lady.
Maybe she was just talking. I looked straight at her. No doubt about it,
she was talking to me. She was waiting for an answer.

"I used to live near some folks who raised them when I was a girl,"
she said. She pointed.

I looked down at the page my book was open to.

What I should have said was: That is quite impossible, madam. This
is a drawing of an extinct bird of the island of Mauritius. It is perhaps
the most famous dead bird in the world. Maybe you are mistaking this
drawing for that of some rare Asiatic turkey, peafowl, or pheasant. I am
sorry, but you *are* mistaken.

I should have said all that.

What she said was, "Oops, this is my stop." And got up to go.

My name is Paul Lindberl. I am twenty-six years old, a graduate student in ornithology at the University of Texas, a teaching assistant. My
name is not unknown in the field. I have several vices and follies, but I
don't think foolishness is one of them.

The stupid thing for me to do would have been to follow her.

She stepped off the bus.

I followed her.

I came into the departmental office, trailing scattered papers in the
whirlwind behind me. "Martha! Martha!" I yelled.

She was doing something in the supply cabinet.

"Jesus, Paul! What do you want?"

"Where's Courtney?"

"At the conference in Houston. You know that. You missed your
class. What's the matter?"

"Petty cash. Let me at it!"

"Payday was only a week ago. If you can't—"

"It's business! It's fame and adventure and the chance of a lifetime!
It's a long sea voyage that leaves . . . a plane ticket. To either Jackson,
Mississippi, or Memphis. Make it Jackson, it's closer. I'll get receipts!
I'll be famous. Courtney will be famous. *You'll* even be famous! This
university will make even *more* money! I'll pay you back. Give me
some paper. I gotta write Courtney a note. When's the next plane out?
Could you get Marie and Chuck to take over my classes Tuesday and
Wednesday? I'll try to be back Thursday unless something happens.
Courtney'll be back tomorrow, right? I'll call him from, well, wherever.
Do you have some coffee?"

And so on and so forth. Martha looked at me like I was crazy. But
she filled out the requisition anyway.

"What do I tell Kemejian when I ask him to sign these?"

"Martha, babe, sweetheart. Tell him I'll get his picture in *Scientific
American*."

"He doesn't read it."

"*Nature*, then!"

"I'll see what I can do," she said.

The lady I had followed off the bus was named Jolyn (Smith) Jimson. The story she told me was so weird that it had to be true. She knew things only an expert, or someone with firsthand experience, could know. I got names from her, and addresses, and directions, and tidbits of information. Plus a year: 1927.

And a place. Northern Mississippi.

I gave her my copy of the Greenway book. I told her I'd call her as soon as I got back into town. I left her standing on the corner near the house of the lady she cleaned up for twice a week. Jolyn Jimson was in her sixties.

Think of the dodo as a baby harp seal with feathers. I know that's not even close, but it saves time.

In 1507 the Portuguese, on their way to India, found the (then un-named) Mascarene Islands in the Indian Ocean—three of them a few hundred miles apart, all east of Madagascar.

It wasn't until 1598, when that old Dutch sea captain Cornelius van Neck bumped into them, that the islands received their names—names that changed several times through the centuries as the Dutch, French, and English changed them every war or so. They are now known as Rodriguez, Réunion, and Mauritius.

The major feature of these islands was large, flightless, stupid, ugly, bad-tasting birds. Van Neck and his men named them *dod-aarsen*, "stu-pid asses," or *dodars*, "silly birds," or solitaires.

There were three species: the dodo of Mauritius, the real gray-brown, hooked-beak, clumsy thing that weighed twenty kilos or more; the white, somewhat slimmer, dodo of Réunion; and the solitaires of Rodriguez and Réunion, which looked like very fat, very dumb light-colored geese.

The dodos all had thick legs, big squat bodies twice as large as a tur-key's, naked faces, and big long downcurved beaks ending in a hook like a hollow linoleum knife. Long ago they had lost the ability to fly, and their wings had degenerated to flaps the size of a human hand with only three or four feathers in them. Their tails were curly and fluffy, like a child's afterthought at decoration. They had absolutely no natural enemies. They nested on the open ground. They probably hatched their eggs wherever they happened to lay them.

No natural enemies until Van Neck and his kind showed up. The Dutch, French, and Portuguese sailors who stopped at the Mascarenes to replenish stores found that, besides looking stupid, dodos *were* stupid. The men walked right up to the dodos and hit them on the head with clubs. Better yet, dodos could be herded around like sheep. Ships' logs are full of things like: "Party of ten men ashore. Drove half a hundred of the big turkey-like birds into the boat. Brought to ship, where they are given the run of the decks. Three will feed a crew of 150."

Even so, most of the dodo, except for the breast, tasted bad. One of the Dutch words for them was *walghvogel*, "disgusting bird." But on a ship three months out on a return from Goa to Lisbon, well, food was where you found it. It was said, even so, that prolonged boiling did not improve the flavor.

Even so, the dodos might have lasted, except that the Dutch, and later the French, colonized the Mascarenes. The islands became plantations and dumping places for religious refugees. Sugarcane and other exotic crops were raised there.

With the colonists came cats, dogs, hogs, and the cunning *Rattus norvegicus* and the Rhesus monkey from Ceylon. What dodos the hungry sailors left were chased down (they were dumb and stupid, but they could run when they felt like it) by dogs in the open. They were killed by cats as they sat on their nests. Their eggs were stolen and eaten by monkeys, rats, and hogs. And they competed with the pigs for all the low-growing goodies of the islands.

The last Mauritius dodo was seen in 1681, less than a hundred years after humans first saw them. The last white dodo walked off the history books around 1720. The solitaires of Rodriguez and Réunion, last of the genus as well as the species, may have lasted until 1790. Nobody knows.

Scientists suddenly looked around and found no more of the Didine birds alive, anywhere.

This part of the country was degenerate before the first Snopes ever saw it. This road hadn't been paved until the late fifties, and it was a main road between two county seats. That didn't mean it went through civilized country. I'd traveled for miles and seen nothing but dirt banks red as Billy Carter's neck and an occasional church. I expected to see

Burma Shave signs, but realized this road had probably never had them.

I almost missed the turnoff onto the dirt and gravel road the man back at the service station had marked. It led onto the highway from nowhere, a lane out of a field. I turned down it, and a rock the size of a golf ball flew up over the hood and put a crack three inches long in the windshield of the rental car I'd gotten in Grenada.

It was a hot, muggy day for this early. The view was obscured in a cloud of dust every time the gravel thinned. About a mile down the road, the gravel gave out completely. The roadway turned into a rutted dirt pathway, just wider than the car, hemmed in on both sides by a sagging three-strand barbed-wire fence.

In some places the fence posts were missing for a few meters. The wire lay on the ground and in some places disappeared under it for long stretches.

The only life I saw was a mockingbird raising hell with something under a thornbush the barbed wire had been nailed to in place of a post. To one side now was a grassy field that had gone wild, the way everywhere will look after we blow ourselves off the face of the planet. The other was fast becoming woods—pine, oak, some black gum and wild plum, fruit not out this time of the year.

I began to ask myself what I was doing here. What if Ms. Jimson were some imaginative old crank who—but no. Wrong, maybe, but even the wrong was worth checking. But I knew she hadn't lied to me. She had seemed incapable of lies—a good ol' girl, backbone of the South, of the earth. Not a mendacious gland in her being.

I couldn't doubt her, or my judgment either. Here I was, creeping and bouncing down a dirt path in Mississippi, after no sleep for a day, out on the thin ragged edge of a dream. I *had* to take it on faith.

The back of the car sometimes slid where the dirt had loosened and gave way to sand. The back tire stuck once, but I rocked out of it. Getting back out again would be another matter. Didn't anyone ever use this road?

The woods closed in on both sides like the forest primeval, and the fence had long since disappeared. My odometer said ten kilometers, and it had been twenty minutes since I'd turned off the highway. In the rearview mirror, I saw beads of sweat and dirt in the wrinkles of my neck. A fine patina of dust covered everything inside the car. Clots of it came through the windows.

The woods reached out and swallowed the road. Branches scraped against the windows and the top. It was like falling down a long dark leafy tunnel. It was dark and green in there. I fought back an atavistic urge to turn on the headlights. The roadbed must be made of a few centuries of leaf mulch. I kept constant pressure on the accelerator and bulled my way through.

Half a log caught and banged and clanged against the car bottom. I saw light ahead. Fearing for the oil pan, I punched the pedal and sped out.

I almost ran through a house.

It was maybe ten meters from the trees. The road ended under one of the windows. I saw somebody waving from the corner of my eye.

I slammed on the brakes.

A whole family was on the porch, looking like a Walker Evans Depression photograph, or a fever dream from the mind of a "Hee Haw" producer. The house was old. Strips of peeling paint a meter long tapped against the eaves.

"Damned good thing you stopped," said a voice. I looked up. The biggest man I had ever seen in my life leaned down into the driver-side window.

"If we'd have heard you sooner, I'd've sent one of the kids down to the end of the driveway to warn you," he said.

Driveway?

His mouth was stained brown at the corners. I figured he chewed tobacco until I saw the sweet-gum snuff brush sticking from the pencil pocket in the bib of his coveralls. His hands were the size of catchers' mitts. They looked like they'd never held anything smaller than an ax handle.

"How y'all?" he said, by way of introduction.

"Just fine," I said. I got out of the car.

"My name's Lindberl," I said, extending my hand. He took it. For an instant, I thought of bear traps, sharks' mouths, closing elevator doors. The thought went back to wherever it is they stay.

"This the Gudger place?" I asked.

He looked at me blankly with his gray eyes. He wore a diesel truck cap and had on a checked lumberjack shirt beneath the coveralls. His rubber boots were the size of the ones Karloff wore in *Frankenstein*.

"Naw. I'm Jim Bob Krait. That's my wife, Jenny, and there's Luke and Skeeno and Shirl." He pointed to the porch.

The people on the porch nodded.

"Lessee. Gudger? No Gudgers round here I know of. I'm sorta new here." I took that to mean he hadn't lived here for more than twenty years or so.

"Jennifer!" he yelled. "You know of anybody named Gudger?" To me he said, "My wife's lived around heres all her life."

His wife came down onto the second step of the porch landing. "I think they used to be the ones what lived on the Spradlin place before the Spradlins. But the Spradlins left around the Korean War. I didn't know any of the Gudgers myself. That's while we was living over to Water Valley."

"You an insurance man?" asked Mr. Krait.

"Uh . . . no," I said. I imagined the people on the porch leaning toward me, all ears. "I'm a . . . I teach college."

"Oxford?" asked Krait.

"Uh, no. University of Texas."

"Well, that's a damn long way off. You say you're looking for the Gudgers?"

"Just their house. The area. As your wife said, I understand they left. During the Depression, I believe."

"Well, they musta had money," said the gigantic Mr. Krait. "Nobody around here was rich enough to *leave* during the Depression."

"Luke!" he yelled. The oldest boy on the porch sauntered down. He looked anemic and wore a shirt in vogue with the Twist. He stood with his hands in his pockets.

"Luke, show Mr. Lindbergh—"

"Lindberl."

". . . Mr. Lindberl here the way up to the old Spradlin place. Take him as far as the old log bridge, he might get lost before then."

"Log bridge broke down, Daddy."

"When?"

"October, Daddy."

"Well, hell, somethin' else to fix! Anyway, to the creek."

He turned to me. "You want him to go along on up there, see you don't get snakebit?"

"No, I'm sure I'll be fine."

"Mind if I ask what you're going up there for?" he asked. He was looking away from me. I could see having to come right out and ask was bothering him. Such things usually came up in the course of conversation.

"I'm a—uh, bird scientist. I study birds. We had a sighting—

someone told us the old Gudger place—the area around here—I'm
looking for a rare bird. It's hard to explain."

I noticed I was sweating. It was hot.

"You mean like a good God? I saw a good God about twenty-five
years ago, over next to Bruce," he said.

"Well, no." (A good God was one of the names for an ivory-billed
woodpecker, one of the rarest in the world. Any other time I would
have dropped my jaw. Because they were thought to have died out in
Mississippi by the teens, and by the fact that Krait knew they *were*
rare.)

I went to lock my car up, then thought of the protocol of the situation. "My car be in your way?" I asked.

"Naw. It'll be just fine," said Jim Bob Krait. "We'll look for you
back by sundown, that be all right?"

For a minute, I didn't know whether that was a command or an expression of concern.

"Just in case I get snakebit," I said. "I'll try to be careful up there."

"Good luck on findin' them rare birds," he said. He walked up to the
porch with his family.

"Les go," said Luke.

Behind the Krait house were a hen house and pigsty where hogs lay
after their morning slop like islands in a muddy bay, or some Zen pork
sculpture. Next we passed broken farm machinery gone to rust, though
there was nothing but uncultivated land as far as the eye could see.
How the family made a living I don't know. I'm told you can find places
just like this throughout the South.

We walked through woods and across fields, following a sort of path.
I tried to memorize the turns I would have to take on my way back.
Luke didn't say a word the whole twenty minutes he accompanied me,
except to curse once when he stepped into a bull nettle with his tennis
shoes.

We came to a creek that skirted the edge of a woodsy hill. There was
a rotted log forming a small dam. Above it the water was nearly a meter
deep; below it, half that much.

"See that path?" he asked.

"Yes."

"Follow it up around the hill, then across the next field. Then you
cross the creek again on the rocks, and over the hill. Take the left-hand
path. What's left of the house is about three-quarters the way up the

next hill. If you come to a big bare rock cliff, you've gone too far. You got that?"

I nodded.

He turned and left.

The house had once been a dog-run cabin, as Ms. Jimson had said. Now it was fallen in on one side, what they call sigoglin. (Or was it anti-sigoglin?) I once heard a hymn on the radio called "The Land Where No Cabins Fall." This was the country songs like that were written in.

Weeds grew everywhere. There were signs of fences, a flattened pile of wood that had once been a barn. Farther behind the house were the outhouse remains. Half a rusted pump stood in the backyard. A flatter spot showed where the vegetable garden had been; in it a single wild tomato, pecked by birds, lay rotting. I passed it. There was lumber from three outbuildings, mostly rotten and green with algae and moss. One had been a smokehouse and woodshed combination. Two had been chicken roosts. One was larger than the other. It was there I started to poke around and dig.

Where? Where? I wish I'd been on more archaeological digs, knew the places to look. Refuse piles, midden heaps, kitchen scrap piles, compost boxes. Why hadn't I been born on a farm so I'd know instinctively where to search?

I prodded around the grounds. I moved back and forth like a setter casting for the scent of quail. I wanted more, more. I still wasn't satisfied.

Dusk. Dark, in fact. I trudged into the Kraits' front yard. The tote sack I carried was full to bulging. I was hot, tired, streaked with fifty years of chicken shit. The Kraits were on their porch. Jim Bob lumbered down like a friendly mountain.

I asked him a few questions, gave them a Xerox of one of the dodo pictures, left them addresses and phone numbers where they could reach me.

Then into the rental car. Off to Water Valley, acting on information Jennifer Krait gave me. I went to the postmaster's house at Water Valley. She was getting ready for bed. I asked questions. She got on the phone. I bothered people until one in the morning. Then back into the trusty rental car.

On to Memphis as the moon came up on my right. Interstate 55 was a glass ribbon before me. WLS from Chicago was on the radio.

I hummed along with it, I sang at the top of my voice.

The sack full of dodo bones, beaks, feet, and eggshell fragments kept me company on the front seat.

Did you know a museum once traded an entire blue whale skeleton for one of a dodo?

Driving, driving.

The Dance of the Dodos

I used to have a vision sometimes—I had it long before this madness came up. I can close my eyes and see it by thinking hard. But it comes to me most often, most vividly, when I am reading and listening to classical music, especially Pachelbel's *Canon in D.*

It is near dusk in The Hague, and the light is that of Frans Hals, of Rembrandt. The Dutch royal family and their guests eat and talk quietly in the great dining hall. Guards with halberds and pikes stand in the corners of the room. The family is arranged around the table: the King, Queen, some princesses, a prince, a couple of other children, an invited noble or two. Servants come out with plates and cups, but they do not intrude.

On a raised platform at one end of the room an orchestra plays dinner music—a harpsichord, viola, cello, three violins, and woodwinds. One of the royal dwarfs sits on the edge of the platform, his foot slowly rubbing the back of one of the dogs sleeping near him.

As the music of Pachelbel's *Canon in D* swells and rolls through the hall, one of the dodos walks in clumsily, stops, tilts its head, its eyes bright as a pool of tar. It sways a little, lifts its foot tentatively, one, then another, rocks back and forth in time to the cello.

The violins swirl. The dodo begins to dance, its great ungainly body now graceful. It is joined by the other two dodos who come into the hall, all three turning in a sort of circle.

The harpsichord begins its counterpoint. The fourth dodo, the white one from Réunion, comes from its place under the table and joins the circle with the others.

It is most graceful of all, making complete turns where the others only sway and dip on the edge of the circle they have formed.

The music rises in volume; the first violinist sees the dodos and nods to the King. But he and the others at the table have already seen. They are silent, transfixed—even the servants stand still, bowls, pots, and kettles in their hands, forgotten.

Around the dodos dance with bobs and weaves of their ugly heads. The white dodo dips, takes a half step, pirouettes on one foot, circles again.

Without a word the King of Holland takes the hand of the Queen, and they come around the table, children before the spectacle. They join in the dance, waltzing (anachronism) among the dodos while the family, the guests, the soldiers watch and nod in time with the music.

Then the vision fades, and the afterimage of a flickering fireplace and a dodo remains.

The dodo and its kindred came by ships to the ports of Europe. The first we have record of is that of Captain van Neck, who brought back two in 1599—one for the ruler of Holland, and one that found its way through Cologne to the menagerie of Emperor Rudolf II.

This royal aviary was at Schloss Negebau, near Vienna. It was here that the first paintings of the dumb old birds were done by Georg and his son Jacob Hoefnagel, between 1602 and 1610. They painted it among more than ninety species of birds that kept the Emperor amused.

Another Dutch artist named Roelandt Savery, as someone said, "made a career out of the dodo." He drew and painted the birds many times, and was no doubt personally fascinated by them. Obsessed, even. Early on, the paintings are consistent; the later ones have inaccuracies. This implies he worked from life first, then from memory as his model went to that place soon to be reserved for all its species. One of his drawings has two of the Raphidae scrambling for some goody on the ground. His works are not without charm.

Another Dutch artist (they seemed to sprout up like mushrooms after a spring rain) named Peter Withoos also stuck dodos in his paintings, sometimes in odd and exciting places—wandering around during their owner's music lessons, or stuck with Adam and Eve in some Edenic idyll.

The most accurate representation, we are assured, comes from half a world away from the religious and political turmoil of the seafaring Europeans. There is an Indian miniature painting of the dodo that now rests in a museum in Russia. The dodo could have been brought by the Dutch or Portuguese in their travels to Goa and the coasts of the Indian subcontinent. Or it could have been brought centuries before by the Arabs who plied the Indian Ocean in their triangular-sailed craft, and who may have discovered the Mascarenes before the Europeans cranked themselves up for the First Crusade.

At one time early in my bird-fascination days (after I stopped killing them with BB guns but before I began to work for a scholarship) I once sat down and figured out where all the dodos had been.

Two with Van Neck in 1599, one to Holland, one to Austria. Another was in Count Solms's park in 1600. An account speaks of "one in Italy, one in Germany, several to England, eight or nine to Holland." William Boentekoe van Hoorn knew of "one shipped to Europe in 1640, another in 1685," which he said was "also painted by Dutch artists." Two were mentioned as "being kept in Surrat House in India as pets," perhaps one of which is the one in the painting. Being charitable, and considering "several" to mean at least three, that means twenty dodos in all.

There had to be more, when boatloads had been gathered at the time.

What do we know of the Didine birds? A few ships' logs, some accounts left by travelers and colonists. The English were fascinated by them. Sir Hamon Lestrange, a contemporary of Pepys, saw exhibited "a Dodar from the Island of Mauritius . . . it is not able to flie, being so bigge." One was stuffed when it died, and was put in the Museum Tradescantum in South Lambeth. It eventually found its way into the Ashmolean Museum. It grew ratty and was burned, all but a leg and the head, in 1750. By then there were no more dodos, but nobody had realized that yet.

Francis Willughby got to describe it before its incineration. Earlier, old Carolus Clusius in Holland studied the one in Count Solms's park. He collected everything known about the Raphidae, describing a dodo leg Pieter Pauw kept in his natural-history cabinet, in *Exoticarium libri decem* in 1605, seven years after their discovery.

François Leguat, a Huguenot who lived on Réunion for some years, published an account of his travels in which he mentioned the dodos. It was published in 1690 (after the Mauritius dodo was extinct) and included the information that "some of the males weigh forty-five pound. . . . One egg, much bigger than that of a goos is laid by the female, and takes seven weeks hatching time."

The Abbé Pingré visited the Mascarenes in 1761. He saw the last of the Rodriguez solitaires and collected what information he could about the dead Mauritius and Réunion members of the genus.

After that, only memories of the colonists, and some scientific debate as to *where* the Raphidae belonged in the great taxonomic scheme of things—some said pigeons, some said rails—were left. Even this nitpicking ended. The dodo was forgotten.

When Lewis Carroll wrote *Alice in Wonderland* in 1865, most people thought he had invented the dodo.

The service station I called from in Memphis was busier than a one-legged man in an ass-kicking contest. Between bings and dings of the bell, I finally realized the call had gone through.

The guy who answered was named Selvedge. I got nowhere with him. He mistook me for a real estate agent, then a lawyer. Now he was beginning to think I was some sort of a con man. I wasn't doing too well, either. I hadn't slept in two days. I must have sounded like a speed freak. My only progress was that I found that Ms. Annie Mae Gudger (childhood playmate of Jolyn Jimson) was now, and had been, the respected Ms. Annie Mae Radwin. This guy Selvedge must have been a secretary or toady or something.

We were having a conversation comparable to that between a shrieking macaw and a pile of mammoth bones. Then there was another click on the line.

"Young man?" said the other voice, an old woman's voice, southern, very refined but with a hint of the hills in it.

"Yes? Hello! Hello!"

"Young man, you say you talked to a Jolyn somebody? Do you mean Jolyn Smith?"

"Hello! Yes! Ms. Radwin, Ms. Annie Mae Radwin who used to be Gudger? She lives in Austin now. Texas. She used to live near Water Valley, Mississippi. Austin's where I'm from. I—"

"Young man," asked the voice again, "are you sure you haven't been put up to this by my hateful sister Alma?"

"Who? No, ma'am. I met a woman named Jolyn—"

"I'd like to talk to you, young man," said the voice. Then, offhandedly, "Give him directions to get here, Selvedge."

Click.

I cleaned out my mouth as best as I could in the service station rest room, tried to shave with an old clogged Gillette disposable in my knapsack, and succeeded in gapping up my jawline. I changed into a clean pair of jeans and the only other shirt I had with me, and combed my hair. I stood in front of the mirror.

I still looked like the dog's lunch.

The house reminded me of Presley's mansion, which was somewhere in the neighborhood. From a shack on the side of a Mississippi hill to this, in forty years. There are all sorts of ways of making it. I wondered what Annie Mae Gudger's had been. Luck? Predation? Divine intervention? Hard work? Trover and replevin?

Selvedge led me toward the sun room. I felt like Philip Marlowe going to meet a rich client. The house was filled with that furniture built sometime between the turn of the century and the 1950s—the ageless kind. It never looks great, it never looks ratty, and every chair is comfortable.

I think I was expecting some formidable woman with sleeve blotters and a green eyeshade hunched over a rolltop desk with piles of paper whose acceptance or rejection meant life or death for thousands.

Who I met was a charming lady in a green pantsuit. She was in her sixties, her hair still a straw-wheat color. It didn't looked dyed. Her eyes were blue as my first-grade teacher's had been. She was wiry and looked as if the word *fat* was not in her vocabulary.

"Good morning, Mr. Lindberl." She shook my hand. "Would you like some coffee? You look as if you could use it."

"Yes, thank you."

"Please sit down." She indicated a white wicker chair at a glass table. A serving tray with coffeepot, cups, tea bags, croissants, napkins, and plates lay on the tabletop.

After I swallowed half a cup of coffee at a gulp, she said, "What you wanted to see me about must be important."

"Sorry about my manners," I said. "I know I don't look it, but I'm a biology assistant at the University of Texas. An ornithologist. Working on my master's. I met Ms. Jolyn Jimson two days ago—"

"How is Jolyn? I haven't seen her in, oh, Lord, it must be on to fifty years. The time gets away."

"She seemed to be fine. I only talked to her half an hour or so. That was—"

"And you've come to see me about . . . ?"

"Uh. The . . . about some of the poultry your family used to raise, when they lived near Water Valley."

She looked at me a moment. Then she began to smile.

"Oh, you mean the ugly chickens?" she said.

I smiled. I almost laughed. I knew what Oedipus must have gone through.

It is now four-thirty in the afternoon. I am sitting in the downtown Motel 6 in Memphis. I have to make a phone call and get some sleep and catch a plane.

Annie Mae Gudger Radwin talked for four hours, answering my questions, setting me straight on family history, having Selvedge hold all her calls.

The main problem was that Annie Mae ran off in 1928, the year *before* her father got his big break. She went to Yazoo City, and by degrees and stages worked her way northward to Memphis and her destiny as the widow of a rich mercantile broker.

But I get ahead of myself.

Grandfather Gudger used to be the overseer for Colonel Crisby on the main plantation near McComb, Mississippi. There was a long story behind that. Bear with me.

Colonel Crisby himself was the scion of a seafaring family with interests in both the cedars of Lebanon (almost all cut down for masts for His Majesty's and others' navies) and Egyptian cotton. Also teas, spices, and any other salable commodity that came its way.

When Colonel Crisby's grandfather reached his majority in 1802, he waved good-bye to the Atlantic Ocean at Charleston, S.C., and stepped westward into the forest. When he stopped, he was in the middle of the Chickasaw Nation, where he opened a trading post and introduced slaves to the Indians.

And he prospered, and begat Colonel Crisby's father, who sent back to South Carolina for everything his father owned. Everything—slaves, wagons, horses, cattle, guinea fowl, peacocks, and dodos, which everybody thought of as atrociously ugly poultry of some kind, one of the seafaring uncles having bought them off a French merchant in 1721. (I surmised these were white dodos from Réunion, unless they had been from even earlier stock. The dodo of Mauritius was already extinct by then.)

All this stuff was herded out west to the trading post in the midst of the Chickasaw Nation. (The tribes around there were of the confederation of the Dancing Rabbits.)

And Colonel Crisby's father prospered, and so did the guinea fowl and the dodos. Then Andrew Jackson came along and marched the Dancing Rabbits off up the Trail of Tears to the heaven of Oklahoma. And Colonel Crisby's father begat Colonel Crisby, and put the trading post in the hands of others, and moved his plantation westward still to McComb.

Everything prospered but Colonel Crisby's father, who died. And the dodos, with occasional losses to the avengin' weasel and the egg-sucking dog, reproduced themselves also.

Then along came Granddaddy Gudger, a Simon Legree role model, who took care of the plantation while Colonel Crisby raised ten companies of men and marched off to fight the War for Southern Independence.

Colonel Crisby came back to the McComb plantation earlier than most, he having stopped much of the same volley of Minié balls that caught his commander, General Beauregard Hanlon, on a promontory bluff during the Siege of Vicksburg.

He wasn't dead, but death hung around the place like a gentlemanly bill collector for a month. The Colonel languished, went slapdab crazy, and freed all his slaves the week before he died (the war lasted another two years after that). Not now having any slaves, he didn't need an overseer.

Then comes the Faulkner part of the tale, straight out of *As I Lay Dying*, with the Gudger family returning to the area of Water Valley (before there was a Water Valley), moving through the demoralized and tattered displaced persons of the South, driving their dodos before them. For Colonel Crisby had given them to his former overseer for his faithful service. Also followed the story of the bloody murder of Granddaddy Gudger at the hands of the Freedman's militia during the rising of the first Klan, and of the trials and tribulations of Daddy Gudger in the years between 1880 and 1910, when he was between the ages of four and thirty-four.

Alma and Annie Mae were the second and fifth of Daddy Gudger's brood, born three years apart. They seem to have hated each other from the very first time Alma looked into little Annie Mae's crib. They were kids by Daddy Gudger's second wife (his desperation had killed the first) and their father was already on his sixth career. He had been a lumberman, a stump preacher, a plowman-for-hire (until his mules broke out in farcy buds and died of the glanders), a freight hauler (until his horses died of overwork and the hardware store repossessed the wagon), a politician's roadie (until the politician lost the election). When Alma and Annie Mae were born, he was failing as a share-cropper. Somehow Gudger had made it through the Depression of 1898 as a boy, and was too poor after that to notice more about economics than the price of Beech-Nut tobacco at the store.

Alma and Annie Mae fought, and it helped none at all that Alma, being the oldest daughter, was both her mother's and her father's darling. Annie Mae's life was the usual unwanted-poor-white-trash-child's hell. She vowed early to run away, and recognized her ambition at thirteen.

All this I learned this morning. Jolyn (Smith) Jimson was Annie Mae's only friend in those days –from a family even poorer than the Gudgers. But somehow there was food, and an occasional odd job. And the dodos.

"My father hated those old birds," said the cultured Annie Mae Radwin, née Gudger, in the solarium. "He always swore he was going to get rid of them someday, but just never seemed to get around to it. I think there was more to it than that. But they were so much *trouble*. We always had to keep them penned up at night, and go check for their eggs. They wandered off to lay them, and forgot where they were. Sometimes no new ones were born at all in a year.

"And they got so *ugly*. Once a year. I mean, terrible-looking, like they were going to die. All their feathers fell off, and they looked like they had mange or something. Then the whole front of their beaks fell off, or worse, hung halfway on for a week or two. They looked like big old naked pigeons. After that they'd lose weight, down to twenty or thirty pounds, before their new feathers grew back.

"We were always having to kill foxes that got after them in the turkey house. That's what we called their roost, the turkey house. And we found their eggs all sucked out by cats and dogs. They were so stupid we had to drive them into their roost at night. I don't think they could have found it standing ten feet from it."

She looked at me.

"I think much as my father hated them, they meant something to him. As long as he hung on to them, he knew he was as good as Granddaddy Gudger. You may not know it, but there was a certain amount of family pride about Granddaddy Gudger. At least in my father's eyes.

His rapid fall in the world had a sort of grandeur to it. He'd gone from a relatively high position in the old order, and maintained some grace and stature after the Emancipation. And though he lost everything, he managed to keep those ugly old chickens the Colonel had given him as sort of a symbol.

"And as long as he had them, too, my daddy thought himself as good as his father. He kept his dignity, even when he didn't have anything else."

I asked what happened to them. She didn't know, but told me who did and where I could find her.

That's why I'm going to make a phone call.

"Hello. Dr. Courtney. Dr. Courtney? This is Paul. Memphis. Tennessee. It's too long to go into. No, of course not, not yet. But I've got evidence. What? Okay, how do trochanters, coracoids, tarsometatarsi and beak sheaths sound? From their hen house, where else? Where would you keep *your* dodos, then?

"Sorry. I haven't slept in a couple of days. I need some help. Yes, yes. Money. Lots of money.

"Cash. Three hundred dollars, maybe. Western Union, Memphis, Tennessee. Whichever one's closest to the airport. Airport. I need the department to set up reservations to Mauritius for me. . . .

"No. No. Not wild-goose chase, wild-*dodo* chase. Tame-dodo chase. I *know* there aren't any dodos on Mauritius! I know that. I could explain. I know it'll mean a couple of grand—if—but—

"Look, Dr. Courtney. Do you want *your* picture in *Scientific American,* or don't you?"

I am sitting in the airport café in Port Louis, Mauritius. It is now three days later, five days since that fateful morning my car wouldn't start. God bless the Sears Diehard people. I have slept sitting up in a plane seat, on and off, different planes, different seats, for twenty-four hours, Kennedy to Paris, Paris to Cairo, Cairo to Madagascar. I felt like a brand-new man when I got here.

Now I feel like an infinitely sadder and wiser brand-new man. I have just returned from the hateful sister Alma's house in the exclusive section of Port Louis, where all the French and British officials used to live.

Courtney will get his picture in *Scientific American,* all right. Me too. There'll be newspaper stories and talk shows for a few weeks for me, and I'm sure Annie Mae Gudger Radwin on one side of the world and Alma Chandler Gudger Molière on the other will come in for their share of glory.

I am putting away cup after cup of coffee. The plane back to Tananarive leaves in an hour. I plan to sleep all the way back to Cairo, to Paris, to New York, pick up my bag of bones, sleep back to Austin.

Before me on the table is a packet of documents, clippings, and photographs. I have come across half the world for this. I gaze from the package, out the window across Port Louis to the bulk of Mont Pieter Both, which overshadows the city and its famous racecourse.

Perhaps I should do something symbolic. Cancel my flight. Climb the mountain and look down on man and all his handiworks. Take a pitcher of martinis with me. Sit in the bright semitropical sunlight (it's early dry winter here). Drink the martinis slowly, toasting Snuffo, God of Extinction. Here's one for the great auk. This is for the Carolina parakeet. Mud in your eye, passenger pigeon. This one's for the heath hen. Most important, here's one each for the Mauritius dodo, the white dodo of Réunion, the Réunion solitaire, the Rodriguez solitaire. Here's to the Raphidae, great Didine birds that you were.

Maybe I'll do something just as productive, like climbing Mont Pieter Both and pissing into the wind.

How symbolic. The story of the dodo ends where it began, on this very island. Life imitates cheap art. Like the Xerox of the Xerox of a bad novel. I never expected to find dodos still alive here (this is the one place they would have been noticed). I still can't believe Alma Chandler Gudger Molière could have lived here twenty-five years and not *know* about the dodo, never set foot inside the Port Louis Museum, where they have skeletons and a stuffed replica the size of your little brother.

After Annie Mae ran off, the Gudger family found itself prospering in a time the rest of the country was going to hell. It was 1929. Gudger delved into politics again and backed a man who knew a man who worked for Theodore "Sure Two-Handed Sword of God" Bilbo, who had connections everywhere. Who introduced him to Huey "Kingfish" Long just after that gentleman lost the Louisiana governor's election one of the times. Gudger stumped around Mississippi, getting up steam for Long's Share the Wealth plan, even before it had a name.

The upshot was that the Long machine in Louisiana knew a rabble-rouser when it saw one, and invited Gudger to move to the Sportsman's Paradise, with his family, all expenses paid, and start working for the

Kingfish at the unbelievable salary of $62.50 a week. Which prospect was like turning a hog loose under a persimmon tree, and before you could say Backwoods Messiah, the Gudger clan was on its way to the land of pelicans, graft, and Mardi Gras.

Almost. But I'll get to that.

Daddy Gudger prospered all out of proportion to his abilities, but many men did that during the Depression. First a little, thence to more, he rose in bureaucratic (and political) circles of the state, dying rich and well hated with his fingers in *all* the pies.

Alma Chandler Gudger became a debutante (she says Robert Penn Warren put her in his book) and met and married Jean Carl Molière, only heir to rice, indigo, and sugarcane growers. They had a happy wedded life, moving first to the West Indies, later to Mauritius, where the family sugarcane holdings were among the largest on the island. Jean Carl died in 1959. Alma was his only survivor.

So local family makes good. Poor sharecropping Mississippi people turn out to have a father dying with a smile on his face, and two daughters who between them own a large portion of the planet.

I open the envelope before me. Ms. Alma Molière had listened politely to my story (the university had called ahead and arranged an introduction through the director of the Port Louis Museum, who knew Ms. Molière socially) and told me what she could remember. Then she sent a servant out to one of the storehouses (large as a duplex) and he and two others came back with boxes of clippings, scrapbooks, and family photos.

"I haven't looked at any of this since we left St. Thomas," she said. "Let's go through it together."

Most of it was about the rise of Citizen Gudger.

"There's not many pictures of us before we came to Louisiana. We were so frightfully poor then, hardly anyone we knew had a camera. Oh, look. Here's one of Annie Mae. I thought I threw all those out after Momma died."

This is the photograph. It must have been taken about 1927. Annie Mae is wearing some unrecognizable piece of clothing that approximates a dress. She leans on a hoe, smiling a snaggle-toothed smile. She looks to be ten or eleven. Her eyes are half-hidden by the shadow of the brim of a gapped straw hat she wears. The earth she is standing in barefoot has been newly turned. Behind her is one corner of the house, and the barn beyond has its upper hay windows open. Out-of-focus people are at work there.

A few feet behind her, a huge male dodo is pecking at something on the ground. The front two thirds of it shows, back to the stupid wings and the edge of the upcurved tail feathers. One foot is in the photo, having just scratched at something, possibly an earthworm, in the new-plowed clods. Judging by its darkness, it is the gray, or Mauritius, dodo.

The photograph is not very good, one of those 3½ × 5 jobs box cameras used to take. Already I can see this one, and the blowup of the dodo, taking up a double-page spread in *S.A.* Alma told me that around then they were down to six or seven of the ugly chickens, two whites, the rest gray-brown.

Besides this photo, two clippings are in the package, one from the Bruce *Banner-Times*, the other from the Oxford newspaper; both are columns by the same woman dealing with "Doings in Water Valley." Both mention the Gudger family's moving from the area to seek its for-tune in the swampy state to the west, and tell how they will be missed. Then there's a yellowed clipping from the front page of the Oxford paper with a small story about the Gudger Family Farewell Party in Water Valley the Sunday before (dated October 19, 1929).

There's a handbill in the package, advertising the Gudger Family Farewell Party, Sunday Oct. 15, 1929 Come One Come All. The peo-ple in Louisiana who sent expense money to move Daddy Gudger must have overestimated the costs by an exponential factor. I said as much.

"No," Alma Molière said. "There was a lot, but it wouldn't have made any difference. Daddy Gudger was like Thomas Wolfe and knew a shining golden opportunity when he saw one. Win, lose, or draw, he was never coming back *there* again. He would have thrown some kind of soiree whether there had been money for it or not. Besides, people were much more sociable then, you mustn't forget."

I asked her how many people came.

"Four or five hundred," she said. "There's some pictures here some-where." We searched awhile, then we found them.

Another thirty minutes to my flight. I'm not worried sitting here. I'm the only passenger, and the pilot is sitting at the table next to mine talking to an RAF man. Life is much slower and nicer on these colonial islands. You mustn't forget.

I look at the other two photos in the package. One is of some men playing horseshoes and washer toss, while kids, dogs, and women look on. It was evidently taken from the east end of the house looking west.

Everyone must have had to walk the last mile to the old Gudger place. Other groups of people stand talking. Some men, in shirt sleeves and suspenders, stand with their heads thrown back, a snappy story, no doubt, just told. One girl looks directly at the camera from close up, shyly, her finger in her mouth. She's about five. It looks like any snapshot of a family reunion which could have been taken anywhere, anytime. Only the clothing marks it as backwoods 1920s.

Courtney will get his money's worth. I'll write the article, make phone calls, plan the talk show tour to coincide with publication. Then I'll get some rest. I'll be a normal person again—get a degree, spend my time wading through jungles after animals that will all be dead in another twenty years, anyway.

Who cares? The whole thing will be just another media event, just this year's Big Deal. It'll be nice getting normal again. I can read books, see movies, wash my clothes at the laundromat, listen to Johnathan Richman on the stereo. I can study and become an authority on some minor matter or other.

I can go to museums and see all the wonderful dead things there.

"That's the memory picture," said Alma. "They always took them at big things like this, back in those days. Everybody who was there would line up and pose for the camera. Only we couldn't fit everybody in. So we had two made. This is the one with us in it."

The house is dwarfed by people. All sizes, shapes, dress, and age. Kids and dogs in front, women next, then men at the back. The only exceptions are the bearded patriarchs seated toward the front with the children—men whose eyes face the camera but whose heads are still ringing with something Nathan Bedford Forrest said to them one time on a smoke-filled field. This photograph is from another age. You can recognize Daddy and Mrs. Gudger if you've seen their photographs before. Alma pointed herself out to me.

But the reason I took the photograph is in the foreground. Tables have been built out of sawhorses, with doors and boards nailed across them. They extend the entire width of the photograph. They are covered with food, more food than you can imagine.

"We started cooking three days before. So did the neighbors. Everybody brought something," said Alma.

It's like an entire Safeway had been cooked and set out to cool. Hams, quarters of beef, chickens by the tubful, quail in mounds, rabbit, butter beans by the bushel, yams, Irish potatoes, an acre of corn, eggplants, peas, turnip greens, butter in five-pound molds, cornbread and biscuits, gallon cans of molasses, red-eye gravy by the pot.

And five huge birds—twice as big as turkeys, legs capped as for Thanksgiving, drumsticks the size of Schwarzenegger's biceps, whole-roasted, lying on their backs on platters large as cocktail tables.

The people in the crowd sure look hungry.

"We ate for days," said Alma.

I already have the title for the *Scientific American* article. It's going to be called "The Dodo Is *Still* Dead."

Special Non-Fact Articles Section

The range of science fiction's speculation about possible realities is bold and unlimited: sometimes science fiction isn't even fiction, quite. Sf writers delight in imagining how such frequently dreary things as business letters or government committee reports might seem if they came from the future or from slightly different worlds.

Herewith, two examples.

SUPERL
Charles E. Elliott

Your request for information [writes Lt. Comdr. Boethius C. Heminstitch, the Public Relations Officer of the Division of Unusual Languages of the U. S. Coast Guard] about SUPERL has been forwarded to me. I hope that you will not take offense because I have not used SUPERL in this letter; it has been a long-standing policy of this office to answer all requests in the language of the request.

As you probably already know, SUPERL is a language devised to replace all of the so-called natural languages. It is streamlined and rationally designed and has every advantage over the "natural" languages.

SUPERL was developed by a team of U. S. Coast Guard linguists on an abandoned oil rig off Santa Barbara. The Coast Guard sponsored this research and development project for obvious reasons having to do with interservice funding. The project stretched over a period of six months and resulted in Coast Guard handbooks in SUPERL Grammar, SUPERL Phonology, and SUPERL Readers I and II. At present an exhaustive SUPERL Dictionary is under preparation. Over five hundred centers for teaching SUPERL have been established, and it is already the official language of several government departments.

The advantages of SUPERL are many. Using it, speakers may talk directly in mathematics, physics, chemistry, spherical trigonometry, and anthropology, without the necessity of an intervening language. It of course makes direct conversion of the foot-pound-Fahrenheit system to the metric-Celsius system, thus relieving users of laborious and time-consuming computations. In its binary mode, SUPERL may be used directly with computers, bypassing any computer languages. With SUPERL a thesaurus is unnecessary: an alphabetical listing *is* a thesaurus. The real relationships of concepts are phonologically represented, and the unwholesome arbitrariness of phonetic symbolization is done away with.

The articulation of SUPERL involves many facial muscles, so that it is impossible to say something illogical in SUPERL without at least a weak smile. Blatant absurdities result in broad grins and repeated winks.

However, while these are major advantages, they might be built into "natural" languages. SUPERL has, in addition, two characteristics that no "natural" language has: truth and compactness.

Grammatical utterances in SUPERL are always *true*. Thus, new truths about the universe can be discovered by babbling. This has obvious advantages. Speakers of SUPERL have at their tongue tip (so to speak) the combined knowledge of mankind, and, what is more, all the facts about the universe they will ever need. The Coast Guard is presently exploiting this characteristic in a unique project. Thirty garrulous people have been gathered in our laboratory in Peoria and instructed to talk about whatever interests them. What they say is recorded and will be compiled into the SUPERL Encyclopedia. We modestly hope that ultimately this will be the Ultimate Compendium of All Knowledge. If it is ever declassified it may prove of interest to scholars and teachers.

The grammar of SUPERL is equipped for many uses. For example, history can be recounted using the past perfect. Count nouns are used for the nobility, and there are mass nouns for the people. And not only does it have a passive voice for the cautious, it even has a future tense for the anxious.

SUPERL is, in addition, amazingly compact. What may be a lengthy exegesis in a "natural" language is often a simple sentence in SUPERL. A classic example of this is B. A. Booper's refutation of stratificational analysis. It was a single word! Whole novels have been written on the back of Howard Johnson menus. SUPERL lends itself quite naturally to poetry. For example:

Gnuj
Wroj

—which shows a height of lyricism not often attained in awkward "natural" languages. The approximate English translation is "As the moon casts silvery fingers (*or* greasy forks) over the spider's (*or* lampshade's *or* fodder's) back, does he (*or* the moon) care, really care? I will return (*or* become nauseous) to my beloved (*or* the general public). Is there any other way? (*or* Do you have any oranges?)" The entire works of Shakespeare are being translated into SUPERL; the result is expected to be a single trilogy of plays. There may be some difficulties with actual production, for, as one writer observed, "The cast is large, but the soliloquies are short."

In spite of the many advantages of SUPERL, large numbers of people still sullenly refuse to say anything in it. We guess that this may be the result of half-baked rumors and spurious opinions about SUPERL. It would be well to straighten out a few expressions of anti-SUPERL sentiment.

Some object because speakers seem to be unable to make jokes in SUPERL. This seems to be a rather pointless objection. Jokes have their place, but there are all sorts of practical jokes that don't require any use of language at all. Let those who cite this as an objection stitch a friend's trouser legs together, or pour olive oil into their wives' cocktail glasses. In any case, to satisfy these spoilsports, we may point out that already a team of United States Coast Guard Transmogrificational Grammarians is at work devising a set of standard jokes that may be recited in SUPERL.

That chimpanzees seem to be able to learn SUPERL faster and better than human beings is not really an objection to the language, either. There is simply a difference between the brains of chimps and the brains of human beings. *Vive la différence!*

The rumor that a recent anthropological finding, an artifact, had no name in SUPERL, and that proponents of SUPERL subsequently smashed and disposed of the artifact, has no truth in it. Speakers of SUPERL have tested this rumor by trying to repeat it in SUPERL. They were able to repeat the rumor, but only with broad grins and guffaws. Thus, even if true, the rumor had to be most illogical.

The most vicious rumor is that it is possible to say "The world is coming to an end soon" in SUPERL without even the hint of a smile. This we must simply discount. If the present trend of diversity in "natural" languages continues to pollute our linguistic atmosphere, we really *are* in for trouble. Let the anti-SUPERLites consider that, instead of carping at a minor inconsistency in SUPERL.

I hope I have given you the information you require. You may be amused to know that there *are* dirty words in SUPERL. In the interests of National Security, however, these words have been classified and may be used only by the highest echelons of the government and the military.

Please write me directly if you are in need of further information about SUPERL. I would also be grateful if you would forward to me the names of any you hear being critical of SUPERL. Please indicate in your report if they are supported by any government moneys.

REPORT OF THE
SPECIAL COMMITTEE
ON THE QUALITY OF LIFE
Eric G. Iverson

30 November 1491
To: Their Hispanic Majesties Fernando II and Isabel
From: The Special Committee on the Quality of Life
Re: The environmental impact upon Spain of the proposed expedition of the Genoese navigator Cristóbal Colón, styled in his native Italian Cristoforo Colombo

The commission of learned men and mariners, established by Your Majesties under the chairmanship of Fr. Hernando de Talavera, during the period 1486–90 studied exhaustively the proposals set forth by the Genoese captain Colón, and rejected them as being extravagant and impractical. In the present year a second commission, headed by the Grand Cardinal, Pedro González de Mendoza, has also seen fit to decline the services of Colón. The present Special Committee on the Quality of Life finds itself in complete accord with the actions of the previous two bodies of inquiry. It is our unanimous conclusion that the rash scheme advocated by this visionary would, if adopted, do serious damage to the finances and ecology of Spain; that this damage, if permitted, would set a precedent for future, more severe, outrages of our environment; that even if successful it would unacceptably alter the life-style of the citizens of Spain; and, most important, that the proposed voyage would expose any sailors engaged thereon to unacceptable risks of permanent bodily illness and injury and even death.

Certain people may perhaps suggest that the sea program of this kingdom is essential to its future growth. To this uninformed view we may only offer our wholehearted opposition. The Atlantic sea program offers extremely high expenses and hazards in both men and matériel for gains at best speculative but most likely nonexistent. Now more than ever, resources need to be concentrated at home, to bring the long war against the heathen Moors of Granada to a successful conclusion. At such a crucial time the state should waste no money on a program whose returns, if any, will not be manifest for some decades.

If funding must be committed to the sea program, they should be earmarked for national defense goals in the Mediterranean Sea, not spent on wild-eyed jaunts into the trackless and turbulent Atlantic. Unless and until we succeed in overcoming the corsair gap now existing, our southern coast will remain vulnerable to attacks from Algeria and Morocco even after the Moors of Granada are brought under our control. Moreover, if we fail to move against the heathen states of Africa, they shall surely fall under the aegis of the expansionist Ottoman Sultanate, with potential profound consequences to the balance of power in the area, as strong infidel forces will then be enabled to strike at our routes to our Italian possessions.

It may be argued that shipbuilding will aid the economy of those areas near ports. This view is superficial and shortsighted. True, jobs may be provided for lumberjacks, carpenters, sailmakers, etc., but at what cost to the world in which they live? Barring reforestation projects, for which funding does not appear to be forthcoming, any extensive shipbuilding venture will inevitably result in the deforestation of significant areas of the kingdom and the deformation of the long-established ecological patterns of the wildlife therein. In any case, it is questionable if shipbuilding represents the ideal utilization of our limited timber resources. The quantity of wood required to construct an oceangoing vessel could better be used to provide low-income housing for whole villages of peasants or could furnish many underprivileged citizens with firewood sufficient for an entire year. Further, especially for long voyages such as that urged by Colón, ships must carry extensive stores (this point will again be alluded to later in the report). The question must be posed as to whether our agricultural industry is even adequate to care for the needs of the populace of Spain itself. Surely an affirmative answer to this question, such as cannot with assurance be made at present, is necessary before expansion can be contemplated and resources diverted for it. We must put a halt to these environmentally disadvantageous programs before they become so ingrained in our lifestyle that their removal presents difficulties.

There is yet another factor to be considered, one closely related to that referred to in the previous sentence. Even if Colón precisely fulfills his expectations, what will the consequences of this success be for Spain? Many substances about which we know little, and which may well be hazardous, will begin to enter the kingdom in large quantities, and control over their sale and distribution will be difficult to achieve. We run a substantial risk of seeing our nation filled with addicts to toxins now unknown. Nor is it possible to discount the dangers of ideological contamination, which is as much to be feared as is physical. It is doubtful if the inhabitants of the distant lands the Genoan plans to visit share our religious and cultural benefits. Yet it is probable that some of their number may settle on our soil and attempt to disseminate their inadequate but perhaps seductive doctrines among our populace. As we are now on the point of expelling the Jews from our state and have nearly overcome the Muslim Moors, why should we hazard the homogeneity we have at last achieved after almost eight centuries of sustained effort?

The sudden influx of new goods will also disturb our traditional economic organization. There can be no doubt that there will be an increase in the monetary supply because of the profit made by reselling Eastern goods throughout Europe, but can a corresponding increase in the volume of goods and services be predicted? If the answer to this question is in the negative, as all current economic indicators would imply, then the "success" of Colón would seem to bring with it a concomitant inflationary pressure that would tend to eat into the profits of that "success" and would make life more difficult and expensive for the average Spaniard. Also, any substantial increase in the sea program would entail the diversion of labor from its traditional concerns to maritime activity. Such a shift could not help but further disjoint our economy, and cannot be anticipated with anything other than trepidation. The dislocation could even be so severe as to cause emigration to the Eastern lands, which would of course entail a drain of the best of the kingdom's populace from its shores.

Finally, if the government of Spain is to approve, fund, and provide manpower for the Colón expedition, it must have some assurance that it is not dangerously imperiling the health and future well-being of the members of that expedition. Such assurance is not at all easy to come by. The dangers of a seaman's trade are well known, and he performs his duties on what can only be described as a diet of "junk food": hardtack, salt meat, and dried peas, with perhaps a bit of cheese. This regimen is manifestly unhealthful, and Colón and the men under his charge would be unable to supplement it except by fishing. They would not enjoy the advantage, as do sailors of the Mediterranean Sea and also the Portuguese in their journeys down the coast of Africa, of replenishing their supplies at relatively brief intervals, but would be compelled to make do once having departed the Canary Islands. Nor is the situation in regard to potables much better, these being restricted to casked water and wine. The probability is extremely high that at least some of the former will go bad; the latter not only faces this danger, but, if drunk to excess, has the potential of severely compromising the efficiency of ship's operations and thereby reducing an already low safety margin. Sleeping arrangements are equally substandard; indeed, for almost everyone they are nonexistent. Ships are so designed that only the captain has a cabin with a bunk, and even this private space is scarcely more than that to be found in a closet ashore. Sailors and underofficers sleep where they are able to find room, in the same clothing they have worn during the day. Thus the life-support systems of any expeditionary force at the current level of technology must be deemed inadequate.

Navigational instruments are also crude in the extreme. Quadrant and astrolabe are so cumbersome, and so likely to be grossly affected by ship's motion, as to be little more useful than dead reckoning in the determination of latitude; dead reckoning alone serves in estimating longitude. For a voyage of the length anticipated by Colón, these factors, in combination with the stormy nature of the Atlantic and the likelihood of meeting unanticipated hazards with no support facilities upon which to fall back, give the Genoan's proposals a degree of risk so high no merciful sovereign could in good conscience allow his subjects to endanger themselves in the pursuit thereof.

Therefore, it is the determination of the Special Committee on the Quality of Life, appointed by Your Hispanic Majesties as per the environmental protection ordinances of the realm, that the proposals of Colón do in the several ways outlined above comprise a clear and present danger to the quality and security of life within the kingdom, and that they should for that reason be rejected. Respectfully in triplicate submitted by

Jaime Nosénada
Chairman of the Special Committee
on the Quality of Life

Mary C. Pangborn's first published story, "The Back Road," appeared in Universe 9. *Here is her second, a wry story of rogues and magic, coshes and sorcery . . . and a surprising curse.*

THE CONFESSION OF HAMO
Mary C. Pangborn

Set down all I tell you, Brother Albertus, and may the devil fly away with you if you bend any of my words from their true meaning. Give them a better sound if you will, you with your book learning, but the truth is strange enough; let there be none of your clerkly twistings and turnings to make either more or less of it. Forty days I'll be here in sanctuary; we have plenty of time.

Yes, I confess myself guilty of taking a life, though I do not admit it was murder, no, for I never meant to hurt that silly fat merchant, only to relieve him of part of his superfluity. How was I to know he had a skull as frail as an egg? But it was robbery on the highway, and so they would hang me. I've no mind to yield myself to that. When my forty days are gone, happen I'll abjure the realm as the law commands, and wade out into salt water each day until there's a ship to take me away. Time enough.

You see no need for my words to be written down? Ah, you *will* see, sir, I promise you. For I have that to tell which might be scoffed at for an idle tale were there only my word for it, yet when it is written soberly in ink on good parchment, it will be known for truth. More, good father: there is a very dreadful sin weighing on me, the telling of which I must approach in fear and trembling; bear with me then, for it may need many words to make all clear.

I'm told I was born in the same year as our valiant King Harry, who killed so many Frenchmen at the great battle of Agincourt some three years past. And they say the King's grace was some eight and twenty years of age when he fought that battle—now God forbid I should name my poor self in the same breath as the King, yet I call myself a true freeborn Englishman even as he is, the saints preserve him. So there is time ahead of me before I can count two score winters; I'm not ready to let them take me and hang me by the neck. And it may be you can feel with me in this, for you cannot be so many years older than I, though you are somewhat fatter.

Where was I? Oh aye, I was born. Hamo of York they call me, and sometimes Hamo the Red, for my hair. I was some twelve years old when my mother died, and I wearied of the kitchen service in my lord's household and ran away. I doubt they ever thought me worth the chasing—a weazened bony snippet of a boy, idler and troublemaker. Here's a handful of sins at the beginning: idleness and mischief, that's sloth, and disobedience, running away from my rightful lord. Eh well, there's worse to come.

Not much to be said of my early years on the road, before I met with Tom—begging, a bit of thieving, lending a hand to the jugglers at fairs —sometimes I'd even work, if my belly was empty enough. It wasn't a bad life. I'd tramped the length of the realm before I was twenty, Lands End to Berwick, and found warm welcome all along the way, from young wenches and honest wives both. . . .

Now, with respect, Brother, that is a foolish question. How could I know? Was I ever in one place so much as two months, to say nothing of nine? How can a man guess how many bairns he may have sired? I'd not be surprised if England is well peppered with my redheads. But I will swear by any godly oath you like, I never took a wench against her will and liking. Willing they were, and pleased with me. I'll not tell you about one or another. I do hereby confess myself guilty of the sin of lechery—*mea maxima culpa*—let one confession stand for all of them.

But this is not what your abbot is hoping I may tell you.

Most kindly the noble abbot received me, when I knelt before him begging for sanctuary; most patiently he heard me as I confessed my crime of robbery. Of that he said nothing; he stroked his holy chin, and eyed me thoughtfully, and he said, "I am told you spent some time journeying with a man known as Moses the Mage." And I said this was true, for how should I deny my friend? Then he said, "It is rumored that this so-called mage has made a study of the art of alchemy, the search for the Elixir, called by some the Philosopher's Stone." And again I said, this rumor is true. Then he said no more except to promise I should receive sanctuary, and that he would send me a confessor to assist me in cleansing my soul of sin. And for this grace, and especially for his sending you to me, I am most deeply and humbly grateful. Now it would be presumptuous in me to suppose I could read the abbot's saintly thoughts, yet it did seem to me he felt that any knowledge of the secret work of alchemy might be too heavy a burden for such a simple soul as mine, and only by divesting myself of that burden, yielding it up to one too holy to be corrupted by it, might I hope to save myself. Wherefore, if you will but hear my confession and write as I bid you, I will reveal to you—for the abbot's ear—all that I know of the making of gold.

Let me first tell you about Moses the Mage.

He had already taken that name when I met him first, but he was baptized Thomas—Tom o' Fowey, a Cornishman. Maybe you know they have a language of their own, not like any other; it would make you wonder if you were in any part of England. When I joined him he was mostly making weather magic, and a marvel it was to hear him lashing out in his strange tongue, all the folk gowking at him—he could switch to priestly Latin fast enough if anyone smelling like a bailiff came near. He'd been raised for a priest, until he decided the life would not suit him, and he had more clerkly learning than many of them, saving your presence. Now the spirits that bring wind and rain surely understood Cornish, for Tom's weather sayings were usually right.

He could make an awesome figure of himself: tall and thin he is, with a mighty beak of a nose, and when he appeared as Moses he wore a black patch over one eye. Folk whispered he had sacrificed that eye in a pact with some evil spirit, in exchange for secret knowledge. Times we'd be in peril of a charge of sorcery, and the bailiff's men would be looking for a tall dark one-eyed man; when they'd find us, I'd be sitting there with the black patch on me, a harmless little redheaded beggar, and Tom with his two great solemn dark eyes whole and sound, a holy pilgrim fingering his rosary; so the fellows who described him would be put to shame. Once it was a near thing, when the sheriff's man pulled off my eye patch, but he backed away fast, terrified and cursing, seeing my eye horribly red and dangerous. We never traveled without an onion.

Weather magic wasn't our only business; we also traded in drugs and herbal mixtures, and sometimes we'd have a stock of the rare alicorn, which is the powdered horn of the unicorn, as you know—a strong cure for all poisons. Now there are rogues without bowels or conscience who will sell you a mess of powdered chalk and call it alicorn. We never did such a thing, though I'll not deny we might have mixed the true stuff with other matters, so as to have enough for everyone. One market day we had our stall set up and Tom was crying our wares in his big voice while I went among the people to take their money: "Here it is," he cries, "the only true alicorn, the one remedy for all poisons, that brave sailors bring you at great peril from strange and far places!" and he gives them a generous earful of Cornish to show how far and strange it was. "Here you see a piece of the horn itself—come close, friends, handle it, see for yourselves!" And then I saw a little man off at the edge of the crowd laughing to himself. Tom saw him too, and flung his Cornish speech at him, and when next I looked that way the man was gone. Scared off, I thought.

Alicorn fetches a good price, and we'd sold all we had, so we were enjoying a good hot supper at the inn when here comes that same little man sidling up to us, grinning and ducking his head at Tom. "Give ye good den, Master Moses," says he, "and will you not drink with me?"

Tom was scowling at him, and I held my breath, for Tom can be a fearsome man in a rage—the gust of his anger will blow you as high as the church steeple, till the sun comes out sudden and he's your good friend again. But this time he only growled a bit. "You'll be a Cornishman?" he says, begrudging it. The fellow lays a finger to his nose and puts his head to one side, as though he had to think about the answer. "Not exactly," says he, "but some of the words I know, yes. Black Jamie I am called, at your service."

Dressed all in black he was, and black-haired he might have been once, but the trifle of hair he had left was all white, only a bit of it sticking up over each ear; a small sharp face with the nose and chin pointing at you like knives, and little no-colored eyes watching from ambush. Still, he spoke us quiet and friendly-like; Tom offered him our salt, and he made a ceremony of taking some of it, to show he meant us no harm. So bit by bit we fell to talking easily, the good ale warming us; we could tell he was one of us, of the company of the road.

Jamie said, "You'll be somewhat of a scholar, Master Moses?"

"Now how would you know that?" says Tom.

"Why, you're too modest, man, you're better known along the road than you think," and Jamie winked at him. Fumbling at his pouch, he got out a little book, a shabby dirty old thing, no more than a dozen pages sewed together. Held it out in his left hand. "I'll warrant you can read this," he says.

Tom took the book over to the light of the torch by the fireplace, grumbling and grunting over it. "Aye, I can read the words," says he. "It is alchemy, I can see that much." We knew about alchemy; we had friends on the road who made a good living at the art, in the way I'll be telling you.

"*Words,*" says Jamie. "Strong magic in grand long words, Master Moses, none knows it better than yourself."

We did know. Tom was trying over the big words on his tongue, tasting and liking them, and Black Jamie watching his face. "I'll be honest with you, my friends," says Jamie (now surely we ought to have been on our guard when he said that!). "I've learned all the words in that book, I do not need it, and if you like, I will sell it to you for one silver penny. And you can lose nothing, for if you do not find you have a good bargain of it, I will buy it back from you for two pennies the next time we meet."

"So you're thinking we'll meet again?" I asked him.

"That shall be as God wills," says he—said it solemn enough, but I did notice he never made the sign of the cross. Tom gave him a penny for the book, and I don't remember that we took leave of him; the next time we gave a thought to him, he was gone.

We spent some days studying the book, Tom reading out the words and I putting them all away in my memory, and true enough there never was a book with finer treasure of long words in it, far more than a penny's worth. Yet they would not be sufficient, as we knew, and I said, "This is all very well, Tom, but it takes gold to make gold."

"I know," he said, and sighed. "Ah, I do wish we had a bit of gold."

Now everyone knows you ought to have a care how you speak those words *I wish*, for there is no knowing who or what may be listening. Yet I will swear Tom spoke no more than those innocent words, so there is no explaining what happened, unless maybe Black Jamie had a hand in it. For it was the very next day we came upon a man dead by the side of the road. A holy pilgrim, by his dress, lying there most peaceful, his hands folded on his breast, never a mark on him; you could tell it was only that his time had come to die, there where he was. His pouch was empty; he had a plain gold cross on a chain around his neck.

I did not like to take the cross off him. Tom said, "Surely 'tis the holiness that matters, not the gold," and he took off his own little wooden cross that had been blessed by Our Lady of Walsingham, and put that on the dead man instead of the gold one; and we went our way. It seemed an honest exchange, and we had done the man no harm. And I will swear neither of us had harbored any sinful thought of calling on the dark powers to help us—not then. . . .

Whatever, we made a good livelihood out of those mighty words in our book, as long as the pilgrim's gold lasted.

Now, Brother, I'd not be surprised if you have heard something of the way this is done. You must find yourself a patron, someone who is well endowed with the world's goods, yet feels he has not enough; a fat burgess is good, or the bailiff of a great lord—but you had best stay clear of the lord himself, he can too easily crush you like a louse between thumb and finger if you do not satisfy him. So, when you have found your man, you converse with him softly, slowly, at length, until you see he is enchanted; you discourse on *lunification,* on *tincture,* on *fixation,* on *dealbation;* on the secret names of Jupiter and Saturn, on the Black Crow, the White Eagle, the King and his Son, the Serpent who swallows his tail, and much more; thus it is beyond doubt that you are an adept, skilled in the lore of the mysterious East. We had an advantage, d'ye see, for if there was danger of being too clearly understood Tom would just speak a bit in Cornish.

Next, your man must build his furnace and supply himself with alembics and crucibles and many rare substances; meanwhile you are living at ease in his house, sleeping soft and eating well, and if you cannot put by somewhat when you go on errands to purchase his materials, you had better choose some other trade.

But you cannot let this go on too long; there will come a day when you must prove your work. You will let him place a bit of lead in his crucible, and throw in a bit of this and some of that, whatever; and finally you bring forth your magic powder. A black powder is good; you can use charcoal, with a sufficiency of powder of lead, and maybe the dried blood of a white cock. You should have him put it in with his own hand, making sure he tips it all in quickly, and then without delay you seal the crucible with moistened clay and place it in the furnace, for as long as you like. After the vessel has been well heated and the molten dross skimmed away, there will be a nugget of gold in the bottom, and why not?—for in your magic powder there was a fragment of gold covered with blackened wax.

Well now, your patron is happy, and so are you. You may decide to make another trial, and the second lump of gold will be a trifle larger than the first. But then, alas, you have only a little of the magic powder left, and you must make a long and costly journey to find the ingredients necessary to make more. He will eagerly help you on your way, and you will generously give him all the powder you have left, with

many difficult instructions on the use of it, so that you shall be long
gone before he despairs of success.

Yes, I know this is not the sort of gold-making your abbot wishes to
learn, but remember it is said: *Blessed are the meek, for they shall be
patient until the end of the story.* You would not have me omit any of
my misdeeds from my confession? And before you lay a heavy penance
on me, Brother, bethink you: this worthy patron I speak of has enjoyed
a rare and strange adventure, and had great pleasure in it; has he not
received good value for his money?

Well; so it went. The time came when all our stock of gold was
gone, and we sat together by our campfire at the edge of a lonely road,
considering what we might do next. We did not see Black Jamie come,
maybe just out of the shadow of the trees; there he was.

"Well met, friends," says he, and sat down by our fire without any
by-your-leave, the dancing shadows making horn shapes out of his two
tufts of hair, and spread his left hand to the warmth of the fire—only
that one hand, and I remembered he was left-handed, a mischancy
thing. We were not wholly pleased to see him, but we did not like to
be unfriendly, so presently we were passing our ale flask back and
forth, and making small talk about the ways of the road; we were two
stout young fellows to one old one, we saw no reason to fear him. After
a while he said, "You'll have had good profit out of your book, I'm
thinking. You'll not be wanting to sell it back to me?"

Tom says, "Nay, that we're not."

"Ah, you've used it well, I'll warrant! But, friends, have you not
sometimes thought of the true art that lies concealed behind all that
writing?"

"We might have put our minds to it," I said, and Tom frowned. But
it needed no warlock to guess that such a thought would have come to
us. For who would labor so mightily at all those mysteries, only to provide a few fellows like us with a chance of trickery? No, we knew there
must be some truth in it. When we had argued this, Tom always said
the secret was buried too deep for us. I was not so sure.

Black Jamie said, "Whatever, you'll be needing more gold."

"Who doesn't?" says Tom, a bit short, and Jamie laughed, a rusty-
screechy noise with no mirth in it, a sound I did not care for. "Ah, a
true word!" says he. "And there's more nor one way of getting it, am I
not right?"

"I've heard so," says Tom.

Black Jamie yawned, like a man having no more to say and thinking of naught but sleep, and he says, tossing it out careless-like—"Well, there's the ancient mounds, and the red gold in them."

Now some folk will tell you those places are entrances into faerie, and if you know the spell you may go in and spend one day in delight at the court of a beautiful elfin queen, but when you come out you will find a hundred years have passed and all your friends are dead. Others say these are only the burial grounds of old-time pagans, not to be feared by anyone who can say his paternoster, and men have broken into such mounds with pick and shovel, finding old bones and sometimes the red gold. You never do hear it told that those men have lived long and happy lives thereafter. I said, "It's known that such gold is accursed."

Jamie yawned again, and stretched out on the grass with his back to the fire. "Ah," says he, "that's because the folk do not know how to get it safely. You will please yourselves, friends, but I am going near one of those places tomorrow, and if you care to walk with me I can show it to you."

Then he was snoring, and it made us feel easier to hear him. A snore is a natural and homely thing; you cannot be afeard of a little bald wisp of a man who makes comical noises in his sleep.

So the next day we went along the road together, and Black Jamie kept us merry with songs and tales of old time, but never a word of himself or his own doings, and we somehow forgot to ask ourselves what manner of man he was. Near dusk he turned off the road into a great moor spreading westward, and we said nothing, but followed him. I will not tell you where the place was. We had lost sight of the highway when we came to the mound.

"Yonder it is," said Jamie, "and I've a notion to camp here for the night. You could join me and welcome, if you cared to."

It was only a hillock rising from the moor; you would think it a natural hill except for the smooth even shape of it. No tree or bush grew there, only the sheep-cropped grass, brighter and greener than common. Nothing fearsome about it. Tom says, "I've spent nights in worse places."

We built ourselves a bit of a fire.

"Ah, there is pleasant," says Black Jamie. The dark was sifting down around us. "It would maybe surprise you," says he, "the things I know that I would not be telling to everyone. But since you have been so friendly as to give me your comradeship, why, here is a secret you will not find in your book of alchemy. You will have heard that the gold found in the barrows is softer and redder than the common metal from the mines. Know, then, that this red gold of the ancient kings is not merely metal such as the goldsmiths use, but the very essence and spirit of gold. It is itself the Elixir."

I asked him, "Why then have the men who found this ancient gold not discovered what it was?"

"Ah, there is the heart of the matter. They have gone in roughly as mere grave robbers, d'ye see, and when the gold is stolen that way, the virtue goes out of it. You must enter the mound gently, humbly, and let the gold be given you as a free gift."

Tom said, "Are you telling us a mortal living man can do that?"

"It is not easy," says Jamie, "but I am the man who can tell you the way of it. Share and share alike, if you can get it."

We sat looking at him, thinking he mocked us, and he went on more urgently, "Of course, there is only one night in the whole month when it can be done," and even while he spoke the great silver circle was rising and peering over the lip of the moor at us. Night of the full moon.

I said, "If you know the way, why do you not get it for yourself?"

"*That* is why," he said, and thrust out his right hand at us, that he'd been keeping hidden. Half a hand it was, thumb and forefinger, three fingers gone. He said, "No one can enter the mound except he be a whole man."

It would have been childish to ask why not. "Well then," Tom was beginning, but Jamie put up that lonesome finger and shook it at him. "Not you." Now Tom had hurt his foot when he was a bairn and had lost the little toe off it: such a small old-time thing he'd nigh forgotten it himself. And Jamie had surely never seen him with his boots off, yet he knew. And now Jamie was studying me.

Let him look, I thought, and I began trying to remember my fights and beatings—scars enough I had for them, but nothing lost. I might now and then have stood in peril of losing an ear or so to the law, for this or that misdoing; still, it had not happened, for they never caught me. "Scars!" said Jamie impatiently. "Nay, how can anyone grow to manhood's years without scars? That is nothing. You could do it."

"I will, then," I said.

Now you see, Brother Albertus, here is that most deadly sin of which I spoke to you. For well I knew this was a trafficking with evil spirits, to the peril of my immortal soul, and yet I did knowingly enter upon it. Wherefore I will gladly suffer penance and go on pilgrimage if I may cleanse my soul of this thing. —Well; you must hear me out, to know how it was.

A black cross was to be set upside down, Jamie said, and he would teach me a spell in ancient Gaelic, and then—halfway through the telling of it he broke off and cocked his head sidewise at me. Smiling, if you could call it that. "There's a thing you ought to know, laddie, before you go on with this," says he. "You'll go in there a whole man, but you'll not come out without leaving some part of yourself in their hands. Whatever they choose to take."

I did not like the sound of that. I could imagine giving up a finger or a toe or two, even an ear, the red gold would be worth it; but there's other parts a man would not like to find missing off him, and I said as much to Black Jamie. "Never fear," said he, "they will play fair with you, they will take no more than you can spare. Even if they take one, they will leave you one," says he, and he let out that screech noise of his, laughter you might call it.

I'll be frank with you, Brother, I did not find much comfort in that reassurance, but it was too late for faint-heartedness. I came back at him cold and quick, the first words I found in my mouth: "Did *they* take your three fingers, then?"

He said nothing, said it in his ancient Gaelic, the little cold eyes freezing into me, and the silence might have gone on until we had all turned to blocks of ice where we sat, if Tom had not spoken. "Eh, well, get on with it, man," he says, "tell us what more we need to do." And so he did.

I had first to learn the words of the old Gaelic spell, and while the moon was climbing the sky Jamie strove most patiently with me to be sure I could say them right. I'd not have ventured to ask him what they meant, and surely he would not have told me—no need for me to know, only to speak them correctly. And at last he was satisfied I could do it. So I went up to the top of the mound and set that unholy cross in the earth, and walked three times widdershins around it saying the words I had learned; and I could not tell them to you now if I would, for as soon as they had served their purpose they went clean out of my head. Then I lay down on my back beside the black cross, and held my eyes open to the full light of the moon. And whether time passed while I lay there, or whether it stopped entirely, I do not know; I was not aware of anything happening, only that I found myself in another place.

I could feel walls enclosing space, and yet there was great distance, and no walls to be seen, nor any roof or sky; there was light—soft, not bright—you could not tell where it came from. Whisper of clean moving air; somewhere a darkness of trees, and a smell of old forest growing more thickly over the land than it does now. And there were men in the forest, though I could not see or hear them.

Then a man was standing in front of me, where there had been no one. He was no giant, but broad and thick, powerfully made, with a great gray beard and fierce old eyes frowning at me. He wore a short kirtle and a wolfskin flung over one shoulder, and held in his hand a bright sword; and around his neck and on either arm he wore heavy circles of red gold. So I knew he was a king.

He spoke, and his voice was a deep rumble like the noise of drums; his words were strange to me, but the air of that place caught them up and twisted them around, the way sunlight spatters through leaves, making new patterns, and I knew what they meant. He said, "Is it time?"

I must have been gaping stupidly, for he moved impatiently, and there was a ringing sound from his sword. "Have you no ears, clod? Have you come at last to fetch me against the enemies of the Land?"

Now in the first breath I thought of great King Arthur, who is to return one day and fight for us; but everyone knows that Arthur is buried at Glastonbury, and moreover he was a chivalrous Christian knight, not a savage clad in the hide of a wolf. Then I saw how there might well be more than one ancient king standing guard over the Land. And at last I found my tongue, and answered him, "Sire, I thank you for your kindness, but I can tell you we've gotten the better of our enemies, for we have a strong warrior as king."

"Ah," he said, and nodded. "That is good. You have driven them back from the beaches?"

"Why, they never came so far," I told him. "It would glad your heart to see it, sir, the way our good King Harry went over the water after them to kill them, and came home to a great triumph."

"Good, very good. Then I may sleep awhile longer." His men had been coming out of the forest behind him; there was a gleam of eyes and a shadow of hands on clubs. He motioned them back. "You must be sure to keep a strong guard on the beaches," he said sternly. "That is the way they always come. . . ."

"We keep guard," I promised him. And then I bethought me one must mind one's manners in speaking to a king, so I went down on my knee and swept off my cap, as I should have done sooner. All this did not take as much courage as you might think, for something about that place made it seem right and proper for me to be there; it was all a part of the enchantment. "Great King," I said, "I have come here boldly to bring you word that the Land is safe, and you may rest in peace. Now in my time, sire, we hold that the bringer of good news merits a reward, and if it should please your lordship to think thus, I would only ask most humbly for a small token of your royal gold."

He smiled; and oh, Brother Albertus, you have never seen such a smile! you could see the naked skull grinning behind the flesh, and I knew that all my secret thoughts and my desires for the gold were transparent to him. Yet it seemed he was not angry. "Be it so," he said, and he drew the gold band from his left arm and gave it to me. The first touch of it burned my fingers like ice; then I felt the living warmth of my hand flowing into it, and it was no more fiercely cold than metal ought to be. I said, "Sire, with all my heart I humbly thank you."

My voice was flat and dull, and I was alone in a small dim space with barely enough light to see what lay before me in the dust, where I was still kneeling: clean old bones, undisturbed, arms straight at the sides; around the neck and the right arm were circlets of gold, but on the left arm nothing—only a fresh scar in the earth under the long arm bone, as though something had been taken away.

Then I was lying on top of the mound in the moonlight, and I would have thought the whole thing a mere vision, but that I held a golden armband in my hands: bright and clean-shining, not like a thing dug out of old earth, and now I could see a swirl of markings on it, like a sort of writing. Down yonder by a fire were the shapes of two men, waiting. In a little, I remembered who they were. I went down to them and said, "Here is the gold," and fell flat on my face.

There was a while I don't remember, and then I was sitting beside the fire with Tom holding the flask so I could drink, and the gold circle on the ground in the firelight.

Black Jamie put out a hand toward it, moving slow and easy, the both of us watching him, Tom with his knife out and ready.

"Given as a free gift, it was," I said.

Black Jamie said, "Yes, I know." He took it into his hands, turning it over as though he could read the old writing. It seemed a long time until he laid it down, carefully, never letting his eyes shift toward the gleam of Tom's knife. "Now," says he, "we must divide it in three pieces."

Not so easy; it was a lovely thing, we did not like to hammer it roughly with stones. Jamie picked up an ordinary-looking pebble and scratched a couple of lines with it on the gold, muttering some of his Gaelic words, and passed it once quickly through the fire. "Now strike it with your stone," he said. I struck it, and there it lay, split cleanly into three pieces. One piece, a trifle smaller than the others, had the greater part of the writing on it. Tom and I sat still, not touching the gold, waiting.

Jamie picked up the smallest piece and tucked it into his pouch. Then he leaped suddenly in the air and clacked his heels together, thumbing his nose at us, and *psst!* like that, he was gone.

We both crossed ourselves quickly, all ashiver, fearing we had dealt with the devil himself. But then I said, "He is maybe a Welshman, or even a Scot, but I think he is not a demon, for then why would he have needed our help? And you must remember how he snored, like any natural man."

"Eh well," says Tom, "we knew he was a warlock."

Whatever he was, we were free of him, and now I told Tom everything that had happened, just as I have been telling it to you. He shook his head and sighed, "Ah, Hamo, Hamo! what a marvelous adventure! Could I but have gone with you!"

Then I remembered why he could not go, and the rest of it, and now my fingers were shaking with impatience to get all my clothes off, Tom helping me. I could scarce breathe till I might discover what had been taken from me. We looked carefully, both of us, and there was no part of me lacking, nothing, not so much as a toenail. Tom laughed. "Ah, I'll warrant he was mocking you—it would seem a merry sort of jest to him, the black-hearted bastard he is, man or demon."

But I could not help wondering: if they had stolen nothing from my outward and visible body, what had they taken instead? I considered myself—not an easy matter, Brother, though easily said—and I felt myself to be the same man I had always been. Ah well; I was accursed, but I did not know it; not yet.

Tom heaved another great sigh, deep out of his guts, and he said, "Think now, Hamo, what a marvelous song it would make! To speak with an old dead king, and win the red gold. . . ."

I knew what was in his heart. It was always his deepest longing to be a bard, a minstrel; not to wrench a livelihood out of the folk by clever trickery, but to win it with praise and joy, as a singer of tales. He could not do it; he had no gift for it, no more than I have myself. What do you think, Brother Albertus? Does everyone cherish some deep unhealing sorrow for the one splendid thing he can never do?

We could not make the song; we only sat quietly there together until it grew light enough for us to see each other's faces, and the two broken pieces of the red gold lying there on the ground between us.

Neither of us moved to touch it. The light grew, and the sun rose, and a finger of sunlight reached down along the mound, pointing at the gold. We'd not have been surprised if it had crumbled into a bit of dust, as they say faery gold does at the touch of morning. But no: it brightened in the sun, it soaked up the light and gave it back in glory, you might think it was a living thing that had suffered from darkness all those years under the earth and now sang with joy. It was ours, the true red gold. . . .

Now am I come to the sad and sorry part of my tale, Brother Albertus, and I ask you to hear me with compassion.

We lost no time in finding ourselves a snug place where we set up our furnaces and crucibles, and we labored earnestly to do all that was said in the book, employing our red gold as the Elixir, of which a tiny bit should suffice to change all the melt into its own pure nature, into true gold. Well. In a word, we could never get back more gold than we put in.

One day I found Tom sitting with his head in his hands, nigh to weeping, and he said, "I am greatly to blame, Hamo, I have made you think me a greater scholar than I am. I can read the secret words in our book, saying *Seize and slay the dragon, lift out his entrails, bring the green lion to the current of the Nile,* and so on, but I do confess to you I have no notion at all what these things mean, nor what the old masters are telling us to do."

I had been wondering about it myself, but it grieved me to see my poor friend taking the whole weight of our failure on himself, and I said, "Tom, I am thinking we ought not to have been so ready to trust yon fellow Jamie."

"Why, did he not have a potent spell? Did it not get you into the mound as he said it would? And surely he knew the value of the red gold, for he desired it for himself."

"He did," I said, "but I am not sure he wanted the gold as much as he did the secret writing on it. Most likely that was some excellent ancient magic."

"Do you mean—? Are you saying—?" Tom was swelling slowly to full fury, his face turning red. "When he told us that the red gold was the Elixir—?"

"I would not say he was lying," says I, "I was only wondering about it."

Tom was not wondering. He crashed his great fist on the table so the spoons jumped to the floor. "Why, that misbegotten limb of Satan! That—that *creature—he* to cozen *us?* I will have the heart out of him with my bare hands, by God's bowels I will! I will hang him up by the heels and cut out his tripes to feed him—I will . . ."

I don't know what more he planned; the rest was in Cornish. I waited until he grew weary and then I said, "We have no power to hunt him down, Tom, well you know it. Here we be two simple fellows trying to make an honest living, and him a warlock."

He did know it, and he sat drained and spent, the way he does when the anger has run out of him, and he said, "So, then, we must go back to our old trade. We have gold. . . ."

And so we did. I cannot bear to spend many words on this, Brother, for the horror is still with me. We found a patron, we sat at drink with him, and Tom spoke with him learnedly, as we had so often done; I, the humble assistant, waited until Tom should turn to me and say, "Now my good man here has somewhat to show you," and I was to unwrap the little bar of red gold and say, "Look you, master, a small bit of the gold we have made."

And I could not do it. I felt the words fighting each other in my throat, and knew what would happen if I spoke; I had just enough wits to fall on the floor, foaming at the mouth, and I heard Tom say, "Poor fellow, he's not had one of these fits for a month," and somehow he got me away. Truly feared for me he was, thinking of poison or some dread illness, for well he knew I never had fits.

Ah, the case was far worse than he thought! For I was accursed; I knew now what dire mutilation the old King had wrought on me. He had taken away my power to lie.

Better, far better, he had stolen an ear or even an eye! Only think, Brother, how easily your welfare or even your life may depend on your ability to lie! Never tell me the monastery is different from the rest of the world in that way, I would not believe it. Could you face even one day in which you knew that you could utter no word other than the truth, however great the need? Would you not be forced to a vow of silence? Can you not pity me, Brother Albertus? Yes, I see you do, I thank you for your tears. I could not have wept better in my evil old days, no, not even with the best of onions. . . .

I have striven against my fate, hoping to find the curse weakening with time. Often, while I have been speaking with you, I have tried to cheat just a little, not wishing to deceive you but merely as one might test a wounded arm to see if it has healed enough for use. All to no avail; the words I sought to bend have come out of my mouth straight, I have not been able to tell you anything except the exact truth. —You shake your head, you think such a thing impossible? But consider, Brother, you have the best possible reason to believe it. Am I not the one who is telling you? And I am Hamo the Accursed, who cannot lie.

Now when I had made Tom understand what had happened to me, I begged him to let me go my separate way, for I was surely no use to him. "My poor friend," said he, "you could never make your way alone in the world under such a curse. Let us think what we can do."

I will not spin you a long tale of those dreary days. In our despair, we thought of setting up an honest mercer's shop, but we had not the gift for it; nothing went right, in no time at all we were deep in debt, and my poor Tom whisked off to the debtors' prison. We still had our red gold, buried in a safe place, but it would not have been enough, and anyway we could not let them have it. There's much virtue in it, even if it may not be the Elixir.

So I gave the sheriff's men the slip, and whispered Tom that I'd make the money to set him free, and then I took to the greenwood, as we ought to have done in the first place. I had almost enough for his needs when I had the misfortune to kill that merchant on the highway, and there, but for the holiness and kindness of your sanctuary, would have been the end of my pitiful tale.

You might think that for a man who has seen such adventures as mine it would be tedious merely to go on living from day to day, but I do not find it so; I am truly grateful for this enchanted world God has given us, and who knows what further joys and wonders I may find in it? So I have decided not to wait out my whole forty days in sanctuary. My good friend Tom is out of prison now—never ask me how it was arranged—and he is waiting for me. We'll try our luck with our comrades in the greenwood, or maybe on the high seas; there's Tom's cousin, captain of his own ship, a free trader—I suppose some folk would call him a pirate.

It's useless to struggle, Brother Albertus, I am stronger than you. I do not wish to hurt you; have we not enjoyed these days and hours of friendly converse? However, I must win time to leave this place quietly, you see, and so I must tie your hands and feet—I hope that is not too tight? Yes, your habit fits me quite well, I knew it would. I am sorry I cannot leave you my breeches, but you may have this old coat to keep you warm until your brothers find you. It will not be long.

Oh aye, the abbot. You say I promised to tell him how he could make gold from lead?

With respect, Brother, that is not what I said. Look back at your writings; you will find my words were: *I will tell you all I know of the making of gold*—and is not this just what I have been confessing to you? One moment; I must tie this cloth over your mouth. I cannot have you crying out too soon. —Very well, you shall learn the final secret. Tell your abbot to take all his silver plate and jewels and his tools of whatever metal, and all his papers that tell of the wealth of the abbey in land and in sheep, and he shall go to the master goldsmith in London town and say, Give me gold enough for these things. Thus he may transmute any object whatever into gold. This is the exact and perfect truth: I, Hamo, have said it.

Does something trouble you, Brother Albertus? Nay then, do not fret your kind heart with fears for my safety, I shall be well away before any pursuit can set out. Farewell; remember me in your prayers. *Pax tecum.*

Artistic genius and the sources of creativity are matters that remain
rather mysterious to the most diligent students of psychology, art . . .
and history. What, for instance, moved Johann Sebastian Bach to write
the Brandenburg concertos? What was in his mind at the time?
Perhaps Carter Scholz has the answer, though we can hope not.

THE JOHANN SEBASTIAN BACH MEMORIAL BARBECUE AND NERVOUS BREAKDOWN
Carter Scholz

—Yes, it's true, I said, I'm responsible for the Brandenburg concertos,
concerti, whatever you like to call them. Pass the ribs, would you
please?

I was at the annual musicologists' picnic in the University of California at Berkeley's botanical gardens. The gardens are laid out by locale
and by era, boasting thousands of specimens, and we were on the
Northern European trail, just south of the Miocene redwood grove.
Since I had come across eight thousand miles and three hundred years
to be there, I was the object of particular attention.

—A pity this can't be put to better use. God made a woman out of a
rib, I said, washing the pungent meat down with Oktoberfest beer.
—With all respect due the ladies present, it pleases the solipsist in us to
imagine a woman made of our own flesh. The fellows up there (and I
nodded in the direction of the genetics lab) know what I mean. But let
me tell you about Bach . . . and with that I cut off any debates on
sexism, incest, or cloning.

—Bach married his cousin Barbara, of course, so he probably had a
touch of the solipsist about him. Most great men have. That, and his
lusus ingenii, the games he played with spelling and numbers in his
works, argues for it. That was my thesis, of course, and I was lucky
enough to get a grant to work it out historically.

—This time hopping is an uncanny business, said fussy Abrams. —If we can rely on Freud—

—Yes, I interrupted my interruptor, for I knew he was about to botch my story. —The uncanny is that which leads back to something long known to us, once very familiar, and forgotten or repressed. The Freudians would say: noninferential knowledge of the future, and less emphatically of the past (and knowledge of distant, current happenings even less so), appear uncanny to us, so to what process of repression may these feelings be referred? I say this. When we are very young, past, present, and future have no meaning to us. Likewise, in the midst of the highest musical experiences we also lose our sense of time's arrow pointing to the impending tonic at the end of a piece, and we live only in timeless moments of sense. As we grow older, the separation of events into a temporal order becomes normal, and the original direct experience unfamiliar. We make signs. Musicians write scores. To reject continuity for the fullness of the moment is not a luxury a mature individual can allow himself, particularly not a historian. Until recently, of course. More beer, please?

—I did a lot of hopping about, so there's no point to saying *earlier* or *later.* . . . Two different continuities are involved, Bach's and my own, and I'll tell you only about the intersections. I flew to the time labs at U.C. Donaueschingen . . . but perhaps you want to know about the process. My colleagues in our little *Kunstgestapo* will forgive my boring them for a moment.

—In this going-back, there are certain requirements of continuity, attention to detail beyond period costume and learning the language. Everywhere I showed up in the past, my name was Johann and I was left-handed. Johann was as common a name then as Lisa is now, so I had a lot of freedom, and of course it's the Germanic form of my own name.

—I hopped first to Leipzig in 1723, as Johann Heinrich Ernesti, rector of the Thomaskirche, where Bach was the new cantor. First I put the real Ernesti under sedation and locked him in a closet, and then strolled out to vespers. It was Good Friday, and Bach was to direct the first performance of his *Johannes-Passion.* You can imagine my excitement. In school my first full-scale analysis was of that work, and in the balmy days of youth, when I still harbored the ambition to compose (didn't we all?), I thought I might write one myself. This was before the impossibility of religious music, not to mention music as a whole, had been made clear to me. I imagined a tribute to John the Evangelist, to John the Divine, to Johann Sebastian, and, naturally enough, to myself. I found it significant that Johann had chosen the gospel of his namesake for his first passion. This was the cornerstone of my thesis— that religious music is the most egocentric, self-reflective of all. Now, you've heard the stories that Bach's first passion was based on Mark, written some fifteen years earlier. I can dispose of that objection. I produced from my attaché case the manuscript and fair copy of the *Mark-Passion,* dated 1709, and tossed it into the fire beneath the barbecue spit.

—Don't panic, the music isn't lost. I lifted this from Bach's study in Weimar, but most of it was reworked into cantatas in Leipzig, from memory. The old boy had an astounding memory.

—It was a fine day in Leipzig in '23. It was spring, the trees were in bloom, and the smell of garbage was kept down by the breeze. I tried to see it with Ernesti's eyes. People thronged to St. Thomas's for vespers. The bells tolled across the square, and you could hear them far down the river, where some few impious strollers enjoyed the late light. The sun sparkled on the water where the banks bent, and threw the face of the church (which is rather ugly) into sharp relief. I reflected on the clouds as symbols of God's love, binding heaven and earth with their sacramental water, until the bells stopped, and then I hastened in to hear the passion.

—On his way to the choir, the Thomas cantor tripped over his robes and lost his wig. The choristers giggled. He practically had to strike them to restore order, and when the music began . . . well! Old Bach was a sight, puffing red-faced over the score, scowling at the players, thrusting warning fingers at the singers, heaving with exertion, trying to hold his wig on. . . . I think he'd been drinking. Speaking of which . . .

—Thank you. The boys had had about a week to practice, and their voices were, well, unremarkable. The instrumentalists fared a little better, but they were occasionally as much as two beats ahead of the choir. It was a travesty. A woman behind me said, "God help us, it's a musical comedy," and I had to agree. On his way out, fuming and muttering, Bach looked straight at me, and it jolted him. He stumbled. I realized that although this was *my* first trip, he might have recognized me from earlier years. His memory was not necessarily confined to musical matters.

—I should have a memory so good, said Olafson, and helped himself to some fried brains.

—Save some for me, I remarked, and helped myself.

—You know, said Olafson, they're tasty, I suppose, but I don't understand exactly why people thought of eating calves' brains, say.

—It's a source of protein, said Lisa McElroy.

—But that's no reason, I put in. It explains more if you allow that
meat possesses some of the qualities of the creature from which it
comes. If there's some chemistry of strong and weak, courage and capit-
ulation, well, aren't the intimate juices of a beast rendered in the fires
and failures of its life, and expressed in its flavor? Why else is some
meat good and some bad? Cows raised on a range taste better than cow
clones force-fed on grain and ash, plausibly because they've had more
chance to live, to explore more fully the possibilities of existence. From
the meat of these cows we might learn something. They might have
their philosophy.

—An animal isn't conscious.

—Perhaps not. But we are. We know that cannibals eat their enemies, to acquire their strength. And if we eat brains . . . well, perhaps
the first man who ate cows' brains was a little dull. Who wants to
ingest the qualities of a cow or a lamb? Now, bulls' balls might have
some value. . . .

—Bull*shit*, said Lisa McElroy.

—My dear, you're welcome to eat cow brains if you like. They might
improve you.

—Taylor!

—Now, now, this is a friendly picnic.

—Quite right, I apologize. Is that what's wanted? We're a little sensi-
tive on this point. Shall I return to my story?

—Yes, go on. It's most interesting.

—Well. After services I filed a formal complaint with the Honoura-
ble and Most Wise Council of the Thomaskirche against the "theatrical extravagances" of the new cantor, Herr J. S. Bach. This was the
start of Bach's troubles at Leipzig. To these I added in subsequent visits.
I went as Johann August Ernesti, the rector's son, later on, and I'd
accost Bach's students practicing on the streets for pennies, and bellow,
"So it's a pothouse fiddler you want to become, is it?" and chase them
off. This was more or less in keeping with Ernesti Jr.'s character, and
the added irritation to Bach was worthwhile. I went back as Johann
Adolph Scheibe in the spring of '37, and wrote an attack published in
Der critischer Musikus. Poor Scheibe. He couldn't remember writing
it, he'd earlier been a student and admirer of Bach, but there it was. He
was vain enough to defend it instead of refuting it, and rose to the oc-

casion splendidly, surpassing me in his later attacks, especially in that very funny letter published in April of '39, supposed to be from Bach himself. Everyone thought Scheibe had a grudge since Bach voted him down for the organist's post at St. Thomas's in 1729.

—Now some of my colleagues in our *Kunstgestapo* disapprove of these tactics. Why harass Bach? they cry. Well, you might imagine the cultivation of artworks as not unlike that of pearls; a little irritation never hurt, as our experiments have shown. Why, look at Webern—we gave him a life of unparalleled peace and leisure, given the circumstances. We smoothed over the roughest spots, got him a conductor's job, a wife, steady money, and what did we get in return? Ninety minutes of music, all told.

—Don't you like the symphony? someone asked.

—Symphony! It's eight minutes long! All full of tiny little amoeba cries. And that absurd serialism he bequeathed to a generation of composers . . . no wonder we had to go back and shoot him. No, it's clear that irritation works better. In any case, the process is far from arbitrary. We have constant feedback from the computers, which know better than we what's what. After every hop I'd check in at Donaueschingen to plan my next move. Oh, the theorists can explain this better than I, all that rigamarole about mean density of necessary events, clear and present realities, temporary temporalities, branches, buds, and whatnot. . . . It started when the National Endowment Against the Arts turned up an increasing probability that the Brandenburg concertos would not be written, and, well, it was my job to save them. You understand that every interpretation of the past changes it, and it changes in ways ever more real as we learn to puncture time's fabric. So if we begin to think the Brandenburgs might vanish, indeed they might, if we don't take measures, and that vanishing would affect our world in turn. This drew my interest. If Bach hadn't exhausted the Baroque instrumental forms, as he did in the Brandenburgs, he wouldn't have gone on to the later sacred music, and the whole individual, solipsistic Western consciousness, the triumph of the mind laboring alone that culminates in music with Beethoven, why, the entire cornerstone of critical inquiry might have been lost. They saw at once that I was their boy. I believe in art, which today must include technology, after all, it's our way to proceed by art—the wit of our minds rather than the strength of our hands. Music became an art when men removed themselves from the dance, took their hands from their instruments, and lifted a pen. That's what we know, and that's why we honor Bach as an ancestor, because he turned from dances and suites to the monolithic church works we know him by. But he wasn't just a man of God, a master solipsist, he was quite a *mensch* as well, as vain, profligate, and unreflective as any jazzman.

—Oh, come, now. . . .

—You think not? Look at his work, look at the title page of the Inventions: "Wherein lovers and students of the clavier are shown a clear way to deal well with three *obbligato* parts; furthermore, not only to have good *invention,* but to acquire a strong foretaste of composition." He was an improviser! He thought the Baroque Age would last forever, and well it might have if we hadn't goaded him to exhaust its forms. Oh, he was perilously close to loving craft over art. And he liked his beer as well. He wasn't unaware that the Latin for Bach is Bacchus. Not that I hold *that* against him . . . yes, thank you . . . but my God! we could be living today in a musical community as primitive as Bali's.

—Would that be so horrible? This came from a young nearsighted ethnomusicologist, whom I marked for a later reproof.

—Yes! Yes, indeed. We have an interest in maintaining our present. Are we what we eat, ladies, gentlemen? History itself is a vast maw. In the words of a popular song (you know I'm a student of the popular arts), "Life is a carnivore." It gorges on all the events of all possible pasts, it has its upsets and its regularities, we're learning that time is not linear, it's infinite, and constantly in flux, and now that we possess the art, it's up to us to regulate it. So if we can influence events . . . alter the Diet of Worms . . . martyr Luther . . . drop stones in the time stream . . . make history with a will and consciousness, *Zukunft zur Kunst,* rather than submit to it as to a flood, well, oughtn't we? Don't we have that responsibility?

I paused to get my breath.

—In any artist's mind is a chaos of experience, past art, possibility, which he organizes in his work in order to get information, whether he knows it or not, about himself. Art is the artist's mechanism of repression. When all the elements of a system are ordered, it's dead—administrative—totally organized, totally communicative, and wholly uninformative. But it doesn't know it's dead until that information comes from a higher state of disorder. So the Baroque Age created the Classical, and that the Romantic, and so on, each exhausting its forms, each subsuming the administrative order of the period before in a higher chaos, extracting all meanings possible, and pointing on to an eventual universal understanding of mind. It's imperative that we maintain this progress, so that we, the scholars and, if I may say so, artists of this future, can rise to a higher, more synthetic level of musical discourse—the job of extracting information not just from tones and forms, but from whole periods.

—But I digress. Next I went to Cöthen in 1720. Bach was happy there. He had forsaken church music, for he had an intelligent, sympathetic patron in Count Leopold; he had full freedom, excellent musicians; his wife drew a salary . . . there were no complaints at Cöthen about the "operatic, too theatrical" nature of his music. He was bound to encounter that from Pietists; in fact, I'd added to his problems in the guise of Johann Adolph Frohne, a Pietist at the Mühlhausen church, oh, about 1707. You can find the formal complaints, in my hand, in the Donaueschingen archives. But there was no conflict at Cöthen, nothing to drive Bach to assert his genius to the fullest. He wrote dance suites, sonatas, sinfonias . . . all very pleasant, but meaningless without the Brandenburgs.

—I went as a doctor. I was the one called when Barbara took sick while Sebastian was away at Carlsbad. I gave her some medications that I knew were useless. And I returned late that night, slipping the latch to let myself in. It was still. All the children slept. The moon shone through the lattice over the window. It was a brooding light, laden with time; the shifting of a billion motes between myself and its source left it cold and placid. And I was poised on the edge of an action that would make a future. Barbara awoke; her eyes were without fear, or even surprise. They simply opened . . . as the doors to the Bach house had opened to me that afternoon to reveal the rooms, furniture, children, alight with life . . . as if she hadn't been asleep at all, or had been dreaming of me and knew she had drawn me there by her dream. Then she shut her eyes. I bent over and pierced her with the hypodermic, alien to the age; her eyes never opened. Then I hopped to Donaueschingen.

—But one thing relies on another. In the time labs the probabilities were seen to have shifted once more. I had to go to Weimar in 1717, as Bach's patron Duke Johann Ernst, and when Bach applied to me for his dismissal to Cöthen, I had him thrown in jail. I stayed on for a month while the real Duke was kept under sedation at Donaueschingen. . . . A dreadful month. . . . The Duke retired at eight, he was crotchety and pious, and his accent nearly wrecked my voice. I couldn't stand it, going to church every morning at the crack of dawn, putting all the lights out at eight, so I took to dropping the disguise and slipping out at night. Strictly against regulations, going abroad without a persona. But I'd been thinking of Barbara; I had already given her a fatal injection, yet that day was three years hence. Can you understand the well of regret, beauty, and inevitability, that derangement of time which is the heart of romantic love, that opened in me? She was thirty-three, my age, she was beautiful—much better preserved than the average German woman of thirty-three—and she was a Bach. I confess it. I wanted to have a Bach. So I wooed her. And before I had to return to my age we were meeting every night. Since Sebastian was locked up the while, I can only assume that the next child, Carl Philipp Emanuel, was mine. He was, of course, the most talented of Bach's many sons. . . .

—Hold it, said Olafson, chewing. Carl Bach was born in 1714. I thought this was in 1717; that was the year before Leopold Augustus was born, the feeble-minded one.

I kept still. Not everything I'd said was strictly true, but it was of the highest imaginative value.

—May I continue? I asked. It's painful to think of Barbara, but I think I should give all the details.

—Before I finished in Weimar, the time boys did me a favor and sent me back to Arnstadt in 1705, when Sebastian was still courting Barbara. I wanted to see her young. As Johann Christian Geyersbach (a kind of pun on goer-back I thought of myself) I went, a musician in the church orchestra. Bach insulted me during rehearsal, and that night I accosted him while he was out with Barbara. He'd called me a *Zippelfagottist*, and, well, for the moment I forgot that *Fagott* is German for bassoon, so I lost my head. I attacked him with a stick and called him *Hundsfott*. And he drew a sword! I cried *"Nicht* fair!" but he kept coming, cursing at the top of his voice and smelling of malt. I held him off with the stick until a couple of classmates got hold of him. Then I made him apologize. I wondered if, those nights in Weimar, Barbara recognized me as the dashing young stranger in Arnstadt.

—There were some other trips, matters of necessity dictated by the computers, too numerous to mention. You may see me chasing Bach through history, showing up now and again in the cursing, capering figures of Johann Martin Schubart, Johann Caspar Vogler, Johann Tobias Krebs, Johann Nicholas Gerber, Johann Philip Kernberger, Johann Ludwig Krebs, Johann Gottlob Krause, Johann Harrer, or a dozen others, for a second, hour, or month, obvious or indetectable, melody or counterpoint, as Bach's tutor, student, patron, doctor, cuckolder, critic, jailer, father, or son, a fugue of Johanns, a *lusus ingenii* surpassing anything the old master ever invented.

—Finally we succeeded. Hounded and harassed, Bach was driven into himself. He marshaled all his genius, with its full complications, to the great religious works we know from the Leipzig period, thereby closing off a still larger realm of possibilities for later composers. His work was complete.

—I saw Bach once more, as Dr. John Taylor of England. An eye expert. The operation, although it had to be repeated, turned out very badly. He not only lost his sight, but his otherwise excellent bodily health was destroyed by it, and by some mischievous medicines and other treatments, so that for a full half year afterward he was continually ill. You can read this in the *Necrology*. It was always a matter of regret that, since there was neither a death mask nor a skull, it was impossible to model a bust of Bach, but the funeral was arranged rather hastily. When the body was disinterred in the 1890s, there was even some doubt whether it was his.

—Of course you're a notorious liar, said Lisa McElroy.

—Oh, in the broadest sense, yes. A lie isn't just a misstatement, but, in the hands of a skilled liar, an assumed personality of presumably greater imaginative value than his own. I did that, certainly. As for variance from fact, you should know by now that facts are always provisional. They're whatever best serves the imagination. If I tell you that Bach finished his *Art of the Fugue*, is that a lie?

—It certainly varies from what we know.

—Here. I displayed the autograph of the last five pages. Olafson gasped.

—He finished it. If not in this reality, in some other. You might prove that I forged this. Or you might prove that one of his sons finished it. But that would be provisional as well. Or, most deranged of all, consider this: that all of us might be fictions, figures in a dream of the ailing Bach. The year is 1749, the only possible present in a solid concept of time, and he is ill, asleep, fevered. He has broken down, the *Art* is unfinished. He invents us. We are the actors in a shameful interior drama of regret, recrimination, and persecution. Here I hold the key to that dream.

And I dropped the papers onto the embers.

Olafson screamed.

—No, I said, restraining him as the pages blackened and curled. —It's best this way. This is what we know.

I considered. Solipsist to the last, he had worked the notes B A C H into his final theme, and died. A signature, a triumph of self-reflection, then *Tod, süsser Tod.* The imaginative value was greatest that way.

The present, after all, is no more than the likeliest collaboration of past dreams. Bach and a million others had collaborated to produce us. No less had we labored to produce them, to make them real to us.

My story was done. A few ashes blew up from the embers. It was dusk, and the lights of Berkeley, Oakland, and San Francisco were coming on. We all admired the view for some minutes.

—Look, said Lisa Davis. —The campanile just lit up. I live a few blocks from there.

—You see, I murmured, we're all self-regarding. When you look raptly at the moon, or study from a height the city where you live, or regard a painting, or gaze into the eyes of a lover, or consider a period of history, what are you contemplating but your absence from that place?

No one answered.

—We have abandoned the creative act. It has been rationalized out of us. So we seek our self-worth in connection with the past . . . to vindicate our own absent presence. We are the children of what parents, what lineage? Now we may choose. That part of the mind which most needs the connection has developed the art to make it. And in that way we become parents of the past, of children who are truly our creation. *They* understand (and I pointed again at the cloning labs) that need for the idea and the reality to close ranks, so that we can have true children, not shared, not born of women, or of history, or of accident, or necessity, but immaculately and without labor. Ours. Ourselves.

The streetlights, laid out in diagonals and perpendiculars, followed the chaotic swells of the landscape, and rose in verticals where the ground would support them. Their patterns mediated the course of the mind through the natural world, as did the vaporous densities of airborne chemicals that colored the western sky red. Jet trails disturbed the smog, cars moved on the streets, man progressed through his own mediations, with no hint of rain. Beyond the Golden Gate lay the ocean, as old and complex as time, as simple as death.

—Well. It's getting chilly here. Everyone had enough to eat? If so, I think I'll take the head. I believe I'm entitled to it.

There were no protests. I put the top back on the skull and took it home. Later I had it bronzed. It stands now on my mantel, between Handel and Brahms.

Here is a fascinating novella that combines a completely fantastic situation with the sort of detailed logic usually found only in "hard science" stories.

Imagine: You're a man who wakes up one morning in a strange room . . . and in a body that's not your own. It's a woman's body, and the muscles are completely uncoordinated. You're in a hospital. . . .

F. M. Busby, whose most recent novel is The Alien Debt, *takes it from there to one surprise after another.*

FIRST PERSON PLURAL
F. M. Busby

First his awareness sneaked up on him; then it sprang and he came awake. His eyes opened. Blinking, trying to focus, he looked around him.

Nothing was right; nothing was what it should be. He saw beige walls, and a pair of french windows with a balcony outside; he saw and heard a blatting TV set. Around him, bathrobed figures huddled in wheelchairs, among them moved white uniforms.

He shook his head. Sure as hell not the motel room, a day's drive short of home, where he had read himself to solitary sleep. Adrenaline sounded Red Alert.

All right; for starters, what time was it? He looked at his watch, or tried to. His arm moved sluggishly, only vaguely to his order; when finally he saw the wrist, he didn't believe it. Fat and flabby and almost hairless, not thin and corded under black wiry bristle. And no watch.

Part of his mind pushed the panic button; another part assured him he had to be dreaming. For the moment he ignored both, and only tried to move the hand he saw. It did not work well; the movement was jerky and inexact.

What's happened to me? He must not scream; that was no way to find out. But his effort, *not* to scream, verged on sheer pain.

He needed to look, to see, and finally his eyes came fully into focus. He tried to catalog the facts at hand. *Item:* he was sitting up, in a wheelchair. *Item:* the TV showed a soap opera, purple faces exchanging slow, breathless platitudes. *Item:* around him people sat or stood or moved; some spoke. *Item:* he wore a loose short-sleeved robe, blue and faded, bulging hugely over his chest. Bulging on each side . . . *now wait a minute!*

And before he could absorb that jolt, he felt, under him, a warm ooze. His anal sphincter did not take orders, either.

When all else fails, Ed Carlain liked to say, *think.* Well, now was his chance, sure as God made Texas and regretted it. The burst of panic ebbed; he felt light-headed and alert at the same time, and his immediate situation became all the universe there was. Ed recognized the feeling from his combat days, in 'Nam; it was a form of shock, and there he had learned to *use* it. Why not now? So, ignoring his body, he looked and listened further.

Some kind of hospital or sanitarium, that's where he was. *He? She?* Again panic nibbled, but he fought it down. He'd worry about that part later; right now, the point was to get some action.

The right kind, though, it had to be. What could he say? He didn't know who he "was," let alone how or why. To hell with that; he needed to talk with someone. Someone who would say things to help him build sanity.

But how to start? Personal experience held no clues. He thought of books he had read, movies and TV plays he had seen. Well, how about the amnesia ploy? It was true enough, God knew! Under his breath he began rehearsing what to say—and found his tongue and lips slow and awkward, as though speech were unfamiliar.

He persisted. Goddamn it, *something* had to work around here. For one thing, he was tired of sitting in his own moist, cooling excrement. So before he was really prepared, he made his try—because a nurse paused nearby, and it might be a while until the next one.

Slowly, with difficulty, the words came. "Nurse? This is silly—but I can't seem to remember—my name. Could you—help me?"

The young woman's eyebrows rose to disappear under her blond bangs. Her lips moved, but silently. She turned and lunged away to Carlain's right, out of the room.

What in hell did I do wrong?

In a few minutes the blonde was back. The big man she brought with her, who did not believe a word she said, she addressed as Dr. Harkaway.

"Nurse Ahlstrom," he said, "you must be mistaken. This patient has never spoken a word in its entire life."

"It has now," said Carlain. Well, it was all or nothing—but he could have wished for a few good leads to work from.

"Who said that?" Harkaway looked threatened, even betrayed.

"I did. I seem to have forgotten my name—and the date."

Somehow, Harkaway's dark, lean features went pale and blobby. He swallowed before he said, "You can *speak?*"

By main force, Carlain fought down a feeling of light-headedness and suppressed the sarcastic retort that came to mind. He said, "Yes. But I can't seem to remember—who am I?"

"This is unbelievable!" *You don't know the half of it, buddy.* "I don't recall your name," Harkaway said next. "Some of the attendants call you 'the turnip.' Because until this moment you've never made a purposeful sound or movement since the day you were born."

The turnip, huh? How about that? All right: "How old am I?"

"A little over eighteen," Ahlstrom said. "And your name is Melanie Blake; I remember that much about you."

Harkaway cleared his throat, and said, "Do *you* remember anything?"

Thinking fast, Carlain stalled. He knew he wasn't enough of an actor to fake total ignorance and go through the ordeal of pretending to learn everything he already knew. So he said, "I do, and I don't. I don't remember *me* at all, until today when I—well, woke up, sort of. But I know things I don't remember learning. They're just *there,* is all." Mentally he crossed his fingers; physically he tried, too, but those fingers were too clumsy.

"TV!" The nurse said it. "TV, and people talking where she could hear. For eighteen years, and on some level it must have registered. So now—" Fervently, Carlain thanked Somebody for the woman's quick intelligence; she had picked up the same "answer" he had thought to use. But he was glad he wouldn't have to; the setup was tricky enough already.

"So now, *what?*" said Harkaway. "What's happened? And how can we *explain* it?" Any irregularity here, his look said clearly, was all Melanie Blake's fault; certainly none of Dr. Harkaway's.

Carlain said, "What's been wrong with me? Does anybody know?" He stopped short. *Don't push so fast, dammit! Keep it plausible.*

The nurse waited; when the doctor did not answer, she spoke. "No one knows, for certain. You're one of the cases old Dr. Reynaud used as an example to show that we *don't* know everything. Body and brain perfect, he'd say—as far as we can tell. Maybe some congenital defect, just a few neuronic connections missing. The way an infant is sometimes short a bowel section, or a kidney." She paused. "I'm sorry, Doctor. I didn't mean to lecture."

Harkaway gestured; no offense. "Yes. I remember the case now. Read the file when I first came here. And old Reynaud's notes—very well put."

Very well indeed, Carlain thought; he could use it. "So you mean, something in my brain that's been wrong all my life, now it's working right? The way it's supposed to?"

"Possibly," the doctor said. "But what caused the change?" Frowning first, then he smiled. "Oh well—if Reynaud couldn't identify the defect, no one can expect me to know what cured it."

And what would the fool do, Carlain wondered, if he *couldn't* get himself off the hook? Ignore the change? Pretend it hadn't happened? *This clown could be dangerous.*

Obviously, though, the doctor was satisfied. "I'll just notify Phipps," he said. "I believe he has charge of this file." Still smiling, Harkaway left.

Ahlstrom stayed. "Uh, Melanie—is there anything you want?"

Carlain tried to smile, but his face did not seem to know how. "I'd like to know the date, and to see what I look like. But mostly, I'm afraid, I need a change of diapers."

She brought an orderly, and the two first cleaned him and then got him to his feet. He could not stand alone; even with support, he felt his heart beat fast at the unaccustomed strain. But finally—nude, at his own request—he viewed himself in a wall mirror.

His eyes still refused to focus precisely, but what he did see he did not like. He was about five-nine, and big-boned; that part was all right. But the body—arms, breasts, belly, hips, and thighs—was gross and flabby with fat. The moon of fleshy face showed no expression; his attempt at a smile was grotesque. The head appeared to be stone-bald. And for now, he couldn't afford to let himself even think about the sex of the creature he saw.

After a moment he said, "Thank you. That's enough," and they got him back into the blue robe and the chair. The orderly left.

Raising a clumsy hand to his scalp, Carlain felt prickly stubble. Without thinking, he said, "Very fetching hairdo."

The young nurse blushed. "You—the ones that can't tend themselves—clippers save a lot of work. Yesterday was the day for it. But now, of course, you won't—"

"It's all right." After all, it wasn't as though he could lose enough weight to look reasonably human in any big hurry—or develop the strength and coordination for mobility, either.

He considered the date she'd told him. June third, and the year was right, too; today followed the yesterday he remembered. Somehow he felt comforted, a little.

The nurse had other duties; he was left to himself. For the first time he had leisure to think about his predicament. He wasn't so sure he welcomed the chance.

For he could find no answers. The problem was that he *knew* the whole thing was impossible—yet here he was. How could this—ego transfer?—visit itself on Ed Carlain when it had never happened to anybody else?

Wait a minute; how could he know that for sure? Consider: what might become of someone caught in this situation? If Ed told the truth, right now, Melanie Blake would graduate from vegetable to schizo; correct? Sure; if we can't explain you, you have to be crazy. And such a person, naturally, would never be heard from, outside.

And if the person did not speak up, but held cover through the initial shock and after, who would ever know? Ed had kept his head down by instinct; surely a fair proportion of others, in the same predicament, would do the same.

Case unproven. The thing had happened, and that was that.

He saved the kicker for dessert, testing it gingerly, a little at a time. His sex: now that the shock had worn off, how did he feel about it?

The answer was, a sense of loss. Not from being female, exactly, but from not being male. Sex was vital to Ed Carlain. He did not question his reasons; he simply *liked* it. And oh, damn it all!—he was going to miss the way it had always been for him.

Then he had to face his real problem: would he ever be able to accept female sexuality? No hurry; the bald moonfaced blob of fat he'd seen in the mirror was about as sexy as a two-hundred-pound beanbag. But sooner or later, a matter of months, he would work his way out of here, and by that time his weight would be down to normal. And then . . .

Would he be good-looking, he wondered, or homely? It didn't matter. Any woman with good health and an outgoing personality could be attractive, if she wanted to. Same as a man could.

The big question was, what was he going to *be*? Straight, gay, or sew it up and forget it? The idea of sex with other men had always repelled him. Oddly enough, female homosexuality had not. Once when he was dating a woman who was ac-dc, her female lover had joined the fun—and he found their activities rather stimulating.

So he supposed he could go gay, all right; it wasn't as though he had anything against standard operating procedures. Funny, to find himself conditioned toward what was now "deviant" for him, and against what would be considered "normal." Then he thought that in a way it would be a shame if he could not adapt fully. For he had always wondered what it was like for a woman. . . .

He still couldn't decide anything; his thinking felt stuck between a rock and a hard place. Then it came to him that he did not *have* to decide now, that in fact he probably couldn't yet. His hormones might have something to say about it; wait and see.

So he shucked that problem off his mind and put thought to the body's needs. Gently, he began to exercise his unused muscles. He flexed his hands, moved his arms, wiggled his toes. At first he was embarrassed at grimacing to loosen the muscles of his face, but decided to hell with that—most of the other patients were obviously retarded and he could explain, if need be, to any staff member.

Also he devoted considerable attention to a couple of sphincter muscles. Toilet training was a top priority. . . .

At feeding time he tried to handle the spoon himself, but his coordination was not up to the job. He had to get Nurse Ahlstrom's authorization before the orderly would leave a spoon so that he could use it, empty, for practice.

The nurse wheeled him out onto the balcony; he had his first look at the outdoors. Before him lay hilly, wooded country—downhill, perhaps a hundred yards, a highway—and just this side of it, for Christ's sake, last night's motel! He had not seen it before from this angle—his room had been on the other side—but he recognized the sign. *Do I lie dead, down there?* He could think of no way, without breaking cover, to find out.

In the motel's patio a fountain caught his eye. He had not seen that before either—or any like it. An abstract sculpture, three nozzles spaced asymmetrically at the top—but the flow pattern was symmetrical, a clockwise precession of maxima and minima. One nozzle spouted higher as the one behind it slacked off, then the progression moved on. Carlain watched until he solved the pattern: it mimicked the voltage curves of a three-phase electrical system, star-connected. Satisfied, he nodded.

Another thought came to him. He had not asked *where* he was—with all the rest of it, location had seemed unimportant—but now of course he knew. Near the Oregon coast, close to Coos Bay. Three hundred and eighty miles from Ed Carlain's home. Well, it *still* didn't matter. . . .

His body tired easily; twilight still prevailed when he first dozed. He woke partially when someone put him to bed, but not enough to notice who had helped him. His final thought before sleep was, *If I'm stuck with this, I'll just have to make the best of it.*

He came half awake, and then—as memory struck like a hammer—woke fully. He didn't want to open his eyes—last night's resignation had vanished and he didn't want to believe the day before. But he did open them.

And then he didn't *have* to believe it! He was in the motel room. As he sat up, nude as he always slept, a tide of relief stopped his breath and brought him close to fainting.

For again he was Ed Carlain—wiry, hairy, thirty-eight-year-old, smoker's-coughing, horny Ed Carlain, balding a little but not much yet, still able to party all night and work all day, if he didn't try it too often.

His breath came back. Grinning, he ran his hands down his torso and thighs; no doubt about it, all of him was present and accounted for.

Then he remembered fully. *What a dream! What a crazy spaced-out dream!* He shook his head, then got up, showered, shaved, and dressed. At the coffee shop he had breakfast—scramble two with bacon, toast, OJ, and coffee-with. He read the paper; the date was correct—June third. So much for "yesterday."

Suitcase packed—he hadn't unpacked much of it—he checked out at the motel office and put the suitcase in his car's trunk. He got into the car, fastened his safety harness, and inserted the ignition key. But he did not start the engine. Instead he got out and began walking around the building.

I haven't seen the other side. And then he did see it. The fountain was there, with its three-phase star-connected flow.

For three hundred and eighty miles, all the way to Seattle, he argued with himself. He'd had a few drinks last night—maybe he *had* seen the damned fountain, and forgot. But would he forget something like that? Well, he *had*; that was all there was to it. Except he really hadn't been all *that* drunk.

Over and over he played it, until there were no more variations left; he was on reruns in his own head. An hour short of home he stopped for a drink—a tall gin and tonic, nothing heavy. He left it half-finished when he found himself wondering what would happen, now, to Melanie Blake. *She doesn't exist, damn it!*

When he reached his sprawling ranch-style home he was pleased, but not surprised, to find only his wife's car in the driveway. Open marriage was sometimes a mixed bag, but Carl Forbes, Margaret's latest, was considerate about being unobtrusive. Sometimes Ed wished he knew Carl better.

He found Margaret—lean, sleek Margaret—in their outsized bathtub. Bubbles covered her to the upper slopes of her small, taut breasts; her hands worked in the denser foam of shampoo that crowned her head. "Hello," he said. And "Hello," and before they kissed he used the little shower hose attachment to help her rinse the lather away. Then he stripped, and joined her, thinking, *We haven't played the bathtub game in a long time—too long.*

Afterward she said, "How was your trip?"

"All right." *The hell it was, but I can't talk about it. Not even to you.* "Any word from Chuck?"

"Nothing new. When it comes to college, sophomores are more expensive than freshmen—and my son is no exception."

"No problem." They went to their bedroom and began to dress. "Just as long as he keeps in mind that the one abortion last summer is the only one I intend to pay for."

"He knows, Ed. He does listen to you; the lesson took."

"Yeah, he's a good kid." Now they moved into the kitchen; he put ice and bourbon into a short glass.

He saw her looking at him. "Anything wrong, Ed?"

He paused to take a sip, thinking. "Not really. I . . . had a dream that bothered me."

"What about?"

He shook his head. "It's gone foggy now." Then, remembering their need for honesty, he tried to patch it up. "It's just that it wasn't—I wasn't *me*."

"And that's important, isn't it? Of course it is." She came to him and rubbed her short dark hair against his cheek, then moved to kiss him. "Don't worry—you're you, all right." Her arms tightened around him.

He laughed. But after dinner, still jumpy from the puzzling experience, he drank heavily. At bedtime, sleep, when it came, was uneasy.

He woke expecting hangover, and saw bare beige walls. Hope split; he worked a clumsy arm free of the covers and saw it plump and flabby. But his head was clear and free of pain.

All right, goddamn it—it's real. His calmness surprised him, and the unexpected relief he felt; he found that he was *concerned* with the problems of Melanie Blake, that fat stubble-headed turnip. Even though, during sleep, her toilet training had not held up.

Later, cleaned and fed—he handled the spoon passably well—he was wheeled again onto the balcony. The thin man who approached a few minutes later reminded him of a small gray rooster.

"I'm Dr. Phipps, if you don't remember. They tell me you don't. This is an absolute miracle; I'm going to be wearing you out with tests, I'm afraid." The thin face bisected itself in a grin, then pinched back to normal. "But of course you can't read yet—can you?"

Think fast. "Yes—yes, I can—some, at least. From TV commercials, it would have to be. But there's a lot I don't know—and I don't know how much."

Phipps nodded vigorously. "Sound attitude. Maybe TV isn't all bad, after all. But you can't write, of course?"

"No. I don't know the motions, and even if I did, my hands don't do what I want, very well."

"Of course not. Well, don't worry. Plenty of time for everything—you're young."

The doctor went inside, brought out a light chair, and sat. "Now tell me, have you begun to plan ahead yet? For your own life?"

Tricky—the answer, not the doctor. "Only a little." Carlain shifted is mind into Melanie's situation. "I have to train my body as well as my mind. And I do know enough . . . well, that I'll have to learn a way to support myself, outside."

Phipps laughed, a warm, high-pitched cackle. "No you won't. You're rich, girl. That won't help you walk, of course."

"Rich?" Then, "I hadn't even thought—why, I must have a family. Do I?"

Phipps blinked. "Your parents are dead, I'm afraid. They used to visit regularly. There's a brother—he's several years older."

"Does he come to see me?"

"No. He's in the East somewhere. But he hasn't come here since . . . well, for some years."

"I can understand that."

Phipps's eyebrows raised. "We must notify him. I'll—"

"No! Not yet!"

"But why? Certainly he should know."

"He might come here." Carlain motioned, indicating his head and body. "I want to lose some weight and grow some hair before anyone sees me. Anyone from outside, I mean."

The doctor nodded. "Yes. I see," and he began a new subject. Relieved, Carlain enjoyed the discussion.

He liked Phipps. The man gave information freely, without dickering for it, explaining how physical therapy kept arms and legs from atrophy, "but you'll need a thorough physical and a *gradual* exercise program, to get you up and walking. Your heart and lungs simply aren't geared for it at the moment." Carlain understood but, impatient, he didn't like it much.

After a break for lunch and rest, Phipps administered an IQ test. Carlain went along with it, but warily, on watch for things that Melanie could *not* know. He remembered that some children's programs taught simple arithmetic, but he wasn't sure how much. By deliberating, leaving blank all doubtful questions, he ran the time out before reaching the "heavy" questions at the end of each section. Phipps said, "These results won't be accurate, of course. We'll retest in a month or two, after you've had a chance to plug the gaps in your knowledge."

Carlain balked at taking evaluative tests such as Personality Inventories. "Dr. Phipps, I don't *have* a personality yet. I have no personal experience; it's all someone else's that I saw or heard. And didn't even know it, at the time. I think maybe I'm just a stack of records—and I hate that." *Does it ring true? Probably; this is as new to him as it is to me.*

Phipps's face showed concern. He said, "You're a person, Melanie, and I like you. We can do the personality tests later."

You like this fat bald statue? I don't. But Carlain said, "Can I have some books? I want to find out the difference between what I know and what I don't. Dr. Harkaway is moving me out of the ward into a room tonight, so I'll have a place to put things."

"Certainly. Any books you want, Melanie." *Nice thought, but I've snowed you. How would Melanie know what she needs?*

At dinner his spoon gave him no trouble, and later his bowels moved by his volition rather than their own. Then, in his room, he looked at the titles of his stack of books, deciding what he would pretend to learn first.

He had already learned the most important thing. This day had been June fourth. Like it or not, Ed Carlain was working a split shift.

According to the terms of the contract between man and alcohol, Ed's own June fourth came complete with hangover. He looked to the other side of the bed; Margaret was up and gone.

He rolled back and dozed for a time. When he got up, his liver had metabolized most of the overdose; his body was sluggish, but his mind functioned clearly. And he knew where he stood, now.

He spent the day catching up on business details, paper work. When Margaret came home with a huge array of bundles from a shopping spree he recognized the symptoms: anytime Margaret felt neglected, she spent money. Instead of complaining, ceremoniously he arranged the packages in a large circle and gently pulled her down in the center of it. What happened next did her dress no good at all, for they did not wait on the niceties of disrobing.

And that night in all innocence they slept cuddled together in only one of their twin beds.

Something—somebody—on top of him, panting, hurting him. What the hell! Then he realized who he was and knew what was happening to him—but not who was doing it. He tried to grab the head above him, in the dimness relying on sound more than sight. The hands didn't go where he wanted—almost but not quite. Finally he caught a handful of hair, held it tightly while he worked his thumb down the forehead— over the brow ridge, then he jabbed! The other screamed and hit him; he jabbed again and the rapist broke free and ran.

The night nurse and orderlies asked questions, but there was not much he could tell them. Eventually the nurse gave him a sleeping pill.

Shaken, Ed woke to deepest night. He turned the bed lamp on, the dimmest setting, and lit a cigarette. His heart beat fast; his hand trembled. He told himself that from where he was, there was nothing he could do about Melanie. After the second cigarette his nerves calmed. He turned out the light and went back to sleep.

The morning of June fifth produced more facts than anyone wanted. Dr. Harkaway swept through the ward, muttering, "That degenerate!" Dr. Phipps moved more slowly, and said only, "Dependable help is hard to find." Ed Carlain was most impressed by the news that he was two months pregnant—maybe by the same stud, maybe not.

"I want an abortion."

"That would require a court order," said Dr. Harkaway. "And your brother would have to sign a consent form."

"Do you want my brother to know what happened here?"

"You can't expect us to do anything illegal!"

He thought. Yes, the information would have been on TV. "Up in Washington State, it's allowed. And eighteen's the age of majority for it."

"But you're not legally competent. Your brother—"

"Oh, for heaven's sake, Harkaway!" said Phipps. "She *will* be declared competent as soon as we can arrange a hearing. But we haven't time for that now. And I don't see that there's any problem. She turns up in a wheelchair escorted by her own doctor. What other doctor is going to ask the wrong kind of questions?" He looked at Carlain. "You'll wear a wig, of course."

"If you want to stick *your* neck out," said Harkaway, "go right ahead. Just don't tell *me* anything about it."

Phipps ignored him. "I'll round up some clothes and the wig, and make a couple of phone calls. Tomorrow, with any luck, Melanie, I'll run you up to Vancouver in my station wagon. But right now, let's give you the rest of that physical exam."

"Sure, Doctor," said Carlain.

The results were better than he had hoped. Heart and lungs were sound; the planned exercise program could proceed. Testing the limits of his strength, they found he could stand for brief periods—first holding on to something for support and then, with practice, by himself.

So they could weigh and measure him: height, five-nine; weight, one-ninety-five. *My God! At least forty pounds to go, maybe fifty!* Then he had an idea.

Dr. Phipps did not own a Polaroid camera, but Nurse Ahlstrom did. He explained, "I have a long way to go; it's going to be discouraging sometimes. But if I have a record—a picture now and maybe once a week from now on—I can *see* how I'm improving."

So he stood nude against the wall and the nurse snapped the picture. At his request she marked date and weight in the margin before handing him the print.

He looked and was repelled. The light-brown scalp stubble did not show in the photo. And the face still showed no expression; he had not thought to try to smile. "Well, at least this will be the worst of them. And thanks."

Ed Carlain as himself had a quiet day. Accepting the fact of his dual existence, now he could get back to work. He sat down to study the query from a San Francisco company, asking about something rather unusual in the way of field communications systems. Shortly he reached for a scratch pad and began doodling possibilities.

Hardware was not Ed's specialty; he was an idea man. Once he roughed out a workable schematic, others would fill in the details. But first he had to sell it, and that meant a trip to San Francisco.

His thought hit a tangent streak. Should he fly, or drive? And if he drove . . .

But what the hell could he *do* at Coos Bay?

Riding to Vancouver made a pleasant change. Dr. Phipps, no speedster, drove carefully; Carlain relaxed and enjoyed the scenery. He was in no hurry; he needed the abortion but did not especially look forward to it. Eventually, they arrived.

Dr. Flores was a woman of about forty, slim and attractive, with black hair in a coiled braid. She first seemed puzzled by her patient's appearance, even a little irritated, until Phipps told her, "Melanie is recovering from a paralytic condition; we think there was a glandular problem earlier, also. Two months from now you won't recognize her."

Without giving details, he implied that the pregnancy was due to contraceptive failure and that the "D. and C."—as both doctors called it —was needed for reasons of health.

Then all too soon the preparations were done and he was on the table. As the cold metal entered him, he flinched. Dr. Flores had wanted to use general anesthesia, but that would have meant staying overnight to recover from the effects. Neither he nor Phipps wanted that delay.

It hurt afterward, but nothing like what he had feared. After an hour's rest on the couch—perhaps longer; he had dozed—Dr. Flores pronounced him fit for travel. But during most of the return trip he lay on an air mattress in the back of the wagon.

Home again, he spent a quiet evening and retired early.

Ed completed his schematic and copied it neatly for presentation, but Margaret was not on hand to help him celebrate; she was spending the evening and night with Carl. The liaison seldom inconvenienced Carlain, but this time, he thought, it sure as hell did.

He thought of calling a redhead he saw sometimes, but looked at his watch and shook his head. Too late in the evening.

He curbed the impulse to take bottle comfort. For one thing, he hadn't decided whether to fly or drive next day, and he did not enjoy driving with a hangover.

He slept well and woke in Melanie's room, clean and dry; his toilet training was winning. At breakfast he attempted for the first time to master the use of knife and fork. Coordination came more easily each day, and after a few mishaps he coped well with the tricky tools.

Then he was introduced to a new piece of apparatus—his "walker," a light metal framework on casters, to aid in support and balance as he stood or walked. Phipps helped him up into it the first time and was surprised at how well he did. Only for short periods, of course—but still "impressive," the doctor said.

"I've been toughening my arms by rolling the wheelchair back and forth a little way until they get tired." What Phipps must not guess, he thought, was that Carlain *knew* how to walk, eat with knife and fork— all the things that a restored Melanie could not know. "I think my legs have had it for now," he said. "Back to the old chair, I guess." After helping him sit again, the doctor left for other duties.

After lunch, Carlain dozed for a time and then wheeled out onto the balcony. A cool breeze refreshed him—off the ocean, probably, yet it brought tree scents, not salt air; a row of hills lay between him and the Pacific.

For a while he concentrated on exercise, then rested, his mind idle. From below, a flash of light caught his attention. He looked; someone by the motel fountain had a mirror—no, it was binoculars—and the afternoon sun reflected off their lenses. He looked away, blinking at the green afterimages. When he looked again he saw the person—a man— wave an arm.

His eyes worked better now; he squinted, to sharpen the focus. Even at a distance the man looked familiar. And then—

Jesus Christ! That's ME!

He looked around, back into the ward. "Nurse Ahlstrom! Do you— does anybody have a pair of field glasses? Binoculars?"

"I believe Dr. Phipps does. Would you like to use them?"

"Please. And, if you could—right away?"

"All right, Melanie"; and the nurse left.

First he seethed with impatience. Then he realized, *I'll know, if he stays—if I stay—that the glasses are on the way. Because of course he knows whether I get them or not. If I do, he won't leave yet.* Then he could wait patiently, if not calmly.

The binoculars were big, heavy; he had to brace his elbows on the chair arms. He fumbled at the focusing adjustments a moment before he mastered them, and then the view came sharp and clear.

Suck in your gut, Ed! I'm not the only one who needs exercise. As though by telepathy, the man did. *That's better. . . .*

The man lowered the binoculars; now his face could be seen fully. He smiled, then raised the glasses again. The viewer above set his own aside, and attempted a smile. The man waved and was answered in kind, then made a beckoning motion and pointed northward. This time the answer was thumb and forefinger making a circle, the other fingers straight. *Right on!* The man waved once more and walked away, around the building and out of sight. The one above sat, wondering, *What was that all about? He knows I have to go to him as soon as I can—because I know it.*

And late, just before sleep, he thought, *Why am I going to do something, tomorrow, that is so totally unnecessary?*

Waking in Seattle, Ed wondered the same thing. He had not de- cided, the night before—his own night before—whether to drive or fly. Now somehow the decision was made for him. But by whom? Not by Ed as Ed *or* by Ed as Melanie.

What if I don't do it? Before the thought was complete his breath caught; fear choked him. *All right, I will—I will!* Still shaky, he got up to a solitary breakfast, and packed. He left a note for Margaret: "Off to rent my brains in San Fran. Four-five days, six at the outside. Will call. Love." Then he was ready to leave.

His preferred driving speed—eight miles over the limit, where traffic permitted—brought him near Coos Bay by midafternoon. He checked into the motel, showered and changed clothes, hung his binoculars around his neck, and walked around to the fountain.

She was up there, all right—a fat, robed shape with dull moon face and bald-looking head. If she saw him, she gave no sign. Remembering then, he moved the glasses, watching the spot of reflected light as he tilted it up the hillside. He waved his free hand.

Did she see him? Yes—now she turned to call to the nurse. He waited. The binoculars came; the girl fiddled with them, then held them steady.

What did she see, now? Oh, yes—*suck in the gut!* He did, lowered his own glasses and smiled, then raised them. She followed suit; was that the way it had happened? They waved to each other; he beckoned and pointed; she signed assent.

That was all he could remember; he waved again and turned back to the motel. In his room, he poured bourbon over ice.

Jesus! Is THAT how it's going to be? Following in his own footsteps with no chance to choose their path? Trapped action! Maybe it wasn't such a good idea, after all, to meet in person.

But he had to, he just plain *had* to. Why? Because she was closer to him than anyone else in the world—closer than his wife or a twin could be. She was himself, one day behind himself.

And maybe in Seattle, able to talk together, they could plan ahead and avoid trapping him this way.

But until then, he decided, he would not see her again. *And that's final!*

He went to San Francisco and sold his schematic proposal. He went home, and this time Margaret was there to help him celebrate. He did other jobs and enjoyed leisure between them, and drank not too much and did sit-ups for the gut muscles and sometimes, when Margaret was off with Carl Forbes, visited redheaded Phyllis Asaghian.

But for the most part, Ed Carlain in his own life was marking time. As days added up to weeks, then months, it was Melanie's life he lived for.

Waking, remembering seeing herself from the fountain, for the first time she thought of herself as "she." Ed Carlain had seen her so, and Ed-in-Melanie now accepted it. Somehow she felt a sense of relief, of a tension vanished.

She spent the day in exercise, in the discovery and practice of bodily skills, interspersed with rest and reading. Her body hungered but she ate only what Dr. Phipps prescribed. She tired less rapidly and stayed awake later; at bedtime she slept without chemical aid and dreamed of vague and pleasant scenes.

Each day resembled the one before it. A week after Nurse Ahlstrom's Polaroid picture a second was taken. Melanie studied it alongside the first and nodded with some satisfaction.

Weight loss was not dramatic, but the body stood more erect, better poised. The belly sagged less; overall, her posture was more *alive*. The face was less moonish and showed a hint of expression, of intelligence— not much, but a start. And this time the stubble on the head was clearly visible. Melanie took a pen and in the lower margin awkwardly lettered "June 12—187 pounds."

June 19—180. Chin was narrower than cheekbones. She could walk without her "walker." The smile looked real.

June 26—174. She had walked up and down a flight of stairs. She could do five sit-ups, but they hurt. She was learning to type; Ed Carlain typed only with two fingers.

July 3—165. The waistline was smaller than the bust. She had begun jogging, outdoors, a few minutes each day. Her face showed hints of contours waiting to be revealed. She experimented with masturbation and achieved orgasm on the third attempt. She was pleased to learn that she could.

July 10—160. A plateau, perhaps? Or maybe the Pill—she was "on" it, since the abortion, to regularize her periods. She took the Personality Inventory tests and checked out "normal" except for a tendency toward masculine attitudes. Her hair was nearly an inch long and gave her head and face a better overall shape. Her breasts and shoulders still carried too much fat but no longer looked gross to her.

July 17—155. Reaching the goal she had first set, she pinched her waistline and still found too much fat. She had endured through hunger and adjusted; she no longer felt its pangs—so why settle, just yet, for a maintenance diet? Her coordination was roughly as good as Ed Carlain's and still improving. She smoked a cigarette; it made her sick. *Who needs it?*

July 24—151. She had strong features, not pretty, but striking. She learned to apply lipstick but seldom used it. With Nurse Ahlstrom's help and instruction, her short hair became a curly, light-brown cap, more becoming than the close-lying straightness had been. She wondered how long it would grow if she didn't cut it. She passed the state examinations for a high school diploma. Dr. Phipps said, "You've certainly done a lot of reading in a hurry, haven't you?"

July 31—147. Close, she thought, to what would be her best weight —and soon now. She obtained college entrance exams from the University of Washington in Seattle and passed well. She agreed with Dr. Phipps that it was now time for her competency hearing, to make her legally a responsible adult.

"Will I need a lawyer?"

"Can't hurt to have one. I'll call mine."

The lawyer, Arnold Zumwalt, was a thin man with a plump face; Melanie liked him. After they had talked for a time she said, "I'd like you to represent me in another matter, also."

"Yes?" And she commissioned him to investigate her parents' wills and her brother's administration of them. "Don't see him personally. I want to know where I stand before he learns of *me.*"

Dr. Phipps said, "Isn't that being a bit paranoid?"

"Maybe it is. But this is my brother Charles who quit coming to see me since well before my parents died, since before he moved East. I don't blame him—who wants to visit a vegetable?

"But I think I know how he's going to feel. This money, however much it is—part of it may be legally mine but for a long time it's been factually his. And now here comes the turnip, with her hand out. You see?"

Phipps nodded, and Zumwalt. Discussion closed.

The judge was younger than Melanie expected. He heard the briefs, then asked, "Melanie Blake, to the best of your knowledge, are the foregoing statements true?"

"To the best of my knowledge, yes." Somehow the lie came hard.

"Your memories begin on June third of this year?"

"That is correct." Not quite a lie, that time. *Your?*

"And all your knowledge at that point came from overheard conversations, television, and so forth, recorded unconsciously?"

"That is what I am told. I have no better theory to offer."

"Well, then." The judge tipped his gavel up on end, then laid it flat again. "I've seen the test results—intelligence, personality evaluation, high school and college entrance exams—I've heard Dr. Phipps's testimony and I've seen and heard you. Obviously, at this time you are legally competent."

He leaned forward. "But what if—what *if*, I ask—you were to suffer a relapse. Tomorrow, for instance. Who would be responsible for you?"

"Legally, you mean?" She thought. "Well—sir, every day people suffer heart attacks or strokes that leave them helpless."

After a moment the judge smiled. "And of course no one is given legal responsibility for any of them, in advance. Miss Blake, you've made your point."

The gavel.

August 7—144, and tomorrow Charles Blake, aged thirty-two and several times a millionaire, would arrive. He controlled the more than six million dollars he had built in ten years from the three million their parents had left them—but half was in trust for her. She could claim it. Reading the gray Xerox of the will, she could sense her parents' stubborn, forlorn hope: "if at legal age or at any later time she is adjudged competent . . ." There were more qualifications, but that was the crucial clause.

She memorized it.

Charles, she decided, looked ten years older than his age because he worked at it. She guessed his executive style glasses with their heavy black frames to be "window glass," for appearance. Dark and stocky, he was at least an inch shorter than she. His obvious embarrassment blanketed any personality he might have displayed, except for his equally obvious resentment of Zumwalt's presence.

She tried at first to make some sort of polite conversation, but he was having none of that. Finally he said, "I don't know who you are or what you're up to, but one thing is clear. You are not my sister." He looked at Zumwalt and at Dr. Phipps. "I suppose you're all in on it. If I'd known what I was walking into, I'd have brought my own attorney. He'll be here tomorrow."

"Fine," said Melanie Blake. "The more the merrier." She stood and loomed above him where he sat. "And now tell me why I'm not your sister. Because my fingerprints, along with the ones on my birth certificate, say I *am*."

It went on and on. She had been willing to settle for half the original legacy, leaving to Charles all the increase he had wrought. Zumwalt had disagreed. "If you had been normal all your life you'd be entitled to your full share. Correct? Why should your previous disability make any difference?" She had been undecided, but now Charles's attitude and behavior swung her to Zumwalt's view. Argue-argue-argue—her brother was intolerable.

But still she wanted an amicable settlement, not a lawsuit. Charles was holding forth nonstop; she cut into his Point Seven. "Charles! I do *not* intend to cause you any trouble."

"As I have said, it is impossible for me to liquidate enough assets to give you your so-called share, without—"

"*Goddamn it, shut up and listen!*" And for a wonder, he did. "If you'll just turn off your mouth for a minute—I've been trying to *tell* you—keep control; I won't tamper. Mr. Zumwalt explained how under the terms of the wills you keep a sizable cash account in my name, to provide for my care and medical expenses."

He started to speak; she swiped a near-slap past his face. "All *right,* Charles. You haven't touched that money for yourself; you can't. I can use it for a drawing account, quite legally, for major expenses. Right?"

She did not wait for an answer. "But I want an income, too, eventually. And the best way to get it—a way that will cost you nothing—is directly from the company you head."

"And just how do you suggest that I rob our company?"

"Who said rob? I'm the second-largest shareholder. So appoint me to the next vacancy on the board of directors."

His mouth fell slack; then he said, "You're not just retarded; you're crazy. Put the competition on the board to fight me?"

She sighed. "Businesswise you're a genius, but with people you're a klutz. No wonder you've been divorced three times. Competition, my dimpled butt! I was going to say, if you'd shut up long enough: Put me on the board and I'll give *you* my proxy. *I* certainly don't know enough to vote it properly."

She saw the renewed confidence in his face, now that he was once again in a situation he knew and understood. "Do you mean that? It could work. Old Showalter's due for retirement soon, and the man next in line isn't exactly on my team."

"I mean it, Charles. I don't want your blood, for heaven's sake. I'd just like to have some of my own."

Luncheon was amicable, but still she was glad when Charles left.

September 4—142, and holding. She had been as low as 140 and could do it again, anytime she wished. Dieting was no longer a problem; she came to meals with good appetite and ate as much as her active body required.

She looked at the latest—and last—of Nurse Ahlstrom's Polaroid prints. *Damned good body, if I do say so myself.* Well, she had worked for it, hadn't she?

Her two-inch growth of hair looked well enough in a mild curl, especially with the reddish rinse she had used on it. The cut was a little too pixieish for her face, she felt, especially on a big girl, but time would correct that. She'd do.

For two weeks she had owned a car; it waited in the parking lot. Her purse contained, among other things, a valid driver's permit.

She had said good-bye to Nurse Ahlstrom and to most of the others she knew at all well. Dr. Phipps had been away for the day, but she would see him at breakfast next morning.

The doctor fooled her. "Mind if I ride up to Seattle with you? We can trade off driving. You haven't driven more than a few miles at a time yet; you'd get tired."

She wouldn't; her driving habits were Ed Carlain's, not the newly learned ones of Melanie Blake. But his consideration touched her.

"You're welcome, of course. But how will you get back?"

"The puddle-jumper plane stops by, every day. We can drop my car off at the airport, on the way out."

She nodded. "Fine. But now tell me why you *really* want to come along. No, it's not just the driving—though I appreciate that, too. But I could do it in short hauls if I had to, take two days for the trip. So, why?"

"Well . . . Melanie, you—your consciousness—is really only three months old. There's so much you don't know, *can't* know. Like a baby bird leaving the nest, and—well, maybe papa bird wants to see you settled on a safe perch."

She felt guilt—because this kindly man could not be told that his anxiety was groundless, and why.

"I worry a little," he said. "You've leased this town-house apartment and had it decorated—a little stark, I thought, when the decorator was down from Seattle with his drawings and samples, but you can change it later if you like.

"Anyway, that part's fine. But when you get there, what's in the refrigerator? You've learned some cooking but you've never been in a supermarket. And other things—so many daily-life things you don't know first-hand yet—I'd like to steer you through a few of them, if I may."

She laughed. "All right. But believe me, I *won't* do the TV-commercial bit—poke into someone's grocery cart and get nosy about their detergent."

His answering laugh was brief. "I know; you seem to have sorted the facts from the garbage all right. But still I'm glad you'll indulge an old man who'd like to monitor your first day of total independence."

"So that it won't be quite so total?"

"You got me that time! But I won't interfere, unless . . ."

"I don't think you'll have to. I hope not."

Alone, she would have driven the distance in about seven hours including stops, but to please Dr. Phipps she agreed to trade seats every fifty miles or so and take a rest stop at each exchange. Also, she drove at his speed, not Ed Carlain's.

While she drove he talked little, but when he first took the wheel he asked her, "Have you thought much—decided yet, among the things we've talked about, what you intend to do?"

"You mean, like work—though I don't have to, of course—or going to college?" She shook her head. "No, not really. Oh, I'll probably take classes at the university, but not right away. I may get into some volunteer work—you know the kind of thing—mostly to meet people. That's what I need, I think—to learn to live with people." She hoped it sounded right, like Melanie, not like Ed Carlain in drag.

"And I need to get to know people of my own age." That, at least, was true. She had forgotten what it was like to be eighteen in company, and today's youngsters were not the same as Ed's youthful contemporaries had been; he was often puzzled by Margaret's son and the boy's friends.

"Yes, I suppose so." The doctor hesitated. "Melanie—there's one matter—you've been rather evasive—your attitudes toward sex. Did the rape . . . ?"

"No. That wasn't—it was something blind and impersonal." She turned to face him. "I know I'm ignorant—all TV ever does about sex is talk around the edges of it—but I've read a lot, and I think I know how people should feel about each other . . . first. Not like Hollywood, maybe, but . . . well, *friends*. Is that close?"

"Perhaps something more than friends, I think. I—"

"Oh, don't worry, Doctor. I'm in no hurry about it."

The hell I'm not. First chance I get, I'm going to try it on with my other body. Because if I can't accept ME, I can never accept any man. And I'd better find out sooner than later.

They lunched at a motel restaurant just short of Portland; at the beginning of the afternoon they crossed the Washington border, somewhere along the bridge over the Columbia. Dr. Phipps had the wheel when, a little ahead of rush-hour traffic, they reached Seattle.

The doctor insisted on driving to her apartment. Melanie gritted her teeth to keep from telling him easier routes—she knew the building and how to get there, because until a few months ago Phyllis Asaghian had lived in the second-floor front. But finally they arrived, and she congratulated him on his superb sense of direction. Actually, for one who did not know the city, he had done well enough.

Her apartment was second-floor rear, overlooking Lake Union and the downtown area beyond. It had nine-foot ceilings and more than eight hundred square feet of floor space, including two baths and a guest room. In the living room a fireplace was set into the tinted glass wall that faced the lake. She had chosen simple decor—solid colors, and furniture without frills. Perhaps a little on the masculine side, she conceded—but damn it, it was the kind of thing she *liked*. She showed Phipps around the place, leaving her luggage in the bedroom to unpack later.

She had no great desire to shop at the supermarket, but the doctor wanted to, so they went. The difficult part was trying to behave as though the experience were new; since the first few days as Melanie she had done no real acting but had merely kept cover. Now she settled for passive behavior, letting him take the lead. And eventually the ordeal ended. She was glad to get "home" again.

Once the refrigerator was stocked—and a couple of items in the liquor cabinet, for Ed's benefit—she said, "I'm too pooped to cook. Tell you what, I'll take you out to dinner if you'll drive. You pick the place —okay?"

He nodded. "All right; that's something else you haven't done. I'll be pleased to accept your hospitality."

He chose a seafood restaurant on the downtown waterfront. She knew a better one, but could not say so. Well, it would do.

And it did. The restaurant situation demanded no acting; she relaxed and thoroughly enjoyed herself.

Back at the apartment, watching the lights on the water—the down-town skyline reflected, boats moving in no apparent pattern, and the occasional light aircraft taking off or landing—they talked. Past reminiscences mingled with future speculations. Finally the doctor said, "Well, I suppose you're as ready as can be managed in so short a time to live independently."

"I'll be all right, really."

"Then I'll call a cab and find a motel."

"You'll do no such thing. I have a perfectly good guest room. And tomorrow I *will* cook breakfast. Then you can drive us to the airport and I'll drive back here. I watched carefully this afternoon; I can find the way." But he insisted on drawing the route for her, on a dog-eared city map from his suitcase, before she could go to bed in her own new, spacious bedroom.

Carlain woke, thinking, *Well, she's here!* Or rather, he amended, on the way—due to arrive in the afternoon.

He felt good. During the past few weeks as Melanie slimmed down to beauty, he—as himself—had avoided thinking of the sexual implications. The situation was too much like a combination of cradle-robbing and incest. He was glad the problem had surfaced, and perhaps solved itself, during the Melanie phase. Somehow his lives had diverged, had become separate entities connected only by his continuing, alternating consciousness. Now it seemed to him that Melanie was a person in herself; even though her ego was his own, it *felt* different.

He had another worry. Subscribing to the ideal of full honesty in marriage, he was not in the habit of keeping secrets from Margaret. But for three months he had kept her ignorant of Melanie's existence. And now push would come to shove. Not on the sexual aspect—by their agreement he had the same freedom she had. But how in the name of ten thousand blue pigs would he ever convince her that he and Melanie were the same person?

He would have to try, was all. And certainly he could not have done so earlier, without Melanie present to speak for herself.

He set the problem aside. He had another schematic to work out— and then to present and try to sell.

He worked late at it.

Melanie's morning omelette came out lopsided, but Dr. Phipps made no complaint. He drove them to Sea-Tac Airport and stopped at "Passenger Load." Before he could begin his good-byes she reached and hugged him, then kissed him thoroughly—in the way that Ed Carlain liked to be kissed. She was testing herself, testing her reactions to a man, and she passed.

After a moment for catching breath he said, "I don't know how you learned that—maybe there is more to instinct than I had thought. But, my dear child—don't kiss a *young* man that way, if you intend matters to stop there."

She laughed, and thanked him "for everything," waved good-bye, and moved over to the driver's seat as he walked away. On the way home she kept the speed limit, exactly. When she entered her apartment she looked at her watch.

Ten-forty. At eleven I will come here.

At one minute after eleven, she opened the door to Ed Carlain.

Ed ate a light breakfast, not hurrying. *Eleven o'clock,* he thought. His watch said nine-thirty. *What will it be like, from this side?*

Time dragged, then speeded as he found unexpected things that needed doing before he could leave. Nervous, though he *knew* he would be on time, he drove fast, keeping an all-around scan for police cars.

As he rang her doorbell his watch read eleven, exactly.

She opened the door.

Once inside, door closed again, the two embraced.

"Was there *ever* such a meeting? It's been forever."

"Three months, really, and a little over. But I know—it was hard to wait until I knew he was gone."

"Yes. Now stand back, let me look. You know? I think . . . from here, I'm better-looking."

"So are you." Laughter. "We need new pronouns, don't we? Funny, though—it does look different, seeing from outside."

"Yes. Do you want a drink now, or afterward?"

"There's no choice. It was after."

"Trapped action? Already?"

"Not really. Or if it is, I did it myself."

A headshake. "I—it seems so idiotic, anything I say, knowing you already remember it."

"Not really, not in detail . . . until you actually say it. Or when I do, for that matter. We'll get used to it. There's a lot we'll have to get used to."

"Of course. I think the hardest part for me will be always wondering what you know that I don't, yet."

"True. But getting hooked into trapped action isn't all that much fun, either—remember? Anyway, we may be able to switch it. I thought of a way, this morning, that might work."

"That could be a good thing. Neither of us can afford dominance."

"Because neither would put up with it for very long."

"No. Even now, I don't feel especially submissive."

"I remember." Undressed now, the two embraced.

"How far are you ahead of me, do you know?"

A pause. "About fifteen hours. Roughly half and half."

"That's not too bad." A laugh. "I'll catch up."

"You always do."

"Except, not really."

But when the one's remembrance met and blended with the other's anticipation, it didn't matter—not any of it.

"Don't get up yet. I want you this way as long as you can."

"Finest kind."

"I was good, wasn't I? I could tell. And you . . . well, you remember how *I* feel, of course." A gusty, exuberant sigh. "Good for our ego—isn't it, though?"

He laughed.

"What's funny?"

"Nothing much. Remembering how we sweat this so much, from your side. And—you recall, in the Army, what people were always telling each other to do?"

She laughed too. "Yes. Little do they know. . . ."

"That anyone really could." Ed yawned. "I'm hungry; let's fix up some lunch."

After eating they sat, talking. He had a beer. She tasted it, decided she did not like it, and had tea instead.

She said, "Being together has more advantages than just the obvious. Remember when you first came in?" He nodded but raised his eyebrows. "And you know how I'd been worried, that maybe I couldn't be heterosexual from this side. Well, the minute I saw you, smiling, I knew it was all right. Because I knew *you* knew."

"I knew that you knew that she knew that he knew—"

"Stop it! Sometimes we have a *disgusting* sense of humor."

"Melanie."

"What?"

"I was just trying it on for size. *Melanie.* We'll have to call ourselves by our body names, in company. I was wondering about the psychological effects."

"Yes, I see. Ed. Ed, Ed, *Ed.* Ed is Melanie plus fifteen hours. Melanie is Ed minus fifteen hours. How old is Ann?"

"You said something about our sense of humor?" He grinned. "All right—we're two personalities, serially connected by the same consciousness, now interacting in the same time and place. But we're becoming more different, aren't we? Is that good or bad? And will using our names hurt or help us?"

She frowned. "I think . . . the more different we get to be, the more we bring to each other. Let's ride along for a while and see, shall we?" Then, "What about what you said at first—about maybe changing phases sometime, so *I* could be the one who knows what's happened? I haven't figured that out yet."

"I know, because I didn't either, until this morning. Of course I'm not sure it would work, but the idea is simple enough." On a paper napkin he drew straight parallel-line segments, zigzag-connected by diagonal dotted lines. "This first solid line is me, living Day Number One. Then dot-dot-dot I zig over and wake up next morning as you. You live Day Two, go to sleep, and zag back to wake up for *my* Day Two. You see?"

"Of course. And so?"

"So." He drew more lines. "Suppose you have one long day while I have two short ones. On Day Three, for instance, you sleep in, get up late, and *stay* up—well into Day Four—noon, maybe, before you sleep and I get *my* Day Three. I get up early, take a short day, sleep again, and wake up while you're still awake from Day Three. Then—"

"Yes—I think I see it."

"Right. After I have Day Three, who am I when I wake? Do I skip all the way ahead to *your* Day Four, or to mine, which is closer in time? If it's mine, we've switched phases; you'll be ahead of me, on the memory angle. If it doesn't, what have we lost, except a little sleep?"

"Do you want to try it?"

"No hurry, I'd think. First we need to figure how to *plan* things, so we don't get stuck with decisions neither of us made, like the time I had to go to Coos Bay because I *had*. I don't like trapped action."

"Yes." She shuddered. "I remember. That was . . . frightening."

They talked, planned, made notes. Obviously, only their meetings and communications were crucial; nothing each did separately could inflict determinism on the other. Neither mentioned the possibility of trying to change something that one had experienced and the other had not.

He looked at his watch. "It's nearly three. Time to call Margaret."

"Margaret? Why?"

"To get her over here and tell her, of course."

"You've figured out a lot of things in the past fifteen hours, haven't you? Tell me about this one."

"Another circular paradox, I'm afraid—more trapped action. You didn't do any of it; I did it all myself. Yesterday—*my* yesterday, as you—I watched *me* call Margaret and she came here. So now on my today we go through the same motions."

"Ed! Maybe we'd better separate, not see each other anymore. This is too scary!"

"Isn't it just? But we're not separating, Melanie—you know better than that." He stared at her until she nodded, then said, "But maybe after today we shouldn't be with or talk with any third party when we're together. Or maybe the later personality—me, at present—must not make decisions without consulting the earlier one first."

"We're messing with causation. That's what scares me."

"I'm fifteen hours more scared than you are. I've had that much longer to worry about it."

"Why didn't you say something earlier?"

"Because—same old reason—I hadn't, so I couldn't." He shrugged. "Look, I have to call Margaret now. When she gets here, you do most of the talking."

He picked up the phone.

Margaret, following Ed along the entrance hallway, did not bother to glance at the mirror she passed; she knew she looked well. Her dark hair was cropped sleek, the front brushed into brief bangs and the crown barely long enough to hold a slight wave. She dressed with understated elegance and ignored fads. Her face, like all of her, was lean and tanned; the full lips accented it. And she moved with grace.

When she saw the girl she knew her own height and slimness made the other a giantess—a healthy, attractive giantess, but still . . . Margaret nodded. She could afford the age difference.

She made the competitive assessment by instinct; she had no fear of losing Ed to any woman. But she was puzzled—why the need for a conference, just because this time he had picked a youngster? She accepted a daiquiri and sat where she could view the lake and the city beyond.

"Lovely apartment, Miss Blake." Margaret thought the decor rather stark for a young girl, but in its own way striking.

"Thank you," said Melanie. She looked at Ed, then back to Margaret. "I suppose . . . I'd better explain. . . ."

"What's to explain? The way you and Ed look at each other, the picture is obvious. My only question is, what's the problem? I'm sure he's told you the terms of our marriage. Of course you *are* a little young for him"—why did the girl grin? Not a smile, a *grin*—"but I don't mind if you don't. So what is it?"

Ed spoke. "Margaret, it's not what you think. Well, that too—but that's not *it*. It's . . . something you won't believe, that we have to convince you of."

"Quintuplets?" seeing their faces change, she felt shame for the jape. "I'm sorry. Go ahead."

Frowning, the girl leaned forward. She turned to Ed. "Damn it, I don't know where to start!"

"Tell her who you are—who *we* are."

Ed's daughter? No—that didn't fit what he'd said. She saw the girl's confusion and felt pity. "All right—I'm listening; go ahead." She smiled. "Melanie . . . if Ed cares for you, believe me, I'm not your enemy."

The younger woman sat straight and breathed deeply. "Okay—here it is, ready or not. Except in body, there *is* no Melanie Blake. Until three months ago, she was a mindless vegetable."

"But—you're *here*. I don't understand."

"I—we don't either. Listen—Ed Carlain went to sleep in a motel near Coos Bay, Oregon—and woke up in this body. And lived a day in it—a terrible day. The next time he woke he was back in the motel, himself again, and drove home to you. And then—"

"Ed! That trip—when you came home and began drinking so hard?"

"Yes. But let her finish."

"He—I—thought it had been a dream, maybe. But I woke as Melanie again, and then as Ed—and ever since, I live a day first as me and then the same day as him. But we're both the same person; there's only the one consciousness and memory between us." She made a lopsided smile. "Now you can call the men in the white coats."

"Or not," said Ed.

Margaret looked hard at her husband, then at the girl. They seemed not only serious but desperate, nothing at all like people pulling a practical joke. But, *this* . . . ?

Slowly she said, "You're right. I *can't* believe it. But—" She shook her head. "I can think of no reason—and take my word, I'm trying to— why you'd tell me anything like this if it weren't true." She paused. "Or if at the very least you didn't *think* it was true."

Neither answered. She thought there had to be another answer—one that made sense. "Ed—you haven't been into drugs, have you? Or hypnosis—anything like that?"

"Nothing. Neither of us. It happened the way she said. We don't know how or why, or if it has ever happened to anyone else. But it did, to us—beginning on June third."

June third? That's three months, and— "And you didn't tell me, until now?"

"How could he?" said Melanie. "You can't believe it now—you couldn't have *begun* to believe it if I'd tried to tell you as Ed alone, without me here physically to back it up. Right?"

"She *is* right, Margaret. I hated the secrecy, but there was nothing I could do. Now . . . why don't you think of questions—anything—that Melanie couldn't know if she were *not* me?"

She was not ready—not so soon, not so easily—to give in. "You could have coached her."

"No way," said Melanie. "You can check. I didn't leave the sanitarium—except twice, briefly, and under a doctor's care both times—until yesterday. I had only one visitor—my brother, Charles Blake, from New York—and no letters or phone calls in or out. So . . . when's to coach?"

With her objection stymied, Margaret set herself to asking questions. Dates, times, places, and people; she ran out of things to ask. Ed suggested she work on trivia, personal minutiae; Melanie knew a convincing percentage. No one remembers everything, Margaret realized— and could think of no further ways to resist.

"All right," she said, "I guess I'm convinced. Not in my gut yet, but in my head I can't deny it. The more we talk, Melanie, the more I hear Ed in you. That impresses me, maybe more than your answers do."

Now that she had said it, her mind cleared; she could *think* again.

"So you are Ed and Ed is you. And it's all right that I don't understand it, since you don't, either. One question, though—just what do you want *me* to do about it?"

Melanie's eyes widened. "Why, *accept* it, is all. Let you and Ed get back to full honesty—take this load off the split-level soul we share. Okay?"

Looking from one to the other, Margaret nodded. "And of course I see why you have to be lovers. No one, not even I, can possibly be as close to Ed as you are, Melanie. Well, I've never been jealous—have I, Ed?—and I'll try not to be now."

Seeing their intent, serious faces she felt tears coming. To break the mood, she laughed. "All right, you two-in-one or vice versa, let's go over to the Carlain abode and have dinner."

"Why not here?" said Melanie. "I've been learning to cook, and there's food. Let me—"

"Not a chance." Margaret shook her head. "Ed and I used to go camping—remember?—and no mere three months could make him a passable cook. Give it a little time—and I'll help, too. But not today. Let's go."

They went.

Melanie thought, *That was easier than I expected.* Margaret liked her—no problem there. Her own feelings toward the older woman? Not quite the same as Ed's; she could feel a difference but could not yet put her finger on it. Meanwhile . . .

Outside, she wanted to take her own car, but the other two insisted they all ride in Margaret's. All right. On the way she lay back with eyes closed, not talking, letting her thoughts roam.

At the Carlain house, Margaret started to guide her, to tell her where things were—then stopped cold, laughed, and said, "I'm sorry; I forgot you've lived here too."

Melanie said, "You can't expect to digest the whole impossible thing in two hours; we have three months' head start on you, remember."

Ed spoke. "And living it, at that. No sweat, Margaret."

His wife smiled and said, "You're right; I'll need some time."

Later, at dinner, the man and wife talked mostly of Carlain family matters; although these were also part of Melanie's own recalls, she felt subtly excluded and did not know why.

When Ed poured wine she said, "You're wasting this. So far, nothing alcoholic tastes good to me."

He grinned. "You like this one; I remember. It's light, white, and dry—you even have one refill."

"You—?" She scowled. "More trapped action, Ed?"

"Not really—it just happened. But if you'd rather, I'll try not to tell you things ahead of time, unless you ask."

"Yes. That might be better." She sipped the wine and found that she did like it; almost immediately she felt its glow. Midway through her second glass she looked and saw Ed's amused smile. "Don't worry, I can handle the rest of this okay. But no more." The alcohol stimulated and relaxed her but did not fog her mind; she followed the conversation and occasionally contributed.

She was neither surprised nor perturbed when all three went to the master bedroom; after all, Ed was Margaret's as well as hers. Later, without thought—out of habit and instinct and long years of loving—she reached to Margaret.

The older woman gasped. "You mustn't—I don't—"

"I'm still Ed—remember? Even in this package."

A shaky laugh. "Well—anything *you* can do . . ."

Ed enjoyed the dinner and the evening but was impatient, waiting. All that happened later moved him deeply.

I love them both so much. . . .

For the first time, Melanie woke to see Ed beside her. She heard kitchen noises; Margaret was already up. She thought of something Ed had told her: "If the one of us—you, for now—who lives the day first is the one to initiate communication, we can avoid trapped action." It sounded reasonable. She reached under the covers and initiated communication.

The funny thing, thought Margaret, was that she did not feel left out or threatened. Closer to each other than either could be to her—but they were both Ed; both loved her. She would never have joined in woman love had Melanie been *only* Melanie, rather than a new Ed with new limitations, new ways.

When she heard the shower running she began cooking breakfast. When it stopped, she called, "It's on the table, nearly. Five minutes—then you have to fight the dog for it." Both beat the deadline and the nonexistent dog.

Over coffee, Ed talked—perfectly good words, but Margaret had a hard time understanding him. "You get it, Melanie? Unless we agree together, a day ahead of time, you have to be the one to decide *anything* between us that affects action. Or else I'm trapped—or you would be, if we ever change phase."

"Yes, I see that."

"And we should know a day ahead where each of us is going to be, separately, so we don't have chance meetings that nail the second half of us."

"Why is that?" asked Margaret.

"I'm talking about how to avoid determinism—in a situation that springs it on us if we don't watch out like a couple of hawks."

"But I don't understand. What's so bad, that you're trying to keep away from?"

Ed told her of the day when Melanie, at Coos Bay, had seen him from the balcony. "And I hadn't even decided to go by that route—I halfway intended to fly down. But she saw me, so I *had* to be there."

"Why? Why couldn't you just fly, anyway?" She saw both turn pale and sag, hardly breathing. "Hey—what did I *say?*"

Fighting to catch breath, Ed answered. "I—I don't know why it is, but we can't even *think* of causing paradox without being practically knocked on our butts. By panic fear, damn it!" He paused. "I think maybe I can talk about it if I keep it hypothetical—yes, that way it only *half* scares the pants off me. Okay, I've read in stories—the far-out ones, with time machines and such—about things that can't happen if they *do* happen. Paradoxes. One story solves it one way, somebody else writes it different. But I think I see how it really works. A person doesn't commit a paradox—*commit* isn't the right word but to hell with that—because something scares the bejesus out of him so that he *can't.*"

"I still don't understand."

"Neither did I, until I felt it. Just take my word."

"And mine," said Melanie.

Finally Margaret said, "Well, if that's the case, at least you can stop worrying about it."

The trouble was, the two found, that the only way to fight determinism was to inflict it on themselves. Each day, almost, revealed new loopholes for "trapped action"; all they could do was to tighten further their already restrictive rules.

And their two roles chafed them. Ed resented being trapped, even when it was all his own doing and none of Melanie's. Melanie complained at having to initiate all phone calls and most decisions. Once they came near to fighting—shouts and a flung dish. When the dish miraculously escaped breakage the fight broke down into laughter. The worst part was having to live through it twice, both times realizing the wrongness: their unity, split in conflict.

"Maybe if we did change phases we could see each other's side of it better."

"But we're each *on* both sides, Ed. Every twice-lived day."

"Not as each other. You *as* you are always a day behind on memory."

"And always first through the grinder, of whatever happens," she said. "It shouldn't matter, should it? But it does."

"Yes." He thought about it. "It's because we are *not* the same person, looking out of your skull, as out of mine. And the difference keeps growing."

"In itself, that's not necessarily a bad thing."

"Of course not. I didn't say it was, did I?"

"No." She paused. "You know the great thing about us?"

"I know a number of them. Which one did you have in mind?"

"Ed—you and I—we *can't* lie to each other."

"Oh? Hmm—you couldn't, to me. But I could, to you."

"Not for long, Ed. In a few hours I'd remember, and catch you out."

"Yes, but then you'd know *why* I did it, so you'd do it too."

"Determinism, you mean. Trapped action."

"Yes," he said. "Back where we started, aren't we?"

"Shall we try to change phases, then?"

"I don't know. Shall we?"

She smiled. "That's right; it's up to me to decide, isn't it? Okay—then I do. If only to see if we can."

Ed nodded. "All right. And since I've had a day to think about it, after you made that decision—"

"God *damn* you, dangling me on a string like a puppet!"

"I had to; you know that. I'm not supposed to predict your actions for you—remember?" He waited for her smile and returned it. "Anyway, I have it figured out, if you agree."

"Tell me."

"First, for obvious reasons we can't see each other or be in touch, after tonight, until the change is made. Or not. . . .

"Now here's the schedule I've worked out. See what you think of it."

The next day, Tuesday, Melanie slept late. She dawdled through breakfast and did not bother to dress. Loneliness muffled her spirits; she wanted to see Ed but knew she must not.

How about Margaret? If she were careful, said nothing to Margaret that might influence Ed? She dialed the number and heard the ringing signal; after twelve rings and no answer, she hung up, puzzled. Then she guessed what had happened—it was so hard to keep track of *all* the complications.

Ed's there, and he remembers. So he wouldn't answer, or let Margaret, either. I suppose he's right, but—damn!

Automatically thinking ahead, she checked her watch. Twelve-forty. So Ed would know which call to ignore . . . and they hadn't spoken, so her lapse didn't really count, did it? Right!

Everything bored her—reading, TV, records, even food. She made a sandwich for dinner but left half on the plate. She tried TV again and still found nothing that interested her. She decided to dress and—well, go out on the town. Why not?

Her hair had outgrown the short-curls treatment and straggled a little; to hell with that. Her slacks were snug, her blouse modest. The compromise satisfied her.

She attended a rock concert and met a tall youth who called himself Barry Giles. Afterward they went—her transport, so his treat, he said—for Herfyburgers. But in the dim corner of the parking lot he put his hand on her and said, "Let's do it first. Drop the pants, okay?"

She took his wrist and pulled the hand away. "Sorry, suggestion overruled. Let's go get the sandwiches."

His face was ugly as he said, "It's not a suggestion. It's an order." And now he grabbed, hurting her.

Without thought, her right hand reached. The nails of her fingers dug in behind his ear; the ball of her thumb pushed hard against his eyelid. He tried to shake loose and gasped with pain and fear when he could not.

Her voice shook; she could manage only a hoarse whisper. "If you want out of here with two eyes, get out *right now!*" She relaxed her grip slightly, enough that he could pull free. For a moment he glared with the untouched eye, rubbing the other. Then, watching her clawed hands, he reached behind him and opened the door. His mouth worked as if to speak or spit, but after a moment he backed away. Outside and standing, he slammed the car door hard, looked at her a few seconds longer, and turned to saunter into the drive-in. She watched him go inside before she started the car.

Driving home, she thought, *Why, that's what I did the other time, too. Sort of. . . .*

Back at the apartment, she ate the other half of her neglected sandwich. *Some night out!*

Reading and records, and TV until it signed off, and a walk in the cool night when boredom pushed toward sleep. By false dawn she knew she could not continue much longer; her body, accustomed to regular hours, demanded sleep.

She had kept coffee in reserve because more than a cup or two gave her jitters and heartburn, but now was the time for it. She drank several cups, black, while she read another book. When she was finished she had no idea what the plot was about.

When the sun rose she went out to the car. Ed had once driven thirty-six hours without sleep; the act of driving kept him awake without much effort. Melanie crossed Lake Washington on the toll bridge, found her way to I-90 East, and drove to the summit of Snoqualmie Pass, about fifty-five miles from downtown Seattle. She parked and got out, and walked perhaps a mile up a hiking trail, breathing tree-scented Cascades air. She started to sit down, then realized that sitting, in this restful place, was one step nearer sleeping. She walked to the car and started back to the city, driving as she had on the way out—conservatively, in the right-hand lane. It was time, not distance, that she wanted to cover.

A little past nine she entered the apartment again. Her thoughts were fragmented, not tracking well, she knew. She looked at the schedule Ed had left her—hours yet before she was supposed to sleep. From the refrigerator she took a prepackaged salad. It tasted good enough but sat heavily in her stomach.

The coffee had worn off, but not the jitters. She stood looking out through the glass wall, down the lake toward the city skyline—the square, high-rising boxes that now passed for architecture. She found herself nodding, dozing on her feet. She squinted at her watch—oh, *no!* Another two hours?

She shook her head. To hell with it—schedule or no schedule, her endurance had reached its limit.

She lay, feeling the nervous irritable jerks of her body—too strained to relax—and waited for the warm blanket of sleep to cover consciousness. But each time the blanket came, the spasms pushed it away. She drifted into a limbo of not-thinking.

A stronger "jump" brought her half-alert for a moment; then she felt sleep coming on her like a tide. Relieved, she sighed.

In the last instant of consciousness she hung above a black abyss. But before she could fall, sleep came.

The alarm clock began Ed's Tuesday early. For most of the day he kept to himself, trying to work. He avoided Margaret because she was curious about the phase change—and some of her questions he could not answer.

If he had known how hard it would be on the kid, he thought, he would have let things alone, scratched the whole idea. *My God! That creep in the parking lot!* Although he remembered the scene, somehow he did not feel that it had happened to *him*, but only to Melanie.

That memory was one reason why he hit the bourbon harder than he had in some time. Another was that he wanted to be physically ready for bed, early. By eight o'clock he was well primed for sleep.

At four, Wednesday morning, his alarm sounded. He turned it off, groaned, and sat up. A little hung over but not badly, he rose to endure, according to schedule, his second short day.

Only then did he think: *Well, it worked!* For the first time since June second, he was the same person two times running.

He hoped it would not be necessary to change phases often.

Again he kept away from Margaret, staying at his work desk but no longer working. When he heard her leave the house he gave a sigh of relief mixed with guilt. Now he could relax. . . .

He felt sleepy—the compressed schedule, like jet lag, confused his body's processes—but he must not sleep yet. Then he thought, sure he could! For he had taken many catnaps—dozes—since Melanie began, and none of those had changed the progression of their lives.

So he lay on the couch and rested, then slept. Vaguely, he dreamed. Then the dream took him to the edge of a black gulf; he began to fall and woke in cold sweat, lunging off the couch and wordlessly shouting.

He quieted himself and looked at his watch. It read an hour past noon.

His clock, the one in his head, was upside down now. He looked for the schedule he had written in duplicate, but when he found it, it made no sense to him. Had it been coherent in the first place? *Look at it, you moron!*

Yes, he thought, it did make sense. But had he followed it? He could not be sure. In his mind the times jumbled, his and hers.

Suddenly he could endure no more waiting.

Driving now, he forgot caution, ignored his own rules for keeping within limits of tolerance, kept no watch for police cars. But luck rode with him; he arrived safely and unticketed.

At her door he rang the bell. No answer; he used his key. Of course! —she would still be asleep, and God knew she needed it. But he had to see her, to talk with her. In silence he approached her bedroom and opened the door.

Even sprawled sleeping, hair tangled and mouth ajar, the look of her caught him, made him pause. Then with a quick headshake, smiling, he moved to sit gently on the bed beside her and stroked the rumpled hair. Her eyes opened, then blinked.

"It worked," he said. "It *worked*. Here we are, and for the first time I have no memory of it, and you do. Tell me, did we have a good day, once you got yourself all the way woke up?"

Frowning, she shook her head. "You're kidding me, Ed—you have to be. It *didn't* work—because I don't remember this at all." Using her elbows, she pushed herself up, half sitting. "Why are you joking with me? What's the point?"

"I'm not—" He leaned to hug her, fiercely, then pulled her up to sit erect. "Are you sure—you're awake now, aren't you?—are you *sure* you don't remember this, being here, being me?"

Wide-eyed, her face showed only concern. "Of course I'm sure. And —Ed!" For a moment she put her hands to her face and closed her eyes, then looked at him again. "Ed, I went to sleep as me and *woke* as me— nothing of you in between. I didn't go back and have your Tuesday at all. I—"

"Wait a minute. Sure you did—you *had* to. Because *I* did. Look, everything was normal—normal for *us*, I mean—through Monday. Right?" She nodded. "And then you had the long haul—I'm sorry it was so rough—and went to bed this morning. Still right?"

"Yes, I have that, of course. But then—"

"And then there was my own short Tuesday and I got up early

today, skipping from me straight to me again, just as we'd planned. And here we are!"

"But I didn't *have* your Tuesday. I skipped straight from me to me, too."

He thought. "Then I guess you're right. It *didn't* work. The mechanism, whatever it is, compensated somehow. Well, it was a nice try. But I guess we're stuck with the way things are, just as before." He stood, and helped her to her feet. "Come on. This needs some coffee, something to eat. Never mind clothes; you look just fine, and it's warm in here."

She laughed, only for a moment, and followed him to the kitchen. "Eggs?" he said. She nodded, and he added, "You're the one short of sleep; just sit while I fix stuff and think out loud. Or . . . do you have any ideas?"

"One. Do you realize, Ed—here we are and *neither* of us remembers it? We're both having it for the first time? How can that be?"

As he prepared food and coffee, he spoke in brief bursts. "How, you ask? I don't know. Any more than how we happened in the first place." He turned the eggs, broke one, and cursed, without emphasis, as though reciting someone else's words.

He wheeled to face her. "But *now* what happens? Where does it go from here?"

"I don't know. Here, the eggs will burn—let me—" She rose and rescued the eggs, slipping them neatly onto the toast he had prepared. Sitting, she said, "What do you think will happen?"

Now he felt his hunger and ate, speaking between bites. "We've never lived a day in parallel before, each for the first time. Maybe next we switch and do it over, each remembering."

"How can we? Because we're both here, and we *didn't.*"

He shook off the chill of threatened paradox. "Then maybe one of us wakes next with both these sets of memories, and then the other picks it up from there." He poured coffee. "In which case we still don't know whether we managed to change phase or not. I wish I knew—it'd be a shame to go through all this for nothing."

She looked away, then back to him. "Whatever happens, surely it hasn't been for nothing—has it?"

He reached and clasped her hand. "What do you mean? What do you think might happen?"

"No." She shook her head and would not answer further.

It was strange, he thought, being and talking with her when her responses were all new to him, when he had not experienced them from her side. He told her so.

"I wouldn't know. I've always been on the other end of it."

He laughed. "That's silly; we've both had both sides."

"But it doesn't feel the same, when I'm you and when I'm me. Haven't you noticed that? But of course you have. I remember it."

"That's good. For a minute there, you had me worried."

But the talk lagged, for now he was acutely aware of the difference between this conversation and any other they had had.

They tidied the kitchen, showered together, and then made love. At first it went well; then came an awkwardness and he realized how much, with her, he relied on subliminal memory to tell him what to do. He rallied and both succeeded. But afterward, even as they lay smiling in embrace, he felt . . . well, a *lack*.

He could not tell her so and did not try. After a time, up and sitting, watching boats move on the lake below, she said, "It's different, isn't it?"

"I guess so."

"How, for you?"

"Well . . . before, I always *knew*."

"Yes. That's what I wanted to experience, from this side."

He hugged her. "And maybe with luck you will. We don't know yet which way it's going to go."

Now he felt they were closer again, the two halves of him. As he left, he said, "Tomorrow, the one who doesn't remember past today should be the one to get in touch."

"Yes. I hope it's you, Ed. I *want* the other side."

"I know."

He drove home as conservatively as Dr. Phipps; Margaret greeted him. "Well, at last! Now can you tell me how your idea worked?"

He held her shoulders and kissed her. "I wish I could." He explained, and added, "Tomorrow we should know."

Eyes narrowed, she spoke. "Ed, you need a drink. Go sit down; I promise not to scant you."

She didn't; they sat, arms around each other while he sipped. She said, "If it would help any . . ." and quoted a very old joke, wrongly attributed to Confucius.

He shook his head. "Not right now—I'll reinstall you as a fixture in the house a little later, maybe. Thanks, though." Suddenly he realized —with Margaret, the lack of "advance" memories had never been a problem. And he said, "Honey, I wish there were some way, sometime, that *we* could be each other."

"I wish I could even begin to understand how that feels."

"And I wish there were words I could use to tell you."

After Ed left, Melanie read awhile, ate a snack, and went back to bed. When she woke in the night and found her identity unchanged, she buried her face in the pillow and cried.

Ed's first morning thought was, *All right, which way is it?* Then, *Straight from my own yesterday; good.* Satisfied, he nodded. So it had worked after all; his loss of one of Melanie's days was not important in the long run. Margaret was up and gone; he made a quick breakfast and went to Melanie.

He could not believe her. *"Nothing?"*

"No. I'm still just me. For the third time, at least."

"Yes. Me too—but I don't see *how*."

They stood in fierce embrace. "I do, Ed. But I don't like it much."

He pushed back, not violently but away from her. "What is it?"

"Oh, stop it! You know; you just won't admit it."

"Admit *what*? What the hell are you talking about?"

"We're not going to be each other anymore, Ed. Not ever, ever again. We're *two* now, not one any longer." She pulled him to her and kissed him, then let him go. She tried to laugh, but a small, gulping sob came instead. "I'm going to miss you—being you—the same way you'll miss being me. And the physical thing, that's only a part of it."

Nausea struck him. He turned away and fought it down, then turned back. "But—but I'd only *begun* to learn how to be you!"

Every day he saw her. Now there were no paradoxes, no traps, only the driving urge to be what he could not be. When they were together he watched her, totally engrossed, trying to see into her mind that had once been his.

But without success. One day he said, "It's as if I had never been you at all. I can't tell what you're thinking anymore—except from what you say, I have no idea."

Melanie smiled. "Isn't that the way it is with everybody? At least we had more, while we did have it." He got himself a drink—he was watering his bourbon these days—and did not answer.

She said, "I do wish we'd been able to switch precedence for a while. It doesn't seem like much, but . . ."

"I know." Then he had to say it. "Melanie, what are you planning to do now?"

She smiled. "You still know me, don't you? And you're right, of course. Because it's *your* memories and attitudes I'm using—how else?—to decide that I have to cut free of my emotional dependence on you. And—and go out and build my own life."

He saw her wince at the reaction he could not hide. She said, "You did see it coming, didn't you, Ed?"

"Yes. But I didn't want to."

"No." She reached to touch him. "Ed—I owe you—I *am* you, or at least built up from what you gave me. But I can't stay around, being your juvenile alter ego when I'm really not. Can you see that?"

"I guess so." He hunched his shoulders, brought them down again. "Hell, I know so. It's just—I hate to lose—your part of me." He grinned at her. "We lasted too quick, is all."

"Maybe if we'd waited longer to try the phase shift. But we were diverging already; it might have happened anyway, splitting apart." She paused. "Ed? Would you like—?"

Thinking about it, he brushed her trimmed bangs back to kiss her forehead, and stroked her hair down the back of her neck. He shook his head.

"No, Melanie. We've had the best of that, between us."

"When we were the same, you mean?"

"And getting used to being separate. That was good, too."

"Then why not—?"

"You just declared your independence, and you're right. So this is no time for you to look back or step back."

"If you say so." She stood. "Well then—you want a good-bye kiss or a good-bye handshake?"

"How about both?" As he walked away after her warm response, as he reached the door and turned the knob, he looked back and said, "Live yourself a good life, Melanie. For both of us."

She heard the sound of his footsteps, outside, diminish. *Was I right? Or is it too soon?* She paced to the glass wall, looked out, and turned away. *I could call him.* She gazed around the silent room.

He had left half his drink. She sat and sipped at the watered bourbon, not liking it much. Her thoughts refused to quiet.

Memories: "the turnip," bluffing her way through that frightening, disoriented first day. Ed's relief at thinking it all a dream, his resignation when he found it wasn't. Dr. Phipps. Rape, abortion. Trapped action, as Ed. The competency hearing. Brother Charles—she should get in touch with him, probably. The slow transformation of turnip into Melanie, the daily counterpoint of Ed's life. The meeting, the time together as one, the split, the time together as two. All of it now ended. The new, unknown beginning. . . .

Remembering, she pitied the man she had been—and would miss. Was she wrong to leave him? Without him, she would have been nothing.

Then realization struck. *All* her feelings for Ed Carlain came from June third and after; for his earlier life she felt no emotional identification at all.

She nodded. All right, it would hurt—it *did* hurt—but what she was doing, she had to do.

Maybe I'll come back sometimes—when I have a life of my own to share.

When he got home he told Margaret, "I'm sorry, honey, but I can't talk. Not yet, anyway. Maybe I need a drink." She went to another room. He poured himself a very large glass of bourbon—no ice, no water. He held the glass and looked at it, took a sip, and then another.

He sat for a long time, his thoughts all of Melanie, before he rose and went to the kitchen. There he poured a little of the liquor into a smaller glass, adding ice and water, and put the larger one aside. Then he went to Margaret.

She looked up and said, "That was fast. All better now?"

"No. But maybe if I try to tell you . . ."

When he was done, she said, "You're two different people now? There's no more connection?"

"That's right. I've lost her. Lost *being* her, and now lost her new self, too."

Margaret paused, then said, "What's the worst part? You were getting to like being a double agent in the war of the sexes?"

"No. I mean, sure, that was a goddamn *revelation*. I—"

"Yes. I've noticed some differences lately. Good ones."

"Okay—it's too bad *everybody* can't make all those rounds, and I'll miss it. But that's not what kills me."

"Then what does? To me, you look pretty healthy."

Eyes unfocused, Ed looked into a lost future. "Age, honey." He shrugged. "We all have to face it; right?" He looked at her and pointed a finger. "But there I was, every other day, *eighteen years old* again. I never said anything about it, but of course Melanie remembers how I felt."

He tried to laugh, but even to himself it did not sound right. "I wondered, you know—what would happen to Melanie and me if I died? After all, I'm twenty years older. Or if one of us got killed, for that matter—would the other just keep going?"

"So being Melanie could add twenty years to your life?"

"All right—*yes*. I thought maybe I had it. And more—because we were living *two* days for every calendar day, remember. And now it's gone; I've lost it. I . . ."

He frowned, trying to put words to what he felt. "It's like . . . when you dream how someone you loved, that died, didn't really die after all. And then you wake up. But this time it's me that was going to die, and then wasn't, not so soon at least—and now *I* woke up."

"And that bothers you."

He nodded.

"Come here, Ed."

He woke when Margaret set an icy glass on his belly. The gambit was familiar; he flinched only a little before taking hold of the glass. He sipped; it was tomato juice, with the added tartness of some lemon squeezed in. He felt his mind coming awake.

Margaret said, "How do you feel now?"

He thought back. "I wish to hell I could have had all of it; I can't *help* wishing that. But nobody ever does—and I had more than most, more than anybody I ever heard of. I'll need a long time, I guess, to figure out what I learned. And maybe that's good."

She did not answer. After a time he said, "It's—it's like I had heaven and didn't realize it, so they took it away from me. But I only had it by luck—I'll never know how. *Melanie.* How could it *happen?*"

She touched his shoulder. "And how *about* Melanie?"

He shrugged. "She'll make it. She has me to work from."

"And you, Ed?"

He grinned. "Hell yes. I can't let the kid down, can I?"